My K-pop Brothers
Book 1: The Guardians

Lina Sonnet

Cover design by Melissa Doughty - Mel D. Designs

Edited by Steve Garton

ISBN: 979-8-218-85719-6

DEDICATION

To my sister

Contents

1

I found you a little sister.

-Manager-nim

Day -7

"Do you need a bag?"

"Huh?"

Hayoon glances up to the person in front of her. He's checking a list on his phone; pointing at each item to make sure he didn't forget anything. *Do all boys eat this many snacks?* She subtly observes him as he looks from his phone to the convenience store worker behind the counter.

"Bag?"

"No thanks."

No bag?

He puts his phone on the counter before shoving the snacks into his pant pockets and hoodie pouch. *Guess he doesn't need a bag... impressive.* Only three drinks and a bag of chips left to juggle in his arms.

"Thanks."

When he moves toward the door, Hayoon moves up to place her drink on the counter. *His phone!*

She looks back but he is already walking through the door. She doesn't dare call out to him. There are half a dozen people in the store who would all stare at her if she yelled. She hurriedly pays for her coffee and runs after him.

She pushes through the door as she sees him approach a charter bus. *What if I don't catch him in time?*

She starts running toward the bus. Her coffee splashes onto her hand but she barely feels it in her urgency to get to the door before it closes. *Wait. Don't leave.*

Without a second thought, Hayoon jumps onto the bus and up the stairs. Her eyes lock onto the snack boy and her hand reaches toward him.

As he looks back, her vision widens and she becomes frozen, her arm dropping lifeless to her side.

The bus is full of handsome, fit, young men. When the snack boy stops midair handing someone else a drink, their eyes all shift to her. Someone in the second row, elbows the boy beside him as he nods toward her. Her eyes start pinging around between the boys like a pinball machine. *Oh my gosh. What do I do?*

Hayoon takes a step back. *Retreat. Retreat.*

The boy in the front row stands up and she panics. *Avoid conversation. Get off the bus.*

"Sorry. I didn't..."

"Are you okay?"

They speak English?!? Her plan to avoid conversation for fast retreat is shattered by their four years of English lessons. *Try again.*

"Rojo. Aprendemos en la escuela. Zapatos. Amarillo." Hayoon holds her breath, waiting for their reaction....*I should've paid more attention in world cultures class.* She doesn't even know what she said but she is hoping they don't either.

The boy standing, who spoke before, turns to the other side of the aisle.

"Did she just speak Italian?"

"I think it was Spanish."

"Gracias is Spanish."

"She didn't even say gracias. How is that useful?"

She steps back slowly as the boys deliberate. *It's working... Oh, the phone!*

She remembers her goal for coming on the bus in the first place. In a hurried manner, she takes two giant steps forward and shoves the phone into his arms.

"Your phone."

She turns in a flurry toward the door.

"She speaks Korean?!?"

The boys are all confused. *If she's Korean, what was that whole mess for?*

The man in the front row rockets out of his seat. He turns to his row partner and exclaims, "It's her!"

He runs off the bus and yells, "Wait!"

She stops on command and pivots slowly to face him. *I'm in trouble now.*

"How old are you?"

Does he want to contact my parents for disturbing them? I didn't mean to. "Nineteen. Almost twenty."

He pulls out a business card from his pocket and offers it out to her. She politely takes it with both hands.

"Do you know who those boys are?"

She looks over to the bus but doesn't have time to answer before he rushes through what he has to say.

"Doesn't matter. They're artists under a performance company. I'm their manager. I would like to offer you a job working with them. You'll get free housing and meals, and a decent salary."

What? I...Uh. She's stunned stupid.

"The boys have a busy schedule the next two days... Thursday. No, Friday. Come by the office Friday at ten. I'll explain everything then."

He starts to back away.

"I.." She tries to refuse his offer but never gets a chance.

"Friday. At ten. Address is on the card."

He boards the bus. The boys all rush back to their seats from crowding the window, watching their conversation. The manager sits and turns excitedly toward the boy beside him.

"I found you a little sister."

"HUH?!?"

The boys bombard him with questions but he swats them away.

"Get some rest. We still have an hour left till we get there."

Day -3

The manager is expectantly waiting for Hayoon to arrive with his bus row partner.

"Do you think she'll come?" The manager asks anxiously.

"How should I know? ... Why does it have to be a girl? Don't you think that'll create problems? A girl living with eight men?"

"What are your fans?"

"Mostly girls in their teens or twenties."

"Exactly. Girls look at things a different way. That's the perspective we want them to see. A little brother won't work. Look at me. I'm nearly thirty, had two girlfriends, and still don't understand what fine but not actually fine means."

Hayoon stands across the street from the company. She pulls her eyes from the business card in her hand up to the building that seems to reach to the sky.

Should I go? I don't even know what kind of job it is. Maybe I should just leave. But it doesn't hurt to go hear what he has to say. What if I'll like the job? ...Okay. Give it a try.

She checks the time on her phone, takes a deep breath, and crosses the street.

She walks toward the front desk as her eyes cloud with apprehension. *What do I even tell them? Hello, I'm here because some weird guy on a bus full of boys told me to come but didn't even tell me for what. Ugh. Talking to strangers is hard. Adulting stinks.*

She slows her step, second guessing herself, when someone yells.

"You came!"

She turns to see the strange guy from the bus. She recognizes the boy beside him, too. They quickly arrive in front of her.

"This is the group's leader, Kim Baekhyeon."

"Park Hayoon."

"Let's go up to my office to talk."

"Why don't we tell you about the group first?"

She nods in agreement.

"We debuted three years ago with eight members. All the boys you saw on the bus are members in our group. The youngest member is nineteen and I'm the oldest at twenty-four. Our group is number one in the company and top five in the country. We've gone on two world tours and have another confirmed for this year."

"The problem we're facing now is that their fan base numbers aren't growing as fast as they used to. So, we want to adopt you."

"Huh?!?" *Adopt me? I'm an adult!* "I'm not a child."

"I know. I know. I know. Let me explain. The group is known for being flawless. Good at everything they do. Make their own choreography. Compose their own music. Never a scandal. Some media have even compared them to Greek gods. Handsome, fit, talented but untouchable. Unrelatable. So, we want you to become the members' little sister. You'll live with them and let the world see what they're like 'off screen' by video recording normal everyday things. Cooking dinner. Playing games. Getting coffee. You understand?"

She just stares at them bewildered. *A K-pop group wants to adopt a little sister? Wants to adopt me?*

The leader speaks up. "Um... you finished school, right?"

"Yes."

"Think of it like you're the foil character that allows the reader to better understand the other characters."

The manager takes over again. "You just need to record clips of the boys at home and backstage at events. You don't have to edit them or release them. The company will do that. Just record normal daily life with the boys. You'll travel with them to events and participate in their reality show, Peak Season. When we go on world tour, the members normally film vlogs so you just need to film their interactions with each other and yourself. Pictures are good, too."

She's listening attentively but her brain is whirling in a million different directions.

"Do you have any questions?" The oldest of her soon-to-be big brothers asks after seeing her expression.

"Um... I think you picked the wrong person."

Neither one of them know how to respond, as in their minds, it was already a done deal. Why would someone turn down an offer like this? This is every fan's dream come true- big house, travel, concerts, decent pay, doting famous brothers. Who would say no?

"What?"

"Wouldn't a trainee or one of their fans be a better choice? ... I don't like places with lots of people or being on stage. Won't I just drag them down?"

Kim Baekhyeon is the first to speak after the silence. "I still think you're the right choice. I'm more sure now. I understand what you're saying but I still want you to join us. The show doesn't have a live audience and you won't be performing at concerts with us. If you're worried about living with us... it's just like living in a college men's dorm."

Hayoon and the manager's eyes widen at his remark. Baekhyeon instantly regrets it.

"Not at all like a college men's dorm. I meant, we're just normal people. A perfectly normal house with normal people that just so happen to be men. Very normal. Very calm."

The manager tries to gloss over it by hastily continuing. "Your housing and food are all free and one of the members, Jihoon, picks up all the daily essentials for the group."

Beakhyeon continues, "You can go with him to pick out what you like. Normally, one or two of the other members will go, too."

Hayoon asks, "How long will I live with them for?"

"Let's start with three months. If it works out, then maybe a lot longer."

"Okay."

"Okay?"

"You agree?"

She nods in agreement. "When do I move in?"

"In three days. In three days, I'll come pick you up. Is that enough time?"

She nods. The manager slides a piece of paper across the desk. "Write down your contact information and address. Take your ID to the desk on your way out for them to copy so we can start paperwork."

She writes it down and slides it back. *Did I seriously just agree to become the little sister of a world-famous K-pop group?*

"I'll message you when I'm on my way to pick you up. Probably afternoon. There won't be time to go back once you move in with the boys so make sure you bring everything with you."

She nods. "I understand. Thank you."

She quietly gets out of the chair and leaves.

The oldest member watches her walk away until she's out of sight. There's a reason fans always say he's the dad of the group. Always worrying. Always making difficult decisions as their leader.

Is she always this quiet? Or is she just nervous? Maybe I should talk to Seojun or Minseong before she arrives. I should talk to Jihoon about her room first. ...We barely know anything about her. What if she doesn't get along with the boys?

"I hope this works."

"Don't worry so much. I have a good feeling about this."

2

"Where should I go?"

-Hayoon

Day 1

Three days later, the members all crowd the bedroom doorway as Jihoon and Baekhyeon prepare Hayoon's room.

"Are we really getting a little sister?"

Jihoon looks up from arranging two pillows on the bed. "No, I just thought I'd practice interior design. Cause we're not busy enough." He adds to his sarcasm with an eye roll.

Seojun gets all giddy. "I'm not going to be the youngest anymore."

"You still are." Baekhyeon comments flatly.

"Oh."

"What about me? Am I going to be a little brother or big brother?"

"Let me think... big brother. Two three months older. She'll turn twenty soon."

"Yes!" He sticks his tongue out at Seojun, flaunting his status.

Baekhyeon sets the final item in place and puts an end to their showdown before it could begin.

"Team meeting. Now. Living room. Go."

Hayoon stood outside of her apartment building, waiting to be picked up. Her bookbag stacked on her duffel bag; her duffel bag stacked on her suitcase.

The manager pulls up and gets out of the car with another man.

"Hello. This is my assistant."

"Hello. Nice to meet you."

"Did you pack everything up to bring with you?" He looks behind her to the apartment entrance, thinking she'll need help to bring the rest down.

"Yup." She taps the top of her bookbag.

"Is this everything?"

"Yes."

Why are they looking at me like that? Should it not be everything? Did I forget something?

"Okay. Hop in the car and we'll load it up for you."

"Thank you."

The assistant slings the bookbag on his shoulder and picks up the handles of the duffel bag. The manager drags the suitcase and opens the trunk.

"This is all of her stuff?"

"Why the heck did I bring you to help?"

"She'll probably spend less than Yunjae on living expenses."

They chuckle and get in to take her home.

Baekhyeon goes to the door to help Manager-nim with the bags. They drop the bags down in front of the members sprawled over the couches.

Manager-nim looks back toward the door. "Come here."

The members all stare as she scurries in to stand between Baekhyeon and Manager-nim. Her eyes scan the group curiously. She didn't get a good look before on the bus.

I think it's going to be okay.

"This is Park Hayoon. Starting today, she will be living here with us."

"Hello." The boys all echo in response. "Hello."

Baekhyeon turns to Hayoon and speaks in a calm tone. "These are the other seven members. We mostly call each other hyung or by name."

He instructs the members, "Introduce yourselves."

As the oldest member, he goes first. "Kim Baekhyeon. You can call me Baekhyeon like the fans or Baekhyeon oppa. I'm the leader of the group and the vocal unit."

"Hakkun"

She can't stop the "huh?" from escaping her mouth. The members all chuckle.

"Yeah... My mom is an author and my dad is a literary professor. You can call me Kun oppa or some of the fans call me Hakkuna."

"Junwoo. Leader of the dance unit."

Ah? Her eyes changed. Was it something I said?

"Jihoon. Leader of the rap unit. I do the shopping for the house. Tomorrow afternoon, you can come with me and pick out what you like. The soaps in the house are men's scents so I put travel size soaps in your bathroom for today."

"Thank you."

"Yunjae. Dance unit. You can call me Yunjae oppa or JJ like the international fans."

JJ? Shouldn't it be YJ? Is it because of his last name? Hmm.

"Jeongu. Rap unit. Thanks for returning my phone."

"Minseong. Vocal unit and dance unit."

They have two units?

"Seojun. Dance unit and vocal unit."

Baekhyeon took over again as leader. "Just call him Seojun. He's younger than you."

Manager-nim informs Hayoon, "When the members leave to record for their show tomorrow morning, you'll come to the company for paperwork. I'll send the assistant you met today to pick you up."

He addresses everyone, "Have a good night. Go to bed early for the show tomorrow. We leave at nine. Jeongu, nine. Not nine thirty."

The members laugh at Jeongu and shout out goodbyes as the manager leaves.

"Alright. We have plenty of time to get to know each other but for now, let's let Hayoon unpack and we'll cook dinner."

Seojun jumps off the couch. "I'll take her to her room."

Seojun grabs her suitcase handle and starts walking off before she has time to react. Baekhyeon nods in his direction and she hustles to catch up. Meanwhile, Seojun is already starting to talk with no signs of stopping.

"Jihoon hyung spent hours picking out everything for your room. Do you like pink? I hope so..."

He's definitely an extrovert.

Hayoon glances back and locks eyes with Junwoo as he gets up from the couch. She whips her head back around to listen.

"Since we're close in age, you don't mind if I call your name, right? Do you like to sing? I'm on two units but I prefer dance. I know in the recording studio we just stand there and sing but I swear I end up more tired than practicing in the dance studio all day."

They arrive at her room. Seojun slides her suitcase in like a bowling ball. He plops on her bed and holds out his hand to take the duffel bag from Jeongu.

"Thank you."

"You don't say a lot, do you?"

Jeongu slaps him on the back of the head. "When did you give her a chance?"

"You see how they treat me?" He swings back. "If anyone bullies you here, tell me. I'm the youngest so I'm used to these idiots."

Hayoon smiles at their teasing. *I'm gonna like this little brother.*

"Do you have brothers or sisters?"

"No."

"Is that why you're so quiet?"

Junwoo and Jihoon appear in the doorway.

"Hyung, I thought you were on cooking duty today?"

"Why don't you let her unpack before you play twenty questions? You're going to scare her. Come help set the plates out."

Jihoon grabs Seojun by the shirt collar and drags him out with Jeongu in tow.

Hayoon looks around the room and smiles faintly with a new found peacefulness she can't explain. Maybe it's because of the simple but intentional design of her room. Maybe it's because of her energetic, welcoming little brother that put her at ease.

Her gaze lands on Junwoo, still leaning against the door frame. *Is it because of him?*

He leaves the doorway to approach her. His arms outstretch to put the towels within her arms' reach.

"Jihoon prepared these for you. Fresh out of the dryer."

"Thank you." He can't help but smile from the tone in her voice. Even her eyes are filled with warmth.

He nods and turns to leave.

"Wh…"

Her voice is barely audible but it was enough to catch his attention. He spins back around to wait for her to continue.

"Which rooms can I not go into?"

"Huh?"

"They didn't tell me. Where I'm not allowed to go."

Why wouldn't she be allowed to go somewhere? It's her house now too, isn't it?

"I don't think there are any. You can go wherever you want. But… you might want to knock before going into our bedrooms if the door is shut. Otherwise…"

She blushes at what he was implying. *Living with boys will be different. That's for sure.*

"Come on. I'll show you around."

Junwoo takes her on a tour of the house. Neither one of them says much but there isn't a need to. She follows behind him, looking into each room but not leaving the hallway.

"…Last room in this hall is Minseong and Seojun's room."

He swings the door open.

"They're the closest to you in age. I'll take you up to the second-floor landing."

His front foot hits the second floor as he turns back toward her to talk. *Where'd she go? She was just right...*

"Can I open it?"

He looks across the landing to Hayoon, with a hand resting on the balcony door handle. He nods, giving her permission. *Is she excited over a balcony?* He strides over to the balcony to join her. His leading foot midair ready to step...

"Junwoo! Come to the kitchen."

"I'll be right back."

She glances back to check if he's left the landing. *Yes.* She takes off her hat and lets down her hair. Her eyes close, with her face upturned to bask in the sunlight with the breeze blowing her hair to the side. *Ahhh. How relaxing. I can't believe I have eight brothers. I hope they like me.* She takes a deep breath. *I gotta do a good job to help them.*

Junwoo looks over to the balcony before his feet reach the top step. His body halts as his gaze softens, captivated by the view before him. *Who is she? On the bus, she was nervous but smart. In front of the boys, she was timid but stood tall. In her room, she looked peaceful and now...*

What if I make her nervous again?

Junwoo yells back, "I'll get her."

"Hayoon! Time to eat."

She puts her hat on and hurries off the balcony, politely controlling the door so it doesn't bang shut.

At dinner, Hayoon waits to sit until the members sit. *What if they have seats they always sit at?*

"Come sit here."

Seojun calls her over to sit to the right of the end chair, beside himself and across from Junwoo. Minseong sits in the seat on the end and Jihoon sits across from Seojun, beside Junwoo.

While the boys are eating, Hayoon watches and listens to their conversations. *Ohhh. So, they are having a comeback. No wonder they're so busy. Does that mean I get to see their concert? Do I get to go to practice with them?*

Across the table, Jihoon elbows Junwoo, nearly knocking the cup out of his hands.

"Baekhyeon asked you a question."

He looks over Jihoon to their leader.

"How many hours do you think it will take to review the choreography for the fan showcase? Will there be enough time the day after tomorrow?"

"Maybe but it won't be as clean. It'd be better to do it the evening before."

"That's fine."

Hakkun speaks up, "Time for dishes. Word play. Everyone ready?"

She looks questioningly around the table. *Word play? The consonant game? Yes!*

"Minseong, you go after Seojun. Hayoon won't play."

Oh. Hayoon tries to control her shoulders from drooping over. *But I love this game.*

Is she disappointed?

Junwoo knows he isn't good at talking like the others but maybe because of this, he's become exceptional at observing people. It's because of his patience and acute observations that make him the group's respected dance leader.

The members start the game with S.

"Snake."

"Sand."

Hayoon tries to hide her emotions by staring at the table. She writes her word on the table with her finger to play in her own way. S-A-D

"Sit."

"Sad."

Eh? Someone said my word. She smiles at her satisfactory answer.

She smiled! She wants to play.

"Out. Jeongu, dishes duty. Next round D."

"Danger."

"Dog."

"Drink."

She writes her word on the table again.

"Dance."

Her eyes dart up. *Again?* She looks at Junwoo across the table. *Was he watching?*

He nods as he glances to her hand, encouraging her to keep writing. They play as a secret team through two more rounds. With each passing round, Hayoon's disappointment drifts away.

Day 2

"Why'd you have to go to the company?"

"Sign the contract, learn the rules, get the schedule. They said I have to get a doctor's check up tomorrow. And told me to film a video tour of the house this week, too."

"We just got ours that day we met you on the bus. We go every six months. I wonder if you'll go to the company's doctor. We only have male groups but I think he sees other patients too."

Jihoon is pushing the cart down the aisle, listening to Hayoon, Seojun and JJ chat.

"I need to get the chicken. You guys take her to get shampoo and stuff."

They split up to get what they need. Jihoon shakes his head, smirking, as he can still hear Seojun talking nonstop. His voice slowly fades away. *I hope Hayoon survives.*

"Did you look at the schedule?"

"For a second."

"When we first debuted, it seemed crazy but now, not so much. Mostly fan events, concerts, our show, or practice."

"Have you seen our show before?"

"Not yet." Hayoon flips open a shampoo bottle to smell it. *Eck, that's awful.*

"Tomorrow, we're recording in an arcade."

Yunjae hands her a bottle. "Try this one."

"...not bad. It's a little strong."

Seojun whispers to JJ, looking down the aisle. "Do you think she'll need *that* aisle?"

"Where?" Yunjae cluelessly looks around.

"You know..."

"What are you trying to say?" He raises his voice to a normal volume in frustration at Seojun's guessing game.

Hayoon looks at them, oblivious to their charade. "This one's good."

Why are they looking at me like that? Did I get soap on my nose when I was smelling it? She touches her nose to check. *Nope. ...Weird.*

Seojun looks over to JJ, hoping his big brother will save him. Too bad he's naive.

He steps closer to Hayoon, whose eyes enlarge at his close approach. He lowers his voice to ask, "Do you need aisle seven?"

"Aisle seven," Hayoon mutters as she looks around.

Seven. Seven. Seven. ...Oh my gosh.

"Um, no, let's go."

On the ride home, Hayoon sits in the back with Seojun. Seojun's ability to make people feel relaxed is unmatched. He could even make introverts have the courage to start conversation.

"Can I ask a question?"

"What?"

"You have eight members and you're all sharing rooms. Did someone have to move so I could live there?"

Jihoon answers first. "No one had to move."

"Well not this week anyway."

"That was supposed to be Baekhyeon's room."

"But he spent all his time in mine and Junwoo's room. We joined the company at the same time and we each lead a unit. Most of our time is either spent leading our units or together."

"So, they just all ended up sharing the biggest room."

That's good. I didn't want one of the members to hate me before I even moved in.

"Oh. Wait. You're a unit leader. But you're number four. Aren't there only three units?" *Dance, vocals, and rap, right? Maybe I'm just dumb.*

"There are three. Kun hyung isn't a unit leader."

"There's no rule that the leaders need to be the oldest members. There are a few groups that have a member in the maknae line leading. But not many."

"He said he wanted to focus on composing. He writes most of our songs."

"He spends more time at the studio than at home."

"You can see his studio when you come to the company with us later this week."

"Have you ever seen a recording studio before?"

"Never."

Day 5

"Is everyone ready?"

Baekhyeon is counting the members before they get in the vehicles to leave. *Eight. All here.*

"Our bus is in the shop and we don't have to go far. We'll divide into two vehicles. Kun and Junwoo will drive."

Hayoon is leaning against the wall by Seojun. She's trying to keep her composure but this is the first time she's left the house with all the members together. The boys all did individual training the day before so she stayed home.

"Let's go."

As everyone is walking out, Baekhyeon walks with Hayoon and Seojun.

"Hayoon, the cameraman is coming to meet you today and give you your camera. He's normally one of the two behind the scenes cameramen we have at all the events but he got assigned to you for the next few weeks."

"Me? Just me?"

Seojun chips in, "He's a really nice guy."

"Why do I need my own cameraman? I thought I was supposed to record you guys."

"We're in a comeback so we don't have a lot of time to record for Peak Season. We recorded a few shows in advance but they want to take this comeback to make a special episode. We'll have a lot more cameramen than usual. Since you won't go on stage with us, you'll be separated from us sometimes."

"Do I have to do anything special?"

"Nope."

Seojun excitedly bounces away as he yells, "I'm going in Junwoo's car."

Hayoon looks back and forth between the cars quickly filling up.

"Where should I go?"

... no answer.

Baekhyeon looks between the two vehicles. *Aish.*

Hayoon takes a step back. "It's okay. I don't need to go today."

"That SUV can fit a third row but we took it out to put our duffels for dance practices. I think the seat is in the storage room..."

He takes a step toward the house but hesitates, looking down at his phone.

"It's okay. You guys will be late. You go. ...I still have some clothes to put away anyway."

She abruptly turns toward the house and leaves before her expression betrays her.

Maybe I should get the seat. What's ten minutes? He looks down to see the manager calling.

"Hello?... We're coming."

He lets her go.

As he's getting in the car, Hayoon reaches the door and glances back. No one realized she was getting left behind.

3

...But no one saw her.

-Dohyun

Day 6

Why does it have to be so early?

Hayoon squints open her eyes to shut off the alarm. She picks up her phone and checks the message from Baekhyeon late last night.

"The back row is at the company. The staff van will come pick you up at 7am. We'll meet you there."

She rolls out of bed to get dressed and runs outside to meet the van right at seven. She jumps in the front row. The sleepy staff, that haven't fallen back asleep, greet her.

They arrive at the venue and everyone piles out. No one says anything so Hayoon follows the crowd in. *I'll just find a quiet corner to sleep until the members come. I wonder if the cameraman will come with the members or the staff.*

"Hey! ...Hey!"

Hayoon looks down the hall. *Me?*

"Come here."

She hurries down to the staff member who called to her.

"You an intern?"

"No. I'm Park Hayoon. The members' new..."

She gets cut off.

"Busy?"

"...No?"

"Go backstage and help the lighting crew."

Backstage, okay.

Hayoon starts to walk away but stops to half turn back.

"Where?"

"Go down this hall, turn right."

Hayoon works diligently with the lighting crew until she hears her name from across the stage.

"Have you seen Hayoon?"

"Who?"

"Park Hayoon. She's the boys' new little sister. They told me she came in the staff van this morning."

"Sorry. Don't know."

Hayoon sets down the crate in her arms and walks toward the man. As he's looking around the stage, his eyes caught on her. He walks in her direction.

"Are you Hayoon?"

"Yes."

"Finally. Nice to meet you. I'm your cameraman, Lee Dohyun. You can call me Samchon, if you want."

They shake hands and he gives her an honest smile.

"Hello."

"Let's go talk about the next couple weeks."

She follows him to a quiet resting area with small tables and chairs.

He gestures to the chair with an open hand. "Please, take a seat."

"Thank you."

Ahhhh. Feels good to sit down. ...If I sit for too long, I might fall asleep.

Dohyun observes her body as she relaxes into the chair. Without asking or telling, he gets up and walks over to the vending machine.

Hayoon doesn't think much of it and examines her hands in his absence. *Will my hands blister?*

Why is she looking at her hands like that? Is she hurt? He returns with more questions buzzing in his head.

"Drink this."

Hayoon looks up to Dohyun and then down to the coffee in front of her.

"For me?"

"Mm." Dohyun confirms.

She quickly opens the cap and gulps down the coffee before remembering her manners.

"Thank you."

Must've been thirsty. Why was she working with the crew?

"What time did you get here?"

"Not sure. Maybe seven thirty."

"Why didn't you come with the boys? I went to their dressing room to find you but you weren't there."

"The third row isn't in the SUV. There wasn't any room."

"Oh. Okay. I'll give you your camera later when you're ready to leave. There are two storage cards in the pack but you only need one. The other you can use for whatever."

"Okay."

"I need to go over a lot more with you but the event is going to start soon. Let's head over and we can talk while it's going on."

She puts the cap on her coffee and slides it into her bag. She sneaks a glance toward the snack machine but gets caught.

"Do you want to buy something before we go?"

"Can I?"

"Go ahead."

Hayoon rushes over to the vending machine. She surveys her options. *I didn't get breakfast. Still a bit until lunch...* She selects a bread and shoves it in her bag with the coffee.

They walk together to the event and choose seats towards the back. He asks her about her first few days and they talk about his job the last couple years. She asks about all the events and things about the boys. He tells her what it will be like having him follow her around. Her conversation with Dohyun is the most comfortable she's been since she arrived. He's calmer than Seojun with the same effect. He's like a walking encyclopedia of the members, too.

"I probably don't need to say much about Seojun. He's like the never-ending energy supply of the group. When you start filming the show with them, stick with him. I promise you'll have fun."

"He was the first one to talk to me when I moved in."

"Baekhyeon, Junwoo, and Jihoon are closest in the group but Seojun is like the child they're raising. Have you gotten to spend much time with them? I know it's busy right now."

"Mmm... I met Baekhyeon at the company when they asked me to live with them. And then he told me you would be my cameraman for awhile but that's about it. I went shopping with Jihoon and Junwoo gave me a tour the first day."

"Junwoo? Junwoo gave you a tour of the house?"

"Yeah, right when I got dropped off before dinner that day. ...Why?"

"Junwoo doesn't talk much. Without a doubt, an introvert. He talks to his team in the dance studio but in shows, interviews, even concerts, he's the quietest member."

Hayoon opens her mouth to speak when the fans all stand and applaud. Dohyun hands Hayoon her coffee, that was sitting empty on the floor, and nods toward the side exit.

"Let's go. Time to eat and rest."

She follows him ahead of the crowd out the door and down the back hallway. They arrive at the room the same time as the boys.

"Hayoon!" She looks up to see Seojun call out to her. "How'd you like it?"

"It was good. I like the choreography to the second song."

Junwoo overhears from behind them. *Choreography?* He smiles in silent pride at her compliment.

"Here. Pass these out."

The manager sets two giant bags in her arms as he blazes past her into the room. Dohyun is already filming behind the scene footage and follows behind Hayoon as she makes her way to the middle table.

She finds the members' lunches in the bag. *Huh. No names. Guess it doesn't matter then.* She starts handing out the lunches in order so she doesn't forget who has one already.

"Baekhyeon."

"Thank you."

"Hakkun."

"Thank you."

"Junwoo."

He walks to her so she doesn't have to go to him. "Thanks, Hayoon."

He said my name.

"Jihoon, JJ, Jeongu, Minseong...Minseong?"

"He went to change. Put it on the table."

"Okay...Seojun."

"Here!" Seojun, with his always smiling face, jogs over to take his food. "Thanks."

And...nothing. Hayoon stares at the bottom of the bag. *Am I supposed to eat somewhere else?* She picks up the empty bags and heads toward the trashcan by the door. Dohyun is still filming as she drops the bags into the trash and keeps going out the door.

Where's she going? Dohyun gets up to do his job and follows her. *Didn't I tell her not to leave her cameraman behind?* She walks down the hall and pauses at the door to the staff room, looking inside.

The staff have a buffet lunch with sandwiches and fruit set out on the table. *Am I supposed to eat here? I'm probably not counted in the staff numbers. What if I eat and there's not enough for someone else?*

Dohyun watches as her hands draw into fists at her side. *What is she doing? Why doesn't she go in?*

Hayoon walks away and disappears into the crowd. He has no choice but to give up the chase after his coworker calls out to him. He heads into the staff room to eat lunch.

After their down time, he heads into the boys' dressing room but Hayoon isn't there. *Where did she go for almost two hours?* She enters the room as the manager gives the signal to head back out to the event stage. They meet up and head back to their original seats.

While watching the boys, Dohyun teaches Hayoon how to use the camera. They watch some of the BTS footage from previous shows and concerts on his phone.

"Give me your phone. I'll add my contact info so you can ask me if you have questions."

"Here. ...Thanks."

"There's someone at the company that's in charge of your videos but they mostly just do the editing so you can ask me."

"Okay. You'll still be at all the events, right?"

"Usually. There's a professional film crew for the show but I still go to film BTS. If they leave the country, I don't always go. We take turns."

"Ohhh... that makes sense. The company said I have to go back soon to deal with my passport stuff. Tomorrow, I think."

"You don't have a passport already?"

"I do but I didn't take it when I went to sign the contract. They need to scan it so they can get my visas for me later."

They talk for a bit longer until the event ends. Dohyun leaves at the same time as the boys but Hayoon waits for the staff van. This time, the sound crew pulls her in.

"Switch out the batteries in every mic pack and in-ear monitor. Put it in the members' order in the box."

"Okay."

I like this one. It's not heavy or difficult. Hayoon switches out all the batteries as told. Right as she's closing the lid, someone hollers at her to help carry tables. She puts her usual, agreeable smile on and gets to work.

Day 7

Uugggghhhhh. I should change my alarm ringtone. The next morning comes too soon as Hayoon rolls out of bed for the second day to catch the staff van. On her way out, she grabs one of Seojun's snacks from the pack. *Four left. Okay. I can take one. Breakfast of champions. Fighting!* She heads out to wait at the curb. *If I don't finish this now, I might not have time later.* She takes a big bite. Luckily, the ray of sunshine little brother had told her when they went shopping, she could eat his snacks. Hayoon chuckles thinking about his comment. He told her he would just make Jihoon buy him more. If he didn't, Baekhyeon would. *Must be nice to have brothers...*

The van comes as the final bite goes missing from the wrapper. She crinkles the wrapper up and puts it in her bag before boarding.

"We need all hands-on deck today. You! Today, don't go to lighting. The stage set up team will need help."

Do they still think I'm an intern? Is that a promotion or a demotion? Stage set up sounds fun.

She follows the hallway down to the stage. She doesn't even have to ask before someone yells, "Come over here and hold this."

She jogs over to a middle-aged man in a baseball cap. He puts a rope in her hand and commands her, "Stay here."

Hayoon looks curiously up to the ceiling and notices a series of pulleys. *Interesting.* Soon, the man comes back with an actual intern.

"You guys are going to be a team today. This stuff is expensive, okay? No matter what, you can't let it drop. When I signal to you, pull it until I yell stop."

Hayoon greets the intern and they set to work. By the seventh rope, Hayoon is starting to sweat.

"Pull!"

"Stop!"

The intern's phone rings and he releases the rope. The full weight of it shocks Hayoon and the rope starts to slip through her hands.

"Grab it!" The man yells from the front of the stage. She holds on to the rope with all her strength, wrapping it around her wrist on one side. Realizing her weight alone might not be enough, she looks around frantically.

She sees Dohyun approach the stage.

"Lee Dohyun!"

He jerks his head up from looking at his camera to her strained face. He sprints over to grab the rope. They work together to pull the stage set piece up.

"Stop!"

"Lock it in."

Hayoon breathes heavy, stretching her hands to recover.

Dohyun notices Hayoon's fatigue and hollers over, "We've got to go."

They get waved away and head down the hall to where they first talked yesterday.

Dohyun sets the camera down and walks straight to the coffee machine. "Coffee?"

"Yes, please."

"How did you end up on the stage crew?"

She quietly answers, "I don't know."

He sets the coffee down in front of her but she just stares at it. *Does she not like this kind?*

Sitting opposite of her, Dohyun can't see what she's doing as she stares at her lap. Hayoon opens her hands to examine the source of her pain.

"You okay?"

She snaps out of it and maintains her positive attitude... even if it's a lie.

"Yup."

She smiles up at him as she picks the coffee up to open it.

Did she just wince? Dohyun takes the coffee from her and takes the cap off, holding it out to drop in her hand.

"Thanks," she says with forced cheerfulness as her hand opens flat to accept the cap. Her hand lifts the bottle to her lips.

Was that rope burn? ...I don't get it. They told me she was going to be their little sister. How did she end up a manual laborer? Something's not right.

Hayoon sees Dohyun check his watch and knows the time is coming to go to the event floor.

"Can I buy some bread before we go?"

"We've got two minutes still." Dohyun nods toward the machine.

"Do you want anything?"

"No thanks."

...

"Got it."

"Let's go."

They approach the doors to the venue floor but get stopped by the group's manager.

"Hayoon, I was looking for you. The boys have a double concert in a few days but the bus won't be fixed by then. We're using the companies van but the boys will need to bring more bags..."

"Do you want me to ride in the staff van?"

"I'll pick her up." *Then she won't have to work for the crew.*

Manager-nim asks Hayoon, "Are you okay with that?"

She shakes her head happily. *Saved.*

"Okay, it's set. Catch you guys later."

Hayoon keeps up with Dohyun's pace as he strides to their seats. "Are you sure you don't mind?"

"No problem."

They sit down right as the boys come on stage. The fans roar around them and Dohyun has to raise his voice to be heard.

"I can take you home tonight, too."

"Really?!?"

He chuckles at her reaction. "Happy?"

She shakes her head heartily in response.

Ohhh, so that's her genuine smile. Cute.

"You look like my niece when I gave her a princess crown." He chuckles, enjoying her joyful reaction.

At lunch time, they go to the members' dressing room only for Dohyun to discover Hayoon is missing ten minutes later. *Is this girl studying magic tricks? Where does she disappear to?*

Unlike the day before, he goes to find her. He checks the stage, the staff room, outside, and even asks a woman coming out of the bathroom if there was someone else in there. *How did she disappear into thin air? ...At least I know she'll come back.*

Dohyun takes his camera into the staff room and grabs himself a plate of food. He plops it down on the table, startling his coworker.

"Something up?"

"You know the boys' little sister, Hayoon?"

"Never met her but I heard she was coming."

"I can't find her."

"Huh? What do you mean?"

"She was with me one minute and then I turned around and she wasn't there."

"She probably just went to chill or play on her phone in the dressing room."

Dohyun shakes his head. "I checked."

He finishes eating and looks at his footage from earlier, trying to find the last time she was in frame.

Gotcha! Woooww, she seriously just slipped out and no one noticed. He rewinds it to watch again. *Wait a minute...* He rewinds it one more time and freezes it when she gets to the door. His gears start turning as he gets out his laptop to pull up the footage from the day before. *Go, go, go, go, stop!* His heart sinks. *She looked back. Both times. ...But no one saw her.* He stares at his screen. Her smile doesn't match the depth in her eyes. Dohyun deep sighs and packs up his stuff to go find her.

He finds her at the intersection of two hallways, going toward the dressing room.

"Hey!"

"Hi."

"I was looking for you."

"Oh, sorry. What's up?"

"I didn't see you in the boys' room so I was wondering where you were."

"Oh..I umm... just found a quiet place to eat. There were a lot of people in there."

Just because there were too many people?

"How was your lunch?"

"Good." *I'm not exactly lying. As far as bread goes, it wasn't bad. That counts...right?*

That's it? Just good? ...Did your stomach just growl? Dohyun decides to leave it alone and not push her.

"That's good. Let's head back in. It should be over before dinner and then I'll drop you off."

"Okay, thanks."

4

She can dance?

-Junwoo

Day 8

Hayoon wakes up before the boys and sets up camp on the couch to watch their content. *Today, I'll knock out music videos and dance practices. Tomorrow, their show. ...Probably can't finish it all. ...The schedule's empty for days after the double concert. I'll finish it then.*

She starts the first music video but taps the space bar when she hears something from down the hall. *Headphones.* She leaves her laptop on the couch to retrieve her headphones from her room.

Back on the couch, Hayoon gets enthralled in watching their videos and doesn't notice Baekhyeon pass behind her. A few minutes later, Junwoo comes out from his room. He stops behind her as she clicks back and forth in the dance practice video. She watches the same ten seconds three times before pulling up the performance video.

Baekhyeon is walking back to his room when he asks Junwoo, "What are you watching?"

Junwoo just nods to Hayoon but doesn't speak. They both watch as Hayoon splits the screen and watches the two videos, same ten seconds, back-to-back.

Without knowing she has company, Hayoon whispers, "He's injured."

Baekhyeon leans over the back of the couch and loudly asks, "Huh?" right in Hayoon's ear.

She gets startled by his sudden presence and tumbles forward. Baekhyeon reaches for her laptop. Simultaneously, Junwoo reaches for her. He caught her at an impossible angle and slowly lowers her to the ground.

She shot up and whipped off her headphones. Instead of speaking, she stares at them. She looks back and forth between them like she's watching a tennis match.

Baekhyeon looks at the laptop in his hand and is the first to ask, "Why compare?"

She hesitantly points to Junwoo and answers, "He's injured."

Junwoo's eyes pop open in surprise. *How did you know?!?*

Baekhyeon hits the space bar to play the video again. One more tap to stop the dance video. One more tap to watch the performance video.

"His left ankle... dance practice."

Junwoo asks, "How did you know?" His pitch rising at the end, not in accusation but in genuine curiosity.

Baekhyeon gives him the side eye, "You really were injured?" His tone edged with disbelief.

Junwoo nods his head in confirmation. "I was in the studio the day before. Rolled my ankle. No big deal."

Jihoon calls their leader from his room. He hands the laptop to Junwoo and walks off.

Junwoo circles around the couch to sit next to where Hayoon was earlier, leaving a space for her. He watches the footage again and motions for his new little sister to sit down.

"My timing isn't off. How could you tell?"

"At first, I wasn't a hundred percent sure so I pulled up the second clip to compare. The difference isn't in your steps or your timing."

Junwoo looks at her questioningly.

"Look." She reaches across Junwoo's lap to take the clip back ten seconds. "The difference is in your weight distribution."

"Weight distribution?"

"Yeah, watch."

She plays the clip and then pauses it, mid step.

"Right...here! Look at the angle of your body. Your weight is slightly displaced to the right side."

"Huh... it is."

What if he gets mad, I pointed out his fault? "It's not obvious. Trust me. No one else will know."

"So how did you know?"

"Mmmm... they told me you debuted three years ago. I'm guessing you danced before that, too. You're on the dance unit and the leader on top of that. Compensating was probably second nature. You didn't even have to think about it because your body awareness and mechanics are better than others."

Is she complimenting me? ... Wait a minute. How does she know so much about dancing?

"Oh." Junwoo responds thoughtfully.

Day 9

"Is everyone going today?" Baekhyeon is holding the two car keys, ready to leave for the company.

If everyone else goes, I don't get to.

"Not us." Jihoon and Jeongu decide to stay at the soon-to-be quiet house.

Baekhyeon asks Junwoo, "Which car do you want?"

He looks to Hayoon and asks, "What unit do you want to go with?"

Ahhhh! I get to go!

Seojun links arms with Hayoon, "Come with us! We get to film a dance challenge for the next release."

She looks to Junwoo for approval, "Can I?"

He doesn't answer her right away but responds to Baekhyeon instead. "SUV."

Baekhyeon tosses him the keys and yells, "Vocal unit, roll out."

Junwoo glances at Hayoon, "Let's go."

Yay! Yay! Yay! I get to go to the dance studio!

Seojun drags her out the door. She practically has to jog to keep up. She can hear Junwoo chuckling and looks back over her shoulder. This time, her smile was real.

Hayoon sits by the front mirrors and watches them practice for the challenge. It's only twelve seconds long but they practice the whole song while they're there.

"You guys change and I'll check lighting."

Yunjae and Seojun pick up their bags to leave but Junwoo stops them.

"Change here. I'll take Hayoon with me."

She practically leaps off the floor to rush after him. He hands her the tripod.

"Can you carry this?"

They walk down the hall a short way to an empty room.

"This room wasn't being used and it's easy to control the light. Set it here."

She listens and sets the tripod down. He attaches his phone and opens the camera to check the background.

"Can you record a few second for me?"

"Okay."

Hayoon smiles as she switches from watching him to the phone and back again. After one attempt, he joins her to watch the recording.

"The light isn't right. Let's try again."

He adjusts the light in the room and tells her, "Switch places with me."

Me?

Her astonished facial expression makes him smile. "You can just stand there." Three seconds in, he says over the music, "I'm going to get the light for the phone. Wait there."

Junwoo exits the room without pausing the music and unbeknownst to Hayoon, without stopping the camera from recording.

It takes all of two seconds for Hayoon to start dancing. Her smile, unintentionally, giving away her true happiness. A smile like that can't be faked. She doesn't stop at the twelve second challenge but keeps going until she hears footsteps approaching, pulling her back to reality.

The door opens and Hayoon appears to be still standing obediently in place where Junwoo put her. He attaches the light and nods in satisfaction.

"Better. We can head back now."

Hayoon follows behind him and then splits off to go find Seojun when they get to the dance studio.

Junwoo stares at his phone to compare the lighting one last time to make sure he made the right judgement call. *Yup...much better.* His finger is hovering over the trash can button when he sees her start to move. He looks up to where she's sitting, chatting with Seojun and JJ. His thumb moves to turn down the volume on his phone, knowing she has no idea the camera was still rolling. He watches her dance, awestruck. *She can dance? Why didn't she tell us? ...Does the company know? Baekhyeon can't know. He would've told me, right?* He rewinds the video to watch it again. His head is spinning with possibilities.

Truth is, they don't know much about her. Ever since he saw her on the balcony, hair dancing in the wind with her face turned up to the sky, he knew her presence wasn't ordinary. Now, his curiosity is intensified tenfold.

Day 10

Dohyun shows up to get Hayoon as the boys load into the van. Dohyun steps out of the car to film her friendly wave and approach. She jogs down to his car and opens the front door. She greets him, "Good morning!"

"Morning." Dohyun matches her energy.

He sets his camera in its bag and hands Hayoon a coffee.

"Thanks!"

She opens the lid and takes a long drink. "Do they always have concerts two days in a row?"

"In Seoul, often. Overseas... depends on the city."

"Must be a long day for you and the staff."

"Yeah, but it's fun, too. Especially watching the fans."

"Like the fan showcase?"

"Better. Fan showcases and events have a lot less people than concerts. The venue is bigger, too. Do you want to watch from the floor or backstage?"

"I can choose?"

"Most likely. If we stand on the floor, we'll stand in front of the barriers that separate the fans from the stage. It's where security and a few staff will be. Backstage, you can pick the side but it's not the best view. You only see their sides and backs."

"Which place has less people?"

"The barrier zone has less people but everyone in the venue is right behind you."

"Hmmm."

He glances over at Hayoon as she debates which one to choose.

That's right. She's an introvert. Doesn't like crowds.

"There's a live feed in the dressing room if you want somewhere quieter. Most staff are needed during the concert so few are left in there."

Hayoon sips her coffee while deliberating.

"How about the barrier? ...But if the fans are too close, can we go to the dressing room?"

"Sounds good."

She's gone? Again?!?

Dohyun scans the room while the boys are eating their meal before the concert and staff are fluttering around in final preparations. But no Hayoon.

How did this happen again? What is she? A ninja?

Manager-nim starts laying out the sleeping pads for the boys to rest on with the time remaining. Junwoo and Jihoon lay down in front of Dohyun.

"Did you guys see Hayoon?"

They both search around the room before answering, "No."

Dohyun picks up his camera and goes on a hunt. He searches for Hayoon for twenty minutes before giving up. *This venue is huge. How am I supposed to find her? ...Would she have left? Ugh. Tomorrow, I won't let you escape.*

Seojun bounces around the room waiting for the concert to start while Minseong chases after him. Baekhyeon and Hakkun were finishing their makeup. Hayoon sits off to the side taking in the lively scene in front of her. *This is like a whole different world.*

"Time to go!"

The boys all pile out of the room with the staff supporting them on all sides. Hayoon follows at a safe distance behind the chaos. She watches as they do the final checks on their mics and in-ears.

Dohyun gives Hayoon the signal to head out to the barrier zone before the boys are set in place. As Hayoon turns to follow him, someone grabs her arm.

"Take this back to the dressing room."

They drop a crate in her arms, causing her to wince. She feels warmth on her hand but doesn't dare try to check for fear of dropping the box. She calls out to Dohyun.

"I'll drop this off and go find you."

He wants to disagree but the fan noise becomes deafening with the countdown. *She's going to miss their entrance.* He shrugs it off and goes down to the barrier so she can find him. *There's always tomorrow, I guess.*

Hayoon walks swiftly down the hall to drop the box on the table. Sure enough, her hand is bleeding. She washes it in the bathroom and heads back into the dressing room. She digs around in her bag until she finds a bandage. She checks the live feed. *I'm missing it.* Hayoon sighs in disappointment but doesn't leave to find Dohyun. Instead, she flips the box on its side to find where it's broken. *What if someone else gets hurt?* She finds electrical tape and repairs the box. She checks the live feed before running out.

She meets up with Dohyun in the barrier to watch the remaining concert. He records her BTS as she keeps her eyes glued to the boys' performance. She becomes uncontainably excited at the dance break. She tugs on Dohyun's sleeve as she jumps up and down.

"Look at Junwoo oppa!"

Dohyun grins from behind the camera at her innocent reaction to their performance. She reminds him of young fans who see them for the first time. *Has she never been to a concert before? Cute.*

Day 11

Is she gonna run?

Dohyun chooses a seat close to the door to be ready to chase. Hayoon is passing out the boys' food like usual.

Manager-nim sets coffee on the table beside her.

"These, too."

Hayoon obeys, handing out all the food and coffee. She picks up the cup carriers and empty bags to throw away.

Dohyun starts to rise off the chair to follow. *Wait…she'll look back first.*

He checks his phone to mask his intentions.

Go! He strides toward the door. Dohyun turns left and quickens his pace. Suddenly, a sizeable group of staff block his view. *No, no, no. Yes!* The staff clear out as he sees the door close to the stairs.

He opens the door to find Hayoon sitting on the third step, leaning against the railing, eating a piece of bread. Her eyes were barely open as she stares at the floor, chewing her 'lunch.'

He sets his camera down, recording, on a table off to the side and crouches down in front of her.

She breaks into a soft smile when he appears in front of her view.

She asks, "Why aren't you resting? Are you hungry?"

She holds out her bread to him. He shakes his head in refusal. Hayoon places her hand on the railing to stand, "I can get you a new one."

Dohyun takes her hand off the rail and tugs it gently to pull her back down. Her smile fades away at his worried expression as she lowers down to his eye level.

"Did you not like the bento box? I can get you something else."

Hayoon's eyes dart to the floor and she shakes her head. Her fingers curl around the bottom of her shorts. Dohyun notices her fist and, after spending multiple long days with her, knows what it means.

"You didn't eat?"

She forces a smile before answering. "It's okay. I brought bread."

She gazes into his prodding eyes. *I should tell him the truth.* "There was no food for me."

"What? Why didn't they order the same number as yesterday?"

She casts her eyes back down and mumbles, "They did."

"What?!?" He stands to angle his body away from her to calm his anger. "And last time?"

She doesn't answer. *Is he mad at me? He's the only person who looks out for me. I hope he's not mad.*

I knew something wasn't right. Why didn't I say anything? Aish. A little sister? What crap!

Hayoon doesn't want him to feel distressed so she smiles up at him to soothe his worries. "It's okay. Yesterday, I wasn't that hungry and today, I brought bread."

He looks down to see her waving her bread as proof. *Little fool. Even now, you're smiling. How could anyone not want you as a little sister?*

Dohyun sighs in an attempt to blow out his anger and avoid talking harshly. He doesn't want her to think his frustration is directed at her. He crouches down again to return her smile.

"Okay. Bring your bread back to the dressing room so you can rest."

He rises to get his camera but she doesn't budge.

"You head back first."

He ruffles her hair. "Okay."

Dohyun leaves Hayoon in the stairwell to confirm a suspicion. He enters the dressing room quietly and counts the resting places. *Eight. No place for her.* He watches the members nap and play on their phones, oblivious to the damage they're doing.

The members start getting ready but neither Dohyun or Hayoon are present. Dohyun opens the doors to the stairwell and again, secretly sets up his camera. He sits beside her and gently taps her arm to wake her up. The moment she opens her eyes, her lips turn up into a smile. That sleepy smile glows when he hands her gimbap and coffee.

"Thanks!"

She hurriedly opens the container but doesn't eat. She picks up the first piece and holds it out to him.

"Want some?"

"You eat. I already ate."

She shoves it in her mouth. Her glowing smile brightens with satisfaction as she chews.

Dohyun watches her happily eat like a real uncle doting on his niece. He takes the cap off the coffee and holds it for her so she can take a sip when she wants.

How are you always so cheerful? Stand up for yourself. Throw a tantrum. Do something. Anything.

She covers her mouth and enthusiastically reports, "It's really good."

"Good. Eat up so we can head back. They'll start to look for you soon."

She responds without thinking, "Don't worry. They won't look for me."

Dohyun finds it hard to keep smiling and hold back his sighs.

"Aren't you mad at them?"

"Why?"

"You're supposed to be a part of the group. A part of their family. But you ended up hungry and covered in injuries."

"You can't blame them."

I should've known she would answer like that.

"Their company decided to give them a little sister. They might not have wanted me. They don't mean to forget me. They're just busy right now. Chasing their dreams."

Seems like she's not ready to stand up for herself.

"What's your dream?"

"Me? Hmmm."

He waits patiently, hoping she will answer. Her eyes' gaze intensifies as she stares into her coffee.

"I want someone by my side who thinks I'm worth it."

"Worth it?" *Worth what?*

She takes a bite and considers how to answer. Dohyun rotates his body toward her, ready to listen.

"Someone who thinks I'm worth their time, their care, their protection. You know when you get sick and you just want someone to hold your hand until you fall asleep. Or when something really good happens to you and you just want to run and tell them. They'll pat your head and compliment you."

Wow. She truly is a good kid. These idiots.

Hayoon's unconventional answer makes Dohyun's heart unsettled. *She doesn't want to travel overseas, high paying job or to perform on a big stage. She just wants someone to tell her, "Good job."*

"Like a big brother?"

She thinks for a second before widening her smile, shaking her head. "Yeah, like a big brother."

"What about your family?"

"Mmmmm..." She shoves food in her mouth before answering. "I don't have any."

He chooses not to ask more and redirects.

"I thought you'd say your dream was to be a dancer."

She cocked her head to the side to question him. "How'd you know I like dance?"

"I saw you doing some of the choreography during the concert."

"Oh."

He tries to be considerate of her shyness and moves on.

"It's about time to head back. Give me that. Here. Take your coffee."

5

They might not want me...

-Hayoon

Day 12

The day after the second concert, Hayoon wakes up to an oddly quiet house. She brushes her teeth and fills up her water cup before heading to the second-floor landing with her laptop.

She pulls up Peak Season to watch before filming with them next week. The groups' intro starts playing…

…Why don't I hear Seojun?

Hayoon pauses the video and sets her laptop on the floor. She walks downstairs but doesn't hear anyone. She knocks on Seojun's door but no one answers. She tries Junwoo's room. No answer. She treks back into her room to double check the schedule. Nothing is written for the next three days.

Where'd they all go? Practice?

She jogs back up the stairs to retrieve her laptop and phone. *He did say I could ask if I questions.* She scans through her contacts to find Dohyun and sends a text.

"Do you know where the boys are? There's nothing on the schedule."

"Japan. There's a different schedule for international events."

…

"Did Baekhyeon tell you they need you to go to the company?"

"No. When?"

"Today."

A new message banner comes down on her phone.

"I just got a text."

"They want me there, too. I'll pick you up."

"What time?"

"11"

"ok"

Hayoon rushes to take a shower and dry her hair. She's slipping on her shoes when Dohyun texts her.

"here"

She pushes the door open and dashes out to meet him.

A company staff member is sitting across from Hayoon at the conference room table. Dohyun is filming from beside her. She still feels strange having someone film her every movement.

The staff taps the papers on the table to straighten the pile. She slides the stack over to Hayoon and briefs her on what's left.

"We missed a few papers last time. Not many. Family emergency contact and measurements are the most important. You can start filling this out and I'll call someone over from wardrobe to take your measurements."

Hayoon asks curiously, "Measurements?"

"There are some episodes of Peak Season where you can't wear your own clothes. Sometimes it's for the activity, like swimming, and sometimes it to separate into teams for competition."

"Okay."

"Excuse me." She leaves the conference room to call wardrobe.

The top paper reads, "Family Emergency Contact List."

Hayoon picks up the pen to write but her hand doesn't move. She stares at the paper with one empty line after another. Her pen lowers to the page but remains still, leaving nothing more than a single dot.

Dohyun moves his face away from behind the camera. *Why isn't she writing? Is she sick?* Suddenly, it dawns on him as he recalls his talk with Hayoon on the stairs. *Idiot. She doesn't have anyone to write down.*

Dohyun places the camera on the table and steps closer. He takes the pen out of her hand and slides the paper over. Hayoon stays frozen, hand hovering, like someone cast a spell on her. He fills in his name and phone number. In the furthest column, he writes, "Samchon."

He slides the paper back in front of her and picks up his camera. Hayoon reads what he wrote and tilts her face up to look at him. Her eyes become glossy with emotion as deep as the ocean. For once, she doesn't force herself to mask it. He forgets the camera and puts a hand on her shoulder in comfort.

She wants to thank him but all that comes out is a whispered word, "Samchon."

She called me Samchon. He blinks the water from his eyes as the staff member comes back in.

"How are we doing?"

"What are you going to get?"

Hayoon and Dohyun are reading the coffee shop menu for a late lunch.

"Mmmm. Sandwich and an americano?"

Dohyun asks, "That one?"

She grunts in confirmation.

"Hot or iced?"

"Hot."

"Okay. I'll order. Go find a seat."

Hayoon curves around the tables to choose one by the window. She stands beside the table and calls out, "Samchon!"

Hayoon points to the table in question. He smiles and shakes his head in agreement. *Exactly who adopted her?* He chuckles to himself and moves up in line to order.

When the food is ready, Dohyun brings it to their table.

"Thank you."

Hayoon helps him take the sandwiches and coffees off the tray. She devours her sandwich as she listens to him tell funny stories about fans.

As Dohyun is finishing off his coffee, she asks, "When do they come back from Japan?"

"In two days. Afternoon flight, I think."

"Oh. Okay."

"Hayoon," he says somberly.

She waits for him to continue.

She didn't tell me about her injuries. Should I play dumb? She calls me Samchon. I can say something, right?

"Take care of your hands, okay? Don't let it get infected."

She slides them off the table even though there's no point in hiding.

He saw.

"While the boys are in Japan, take care of yourself. If you need me, call me."

"I will."

Day 14

"Hayoon!"

Hayoon comes briskly down the stairs to greet Seojun. "How was Japan?"

"We won."

Most of the boys pass by without saying anything while Seojun tells her about their music show victory. Baekhyeon hollers from the back of the group. "Don't forget about unit practice tomorrow. We leave at ten."

Junwoo momentarily stops in front of Hayoon. "You're coming with me tomorrow, right?"

"Is that okay?"

"You can always come with us."

"Really?"

"If you want to."

There it is. Her real smile.

Seojun puts his arm around her shoulders and answers for her, "She does."

Junwoo can't help but smile when he sees her sincere happiness. "I'm going to unpack. See you tomorrow."

Day 15

Hayoon slides her shoes on beside Seojun and Minseong. She finishes first and heads out the door, steps ahead of them.

Seojun asks Minseong, "Are you going to dance or vocal unit today?"

Baekhyeon answers for him as he shoves them out the door, "Dance."

Thunk. Minseong runs into a halted Hayoon. Seojun dodges right to avoid the collision.

"Hayoon?" Baekhyeon comes up from behind to place a hand on her shoulder, bringing her out of the haze.

"Sorry. You okay?"

Junwoo is the last out the door and shoos away their youngest members. *Why isn't she getting in?*

There's not going to be room for me.

"Hayoon, come on."

Baekhyeon takes a step toward the van. His hand slides off her shoulder as she steps in the opposite direction.

Why did she move back? Junwoo moves his gaze from her feet to her face; her eyes meeting his. *Hesitancy? Worry?*

"I..." *What excuse can I make?*

"Let's go." Junwoo encourages her, puzzled by her actions.

She reluctantly trails behind Baekheyon as he leads the way. She arrives at the van door a foot in front of Junwoo.

"Do you want shotgun or the back?"

"Huh?"

Junwoo opens the front door. "Baekhyeon's driving. Where do you want to sit?"

Inside the van, Seojun hilariously boots Yunjae out of his seat. "Hayoon, sit here!"

Yunjae's knees hit the ground with a thud. "Seojun!"

Hayoon occupies the newly vacant seat. *How could I ride with them now but not before?* She stretches her neck to look around. *Is it because they have no bags? ...Whatever.*

The company comes into view up ahead and she can't stop the smile from spreading across her face. *I wonder what choreography they'll be practicing today.*

Junwoo abruptly stops dancing mid song. The rest of the dance unit looks to him for guidance. He stares at himself in the mirror trying to come up with a solution.

Minseong leans over to ask Seojun in a whisper, "What's wrong?"

All he gets in return is a shoulder shrug. Yunjae, being three years older than Seojun, clues them in. "It doesn't fit."

The two youngest dancers are still confused.

Yunjae rolls his eyes and expands his previous comment. "The choreography isn't matching well with the music. After Jeongu's rap and we change positions, we start on an odd beat."

"Perfectionist," Minseong says teasingly.

Junwoo hears their chatter and asks, "Any ideas?"

They all work on it individually; trying to change the choreography before, choreography after or even members' positions. Junwoo sees them struggling and calls a break. "Give me a minute. You guys take five."

Yunjae, Minseong, and Seojun rest close to Hayoon, where their drinks are.

Hayoon observes Junwoo as he replays that part of the song twice. She respects Junwoo's leadership and trusts his talent but still...

Should I tell him I can fix it? What if he gets mad at me for overstepping? Besides Seojun, he's the only one to ask what I want. She squirms on the couch, readjusting her legs in indecisiveness. *I can't just sit back and watch him frustrated.*

She leans over to tap Yunjae on the shoulder. He spins around to face her.

"Why don't you add a step back after the position change?"

"What?"

"The choreography isn't perfectly syncing with the music, right?"

"Yeah...?"

"After you move positions, why not add a left-right step back? Take a count from the transition. Legs step back left-right, arms opposite, swinging up to start position of the next dance section."

Yunjae stays seated but moves his arms through what she instructed to verify. She reaches out to adjust his right arm to move more fluidly into the next step. "Ahhh, I get it." Yunjae stands up to combine feet with arms. "It really works!"

She gestures toward Junwoo. Yunjae jogs over to him.

Hopefully, he doesn't find out it was me. It's better that way.

JJ shows Junwoo her idea and they try it together with the music. Junwoo's stressed expression is replaced with happiness mixed with relief.

He likes it.

She goes to the bathroom to avoid his possible suspicion and save herself from explanation.

On the other side of the studio, Junwoo pats Yunjae on the back.

"Good idea."

"It wasn't me..." Yunjae points to the couch but no one's there. He murmurs, "She was just here."

Hayoon? ...Looks like I wasn't wrong.

The boys run through the choreography in its entirety several times, fixing small details. The third time through, Junwoo observes Hayoon in the mirror while they dance. She doesn't look like a typical fan watching them perform. Her eyes were locked in, focused on each step.

Junwoo calls it quits for the day. He shuts down the audio system as the other three boys collect their drinks by Hayoon. She takes her place behind them as they start walking towards the door. Seojun and Minseong are betting on what Jihoon is going to make for dinner. JJ couldn't care less about dinner as he's flipping through social media.

Junwoo catches Hayoon's wrist from behind, startling her. She looks down at their hands before raising her head to meet his eyes.

"Thank you."

Junwoo releases her wrist and quickens his pace to pass her to join up with Yunjae.

Hayoon is left confused. *For what? ...Does he know about earlier?*

Day 16

"Baekhyeon, Junwoo, Jihoon, and Seojun in group one. Kun, JJ, Jeongu, Minseong, and Hayoon in group two."

Sigh. Junwoo and Seojun are both on the other team. Oh well. I can do this!

Hayoon listens attentively to PD-nim explain the rules to the competition. She doesn't want to drag down her team in her first episode.

"Today's Peak Season competition is divided into two stages. Stage one. Solve riddles to win item cards for the second stage scavenger hunt. Each riddle your team solves will allow you to collect one more item in the scavenger hunt. One point for each riddle and one point for each item. You have to make it back to base camp before forty-five minutes is up for your items to count."

Jihoon asks the question everyone is wondering, "How do we get to the scavenger hunt from base camp?"

"You run."

"What?!?"

"From here to the grocery store is only slightly over a mile."

"Only?" Jihoon and Jeongu ask simultaneously.

"Everyone ready? Forty-five-minute count ready? ...Go!"

The teams run to their game zones to start solving riddles. Hayoon scans the table and instantly solves two out of eight riddles. She reaches out her hand but retracts it swiftly.

If I answer, the camera will only be on me. ...but if I hand it over...

Hayoon picks up the riddles and hands them to Kun who stands beside her. She blurts out the answer and he takes off to the table of item cards.

Jeongu and Minseong each solve one at the same time and race over to get cards together. Hayoon gets another and shoves it in Kun's hand right as he returns from getting the first cards. She gets two more and gives them to Yunjae. There's only one left on the table. She reads it over and over again but can't make sense of it.

The other team leaves base camp as Minseong and Kun return.

"They're leaving," JJ exclaims from the card table.

Kun speaks logically, "They still have a card they didn't get but they're probably worried about time. We only have 32 minutes left and the store is a mile away. Even if we run a ten-minute mile there and back, we'll only have twelve minutes to find the 7 items. Forget it. Let's go."

They ditch the last riddle and start running to the store with seven out of the eight item cards in their hands. As they're running, Hayoon keeps repeating the riddle in her head.

While running, her team discusses their strategy.

Jeongu suggests, "Let's get the items in the order of the aisles so we don't have to run all over."

As oldest, Kun has a rational suggestion. "Why don't we divide and conquer?"

Jeongu agrees, "That'll be faster. Who can take two cards?"

"Whoever has two, they should be close to each other."

Kun reads all the cards in his hand and gives his team members their items. He gives himself and JJ two cards and everyone else one.

Hayoon reads her card to submit it to memory as they run.

Oh! I got it! I know the riddle. ...If we make it back in time, maybe I can get the card.

They enter the store and split up to search. She sees Junwoo chase after Seojun with the item she needs in hand.

Better hurry.

She shoves down her fear of too many people staring at her and runs through the store. She finds the aisle and her eyes scan the shelves in laser focus.

No! They're out!

She looks around frantically. *Samchon?* She looks to her shadow of a cameraman but knows he can't help. Her sight lands on an employee and she jogs over to him.

"Do you have any more of this in the back? The spicy crawfish flavor?"

"Uhhh... let me check."

The store employee pulls out his scanner and checks stock.

"...It says we have eight... They might still be in the back. We got a delivery truck this morning."

"Can you get me one?"

"The pallets are on the top shelf for the night crew. I can't get to it."

"Can I see?"

Her urgency and desire to win for her team members temporarily overrides her introverted personality. Watching her persist causes Dohyun's eyebrows to rise in surprise.

"We're not supposed to..."

"Please," she begs.

"Okay. Come with me."

She follows him hopeful and sees Kun two aisles down. She raises her voice to get his attention, "They're out. I'm going to the back. I'll catch up to you guys later."

Hayoon arrives at the pallet and stares straight up to the mountainous storage shelf in front of her.

"It should be on that pallet on the top shelf."

Although it's only three shelves high, they're industrial metal shelves five feet tall.

Hayoon doesn't think twice before asking, "If I can get it, can I take it?"

Dohyun nearly drops his camera in shock. He grabs the bottom of her shirt as she steps forward. Hayoon ignores him, waiting for the employee's reply.

"Heck, if you can get it, I'll give it to you for free." His sarcasm is completely lost in her one-track mind.

Dohyun lets his hand release as she approaches the shelf. The employee's mouth gapes open as she pulls herself up to the second level.

One minute later, her feet hit the floor, face full of pride.

"Got it. Let's go."

She turns back to yell at the employee, "Thanks!"

Daebak.

Hayoon and her shadow reach the front of the store. *They must've left already.*

She sprints out of the store to catch...*BOOM!*

"Hayoon!" Dohyun screams as Hayoon is hit by a car. She's thrown to the ground and rolls several feet before coming to a stop. Facing down, Hayoon pushes herself up to her knees. Dohyun reaches her side and helps her stand. The car owner steps out of his vehicle to check her condition.

"I'm okay. I got to go."

She jogs a handful of steps before Dohyun grabs her arm.

"Stop!"

"I can't."

She shakes her arm free and picks up her jogging pace. Dohyun continues trying to reason with her.

"Hayoon, you just got hit by a car. You're bleeding."

"Nothing's broken. I need to catch up. I know the last riddle."

"Why are you doing this to yourself? They didn't even tell you when they left the country! They left you behind!"

"They might not want me but they need me to win. I can't let them down."

Dohyun can see her determination and surrenders. He chases after her, struggling to keep up with her pace.

Half a mile in, she catches up to her team and matches Minseong's cadence.

"Give your apple to Jeongu. I know the last riddle. We can get one more point."

They both hand over their items and split from the group as they enter base camp. Hayoon goes with Minseong to get the last card but then drops behind as he rejoins their team. Minseong hands over their winning point to PD-nim. PD-nim accepts the last-minute card and declares them as winners. They jump up and down, cheering, in victory.

We won. She sighs in relief. *They look happy.* Her weak smile, a stark contrast to the pain in her eyes.

Hayoon makes her way, seemingly unnoticed, into their base camp house for the night. She sits on the floor of her bathroom to check her injuries. *Thank goodness I wore black sweatpants. Can barely tell.* Taking her pants off with care, she winces at the pain. *Probably faster to clean it in the shower.*

She turns on the water to warm and steps in the shower. As the first drop of water hits her injury, she jerks back, sucking air in through her teeth.

Hayoon grabs a hand towel and puts it in her mouth. She bears down on the towel and steps fully into the shower. She stares at her legs as the blood streams down and pools around her feet before going down the drain.

6

You finally stopped hiding.

-Junwoo

Day 17

"Hyung, I don't think there's enough time. Seojun goes further than me and I almost didn't make it."

Hayoon leans against the front mirror wall observing Junwoo's reaction to what Yunjae said. Junwoo's eyes zigzag across the floor, running through the choreography in his mind. His mind slows as an idea occurs to him.

Time to find out if I'm right. Junwoo meets Hayoon's eyes as his slow stride closes the distance between them. He crouches in front of her and asks, "Can you mark through Seojun's dance positions for us?"

"Me?"

"You don't need to do all the steps, if you don't want to."

Junwoo reaches out to Hayoon's arms and lightly lifts her off the ground. She allows herself to be led to Seojun's position.

"Seojun isn't here. I need to see if there's enough time for him to reach his position."

She nods hesitantly.

"You only have to do as much as you want to," he says reassuringly.

He wants me to dance? What am I going to do?

Junwoo orders Yunjae and Minseong, "Let's take it from the third position."

The music begins and Hayoon's internal conflict grows. *Do I dance or not?* She glances over to Junwoo poised in anticipation for the first step. Her frustration dissipates when her foot meets the dance floor in the first move. By the second move, she's so immersed in the dance that she doesn't notice the boys' facial reactions.

Hayoon can dance!

Daebak! ...How does she know the steps?

All three boys' expression registers shock but only Junwoo's rapidly switches to a smirk. *You finally stopped hiding.*

He stops the music after the position change in question. Junwoo immediately cuts off any opportunity for the members to react and cause Hayoon to withdraw. "Was it enough time?"

"Mmmm. His legs are a bit longer than mine but I think it'll still appear rushed."

"Solution?"

Hayoon walks around, lost in thought, looking at the markers on the floor. While she's distracted, Junwoo signals for the boys to shut up and control themselves.

"Second position, this is Seojun and Baekhyeon, right?"

"Yeah. But the second position isn't the problem. It's the fourth."

Hayoon explains, "But it's Baekhyeon who's singing at the end of second position before the transition."

"Yeah..." Junwoo tries to keep up with her thought process but doesn't see it yet.

"Right now, he doesn't move out of position for his dance steps, since he's singing center. But he can. Just a little."

"Ohhh." Junwoo starts to see the bigger picture. "Which means they can swap third positions so Seojun is two markers closer for the fourth."

"Do you think it'll work?"

Junwoo points to Seojun's position. "I'll be Baekhyeon. You dance for Seojun."

They get ready in their respective positions, forgetting the existence of the other two who stand back to watch.

While watching them dance, Minseong jokingly asks Yunjae, "Why does it seem like those two are a duet and we're outsiders?"

Junwoo and Hayoon pass the tricky transition but don't stop until after the fifth position dance break. Neither Hayoon or Junwoo can prevent their smiles or hide their enjoyment. When the dance break ends, Junwoo gives her a double high five, clasping her hands for a second before releasing them.

"It works!"

She smiles proudly, giving the boys a glimpse into the real her. For just a second, Junwoo can see the girl he saw on the balcony the first day.

"Okay, let's run it all together one more time before we go."

Minseong takes a gulp from his drink and asks Hayoon, "Why didn't we know you could dance?"

Luckily for her, she doesn't have time to answer before Yunjae asks, "Hyung, why didn't you seem as surprised as we were?"

She looks over to Junwoo wondering the same thing. *He said before if I want to dance, not if I can. Did he already know I could?*

He evades their questions. "Enough questions. If you're done stretching, let's go home."

They switch topics on the way out and their earlier questions are forgotten. Everyone else moves on but Hayoon.

As they get out of the car, Hayoon lets Minseong and Yunjae take the lead ahead of her. She wants an answer.

"You didn't really need me today, did you?"

Junwoo pretends to be innocently oblivious to what she is asking.

"You didn't need me." This time, it isn't a question. "Your position was irrelevant. You could have danced in Seojun's position."

He losses control of his expression, exposing himself.

"Why?"

Junwoo stops walking and faces her. "I wanted to see what you would do."

Her expression is demanding more.

"I wanted to see you dance."

Shoot. She turns to walk away in stubborn avoidance.

Junwoo won't admit defeat and grabs her wrist. "Why didn't you tell us you could dance?"

She returns his questions with another one. "How did you know I could dance?"

He smirks. *Fine. Challenge accepted.* He lets her wrist fall back to her side and takes his phone out of his pocket. As he's searching on his phone, he reveals her answer.

"I dance with the members nearly every day but they never knew I was injured. You knew. You told me an experienced dancer would naturally displace their weight to not compromise the step. Only another dancer would know that. And then earlier this week, that transition wasn't working when Yunjae gave me the idea to add the step back. That step was yours. I've seen the look in your eyes when you watch us dance. I thought you were focused because this is all new to you but that isn't it. You weren't watching, you were learning our choreography."

He finds the right video on his phone and hands it over. "This proves it."

She takes his phone and lets a small gasp escape her lips as she sees her accidental recording of the dance challenge while helping him set up. *The phone was recording?!?*

"This music video hasn't been released yet. The only way you could know how to do it was by watching us."

It's too late to deny it now, right? She looks up into his eyes with a guilty smile that accepts surrender. "Oh," is all she could say.

Cute.

Junwoo puts his hand on the back of her head and ruffles her hair. He pushes her toward the house, moving his hand to her neck.

"It's time you start dancing, little sister."

Day 18

"Why does it have to be so early?"

Junwoo drags a sleepy, cranky Seojun to get in the van for their interview. He pushes Seojun to the second row and sits next to Hayoon in the back. He nudges her with is elbow to get her attention.

"Seojun and I are going to the studio after the interview. Can you come with us?"

Previously half asleep, Hayoon perks up at his request and agrees.

Baekhyeon cuts off their conversation, "It'll take us two hours to get there. The staff has prepared breakfast for us. Eat while getting ready."

He switches seat with Jeongu to sit closer to Junwoo and Hayoon.

"Hayoon, they liked your footage from the house but want you to film more at events. It doesn't have anything to do with you, but there wasn't much of Jeongu or Hakkun in the last BTS episode so they're hoping you can make up for it in your videos."

"Okay. I got it."

Baekhyeon heads back to his original seat and Hayoon checks the storage card.

Junwoo leans his head over in her direction to say, "We have a long way to go. Get some rest."

"Mmm." She hugs her bag on her lap and rests her head back against the seat.

Knowing the routine by now, Hayoon walks straight for the table with the members' food to pass it out.

Dohyun stands to the side recording, waiting to see if she gets a breakfast, too. He studies her expression but there isn't even the slightest change. *No expectation. No disappointment.* He can't do anything but watch as she hands out the last breakfast and moves over to the coffee. She takes one look at the coffees and pulls her phone out of her pocket. *What's she doing?* Dohyun moves covertly to stand behind her to see what she was reading.

Hayoon sets her phone on the table, picks up an americano, and scans the room for Baekhyeon. He's sitting next to Jihoon and Junwoo on the couch, reading through the interview script questions. Instead of walking over, she refers to her phone again. *Jihoon, hot latte. Junwoo, iced americano.* She picks up all three drinks and carries them over.

Dohyun takes the opportunity to look at her phone and finds a list of all the members' likes and dislikes. *Wow... should I be impressed or sad?* As he flips through, he finds a dining table diagram, members' personalities, what they like to eat and drink, and even their strengths in the group.

Hayoon comes back from delivering drinks but isn't fazed by Dohyun occupying her phone. On the contrary, she enlists his help. "Hakkun?"

"Huh? Oh. Uh. Hot americano."

"Jeongu is hot latte with coconut milk, right?"

"Yeah."

Hayoon continues to pass out the drinks until they're all gone. She throws away the empty drink carriers and sits off the side, out of the way.

"Time to roll."

The boys file out of the room to shoot the interview and she falls in line behind Dohyun. Halfway out the door, a staff member from the host company stops her.

"We forgot to put a trash can in the dressing room. Here." She pushes a trash can on wheels to Hayoon. "You can put their breakfast boxes and empty cups in here. We'll pick it up later."

Dohyun realizes Hayoon is missing and retraces his steps to find her. He rounds the corner as she pushes the trash can into the dressing room. He keeps filming as he stands in the doorway, watching her pick up the boys' trash to throw away.

Sigh. Dohyun calls to her, "Hayoon."

She puts an empty cup in the trash before looking up. "Samchon."

"Come on. We can do that later."

He reaches in his bag and pulls out an apple. He holds it toward her like he's bribing a child. "Come on."

She jogs over to him and takes the apple. "Thanks," she says as they turn to leave.

Hayoon and Dohyun arrive at the set stage and stand off camera to the side. She listens as the host proposes a game to win a special prize.

"If you can complete two full cycles with the same starting consonant, each of you will get a 'sleep in' card that can be used at anytime to arrive late to practice without penalty. Approved by your company."

The boys chatter in excitement and Hayoon looks on in suspense. *It's the same game they play at home; can they do it? They'll have to come up with 16 words.*

The host takes command, "Let's try a practice round first."

Hayoon counts on her hands as she thinks of words. Her fingers count up to nine when the boys fail on number seven. She drops her hands, reminding Junwoo of her presence.

Junwoo sees sudden movement beside the camera. *Hayoon!* He recalls the first night she arrived when they played as a secret team. He grabs Seojun and pulls his shirt over to whisper in his ear. Seojun listens intently and leans over to Minseong, who has never been good at word games. Minseong looks around Seojun to Junwoo who nods in affirmation. Minseong returns the nods in agreement.

Seojun yells out, "Can we sub players?"

The host is clearly confused but he's not the only one. The rest of the members, Baekhyeon included, look at Seojun. *What is he doing?* Seojun, Junwoo, and Minseong don't notice the unspoken question of their leader because their eyes are all on Hayoon.

She steps back, tripping over a cable. Dohyun steadies her. *Why are they staring at me?*

The host sarcastically says, "If you can come up with another group member in the next ten seconds, why not?"

Seojun ignores his sarcasm and exclaims, "Great!"

Hayoon takes another step back as Seojun runs straight for her. *No, no, no, no.*

Minseong runs off screen to help Seojun. They both grab one of her arms and pull her to the group. She looks back over her shoulder to plead for Dohyun's help but he's enjoying every second.

Once with the group, she tries to find an exit but Yunjae blocks her path.

Seojun holds his hand, palm up, under Hayoon's face. "Our nineth member."

The host doesn't know how to react. He stupidly says, "She's a girl."

The boys all laugh at his obvious observation.

Baekhyeon clarifies, "Hayoon joined our group a couple weeks ago. So far, she's only appeared on our show and in some backstage footage. She lives with us and attends all events as our nineth member." He jokingly adds, "I guess you don't watch our show."

The host becomes selfishly interested in their story. *Not many people know about this. I can use it to boost views.* The host double checks with the producer before approving the substitution. "Who is she subbing for?"

Minseong shoots his hand in the air, "Me!"

Baekhyeon holds his hand out to Hayoon. *She's barely spoken since she came. Can she do it?*

Hayoon warily takes his hand, still unsure of her own ability. *What if they fail because of me?*

Baekhyeon guides her over to stand between himself and the host, without dropping her hand.

The host introduces himself and waits for Hayoon to do the same. She speaks quietly but assertively.

The host turns toward the camera to remind the audience of the rules as the boys rearrange their order.

Baekhyeon places Hayoon between Junwoo and Jihoon, his best friends and unit leaders. Junwoo gives her hand a squeeze of reassurance, boosting her confidence.

The game starts and Hayoon passes the first round effortlessly. Junwoo taps the side of her leg with his finger, undetected by others. His eyes dart toward Seojun on his other side. *He doesn't have a word.* She meets Seojun's eyes before looking at her hands. She uses her finger and writes a word on her inwardly turned palm. Seojun looks back to the game to avoid suspension. On her other side, Jihoon nudges her legs with his own. *He needs a word, too.* Jihoon is already looking at her palm, waiting. She writes while her eyes are locked on Jeongu, who's currently answering.

Because of Hayoon, the members pass two cycles, winning their late card. Her new brothers celebrate their win and rush the staff with their hands out for the card. The host has to raise his voice to get Hayoon's attention. She walks closer to hear him.

"Good job. Is this your first interview show with them?"

Hayoon opens her mouth to answer when someone yells, "Gather around for a group picture."

She picks up her foot to join the group but stops herself, setting it back on the ground in the same place. *Group picture. Not me.* Hayoon stays next to the host, watching from the sidelines.

Dohyun zooms in on her, alone. Then, he slowly zooms out to get the boys in frame as Manager-nim finishes rounding them up. "3, 2, 1."

Under his breath, Dohyun says bitterly, "She's the reason they won but isn't in the picture." *Sigh.*

Day 19

The doorbell rings but Hayoon is distracted with recording the boys cooking breakfast. Today is Minseong and Seojun's turn to cook. It's bound to be a good show. Seojun is notorious for being the worst cook and Minseong for being the clumsiest. Hayoon focuses the camera on Minseong as he cracks an egg too hard and it runs down the side of the cabinet. She can hardly contain her chuckle from behind the lens.

Yunjae opens his bedroom door to yell, "Can someone get the door? It's my mom."

Seojun asks Hayoon, "Can you go?"

Hayoon walks to the front door and swings it open. The two women abruptly stop their chipper conversation when their eyes land on Hayoon.

The woman on the right startles Hayoon with her energetic greeting. "I'm Yunjae's mom. This is Jeongu's mom. You're Hayoon, right? We watched the new Peak Season from two days ago."

She reaches out to take Hayoon's hand not holding the camera. "Welcome!" She claps Hayoon's hand between hers and gives it a pat.

Hayoon isn't sure how to respond. "Hello, nice to meet you. Come in."

She opens the door wider for the women to enter and asks, "Would you like to sit down?"

Jeongu's mom answers, "Thank you."

Hayoon pulls out a chair for them and offers to get the boys.

"That's okay. They'll come out in a minute. Come sit with us."

Hayoon pulls out a chair for herself, leaving a space between them.

"How long have you lived here? My son never tells me anything. I only found out about you from the show."

"Yunjae told me you're a little older than Seojun, right?"

"I moved in almost three weeks ago. Yunjae was right."

Jeongu and Yunjae walk out, ready to go.

"Next time we come to see the boys, you should come out with us."

The mother-son duos head to the door to go out for breakfast. Hayoon walks them out to lock the door. She keeps staring at their backs, observing their interaction, as they get further away. *I almost forgot what it's like to have a mom. They seem happy.*

Distracted by her own thoughts, Hayoon trips on a shoe in the entryway. She falls forward to her knees and yelps in pain. Luckily, the scrapes on her arms are okay but her knee's injury reopens, staining her grey sweatpants. More blood seeps through with every second. Hayoon picks herself up and scurries to her room. She takes her pants off to hand wash them in the sink.

Maybe I should've never come. The days of physical pain make it hard for her mental state to remain bulletproof. She scrubs the blood stain, trying to calm her breathing. *I've got to get control.* She knows, once the first tear falls, she might not be able to stop. She tries to push her emotions away. *They've been together for years. If I wait a little longer, try a little harder, maybe they'll want me in their family.*

7

She doesn't seem okay.

-Junwoo

Day 20

At first light, Junwoo takes Hayoon to the dance studio to help with choreography for their next album. On the way to the studio, Junwoo uses the opportunity to ask Hayoon the questions that have been persistently bothering him.

"When did you learn dance? Were you a trainee before?"

"No. I took dance for my elective course in school. But it wasn't K-pop."

"What form of dance did you learn?"

"Contemporary."

"In high school?"

"And last year of middle school."

"Did you go to a fine arts boarding school?"

"It was a normal boarding school. My teacher came from the ballet company down the street."

"Did you go there for class?"

"The school had its own dance studio. Did you learn dance at school?"

"No. I started dance classes after school when I was eleven. Started training at the company in my last year of high school."

"Did the rest of the members do that, too?"

"Minseong and Seojun joined the company before they graduated. When we debuted, Minseong was seventeen and Seojun only sixteen. So, they shared a tutor. The rest of them went to school like me. Not all of them started dancing early. I think Seojun started dancing a year before he started as a trainee. Everyone's different."

"I don't know what I can help you with. You've been dancing way longer than me and I didn't even learn K-pop."

"It's okay. We'll learn from each other."

Junwoo and Hayoon enter the house late morning before lunch. Junwoo tells Hayoon, "You should have enough time to shower before lunch."

"Take Hayoon!"

Huh? She peeks her head around the corner into the living room to find the source.

Baekhyeon tells her, "Jeongu is going to pick up coffee. He needs help carrying it."

She slides her right foot back in her shoe and follows him out the door.

Hayoon drops the coffee on the table and heads to her room. At dinner, she comes out to eat but something feels off to Junwoo. She talks to Seojun and smiles like usual but her emotions feel forced. During dishes duty, he asks Jeongu about it.

"Did something happen when you guys went to pick up the coffee?"

"What do you mean?"

"Did something happen to Hayoon? She doesn't seem okay."

"I don't know." He shakes his head uncertainly. "I saw some man talking to her when I got out of the bathroom but then he left."

"What did he say to her?"

"I don't know. He didn't look happy."

"You didn't ask her?"

Jeongu shrugs and puts the plates on the shelf.

Junwoo finishes the dishes and heads to the living room. He wants to ask Hayoon but she's listening to music on her laptop, with headphones. Instead of disturbing her, he stays close without being obvious.

Hayoon can feel herself on the edge of losing control. She whips off her headphones and turns toward Junwoo.

"I forgot my sweatshirt at the studio. Can you give me your door code to get in?"

"Give me your phone."

She hands it over. He adds his contact and sends himself a message with her phone. He returns her phone and picks up his own to message her the passcode.

"I'll go with you."

"That's okay. I can go alone." She doesn't wait for his response but heads to her room.

Wasn't she going to the studio?

Hayoon flies out of her room and straight out the door.

Why change to pick up a sweatshirt? Junwoo can tell something is off but tries to give her space.

An hour passes and Hayoon hasn't come back. He loses patience and goes after her.

The company was pitch black, except for the light radiating out from a single door. He follows the light and soon hears music. The music grows louder with each step. Before pushing the door open the rest of the way, he peers through the one-inch gap.

Hayoon's shirt is soaked in sweat by the neckline. Her shoes are discarded off to the side.

Junwoo forgets his intent to bring her home once he sees her dancing. Earlier, he thought he had, on some level, figured her out. But now, he realizes he knows nothing. He watches as she lands a round off back handspring. *There's no way she learned that from an elective course.* She looks at her own reflection with a fierceness he didn't know she possessed. *So much power.* His eyes are glued to her, unable to look away. *I've never seen anyone dance with such strong emotion.* He sighs. *I wonder what happened to make her able to dance like this. ...Are those scratches on her arms?*

Hayoon falls to the ground, rapidly breathing from exhaustion. Junwoo watches her chest rise and fall as she lays on the floor. A minute later, she stands up and shuts off the sound system. She gets halfway across the room to leave when Junwoo walks in.

"You find it?"

"What?" Hayoon completely forgets the lame excuse she gave him to get the passcode.

"Your sweatshirt?"

"Oh. Right. I was wrong. It's not here."

Junwoo takes off his sweatshirt and hands it to her. "You'll catch a cold if you go outside like that."

She looks down at her shirt, realizing he was willingly playing along with her lie. He turns around as she takes off her wet shirt and replaces it with his hoodie.

"It's getting late. Let's go home."

On the ride home, Junwoo asks, "Need to stop anywhere before we head home?"

"I'm good."

After a few minutes of silence, he offers, "If you're not good, you can tell me."

She knows he isn't talking about whether or not she needs to stop. *If I tell him what happened, he might find out about my parents. I hate people's pity. But still...*

They ride in silence and Junwoo gives up hope of her telling him. They make the final turn onto their street when Hayoon opens her mouth to speak.

"Today..."

Junwoo passes their house and keeps driving.

"I was with Jeongu getting coffee when some guy started yelling at me. It wasn't even my fault. When he started yelling, everyone was staring at me and then he..." She clenches a fist full of her pants. "He said my parents didn't raise me right. But my parents... they..." Her voice cracks.

"It's okay." Junwoo hesitates for a split second but then reaches over to hold her tight fist. "You don't have to say it."

She nearly loses her breath at his touch but surprisingly, her body starts to relax. She releases her fist under his hand.

He tries to comfort her without knowing how. "Don't listen to him. You said it wasn't your fault. Even if it was, he has no right to yell at you. Don't be sad." He releases her hand to rub the back of her neck. "It's okay. If you cry, we'll worry about you."

You will?

He returns his hand to the steering wheel to turn. "Next time, take me with you. It's not safe for you to go alone."

He's not as stone hearted as everyone says.

Day 21

"What are you going to do?" Seojun and Hayoon walk into the gym behind the other members.

"Run."

"We had to run on the treadmill while singing when we were trainees."

"Seriously?"

"It helps for when you try to sing and dance."

Hayoon selects a treadmill and Seojun jumps on the one next to her. She warms up by walking for three minutes before she turns the speed up. Seojun matches her pace.

A mile and a half in, Seojun clicks the down button to return to walking for two minutes before he stops. He steps down into the gap between his and Hayoon's treadmill.

"I'm going to lift weights."

"Have fun."

Before she knows it, Seojun is back at the side of her treadmill.

"You can really run! How far will you go?"

"I don't know."

"You don't know?"

"Couple miles maybe. I normally run outside. When I'm tired, I stop." Hayoon notices several of her big brothers cooling down. She asks Seojun, "Are we leaving soon?"

"Minseong is done. Junwoo hyung, Jihoon hyung, and Kun hyung are cooling down."

Hayoon turns the speed down to a walk. She always accommodates them and doesn't want anyone needing to wait for her.

Seojun asks, "Are you going to stretch? I'll go with you."

"Let's go."

"Aren't you hot wearing sweatpants while running?"

"A little but it's not bad." Little did Seojun know, she was covering her injuries that were still visible. Otherwise, she would be wearing shorts, too.

They sit on the mat near Junwoo for stretching. "You guys want to grab some lunch and coffee and head over to the dance studio? I need three people to try a new move."

Hayoon agrees eagerly. *If only I could spend every day in the studio. When it's only the boys and me, I get to eat, too.*

Day 22

"Is it supposed to rain today?" Jeongu looks up to the grey, cloudy sky through the bus window.

As they pull up to the day's event venue, the rain drops begin to fall. Hayoon gets off the bus with Seojun, following behind Junwoo.

Jihoon and Baekhyeon are leading the way when Jihoon stops in his tracks. Junwoo puts out his arm to prevent Hayoon from running into them.

"I forgot my bag."

Hayoon cheerfully offers, "I'll get it."

Before anyone has a chance to oppose, she thrusts her bag at Seojun and runs in the opposite direction to reboard the bus.

Baekhyeon pats Jihoon on the shoulder. "Let's go."

They leave Hayoon behind to enter the building as the rain intensifies.

On the bus, Hayoon flies back to where Jihoon was sleeping earlier. "Got it," she says to no one but herself. She smiles at her mission success and hurries down the aisle to catch up.

Hayoon jogs over to the walkway awning, leading up to the entrance.

"You can't enter." A security guard holds out his arm to prevent her from passing by. "This entrance is for guest personnel only."

"I came with MPeak."

"Back up." The guard's fierce tone frightens Hayoon into stumbling back.

She peers around the guard to the door up ahead. *I have to get in. Jihoon's waiting for his bag.* Hayoon shoves the bag under her sweatshirt to keep it dry and tries again.

"I swear I came with them. I went back on the bus to get Jihoon's bag. Didn't you see me get off the bus over there?" She points toward the team's travel bus.

"You think this is my first day? Fans will say anything to get close."

She reaches to get her phone out of her pocket. *Sigh. I don't have my phone.*

"Can you give them a call? Please. His bag is going to get wet."

The guard remains a statue, unwilling to budge.

The rain becomes a downpour and she's getting wetter every second she stands out there. She puts the bag under her shirt and tucks the shirt into her pants to protect it while taking off her sweatshirt. She wraps the bag in her sweatshirt and kneels down on the ground to shelter it from the rain.

Inside, Dohyun is filming BTS when he realizes Hayoon isn't there. He checks the time on his phone and decides to give her a few minutes. Five minutes pass by and he nonchalantly walks around while filming, thinking she might be helping someone. Fifteen minutes pass by and his search become intentional, asking staff as he goes if they've seen her. Twenty minutes pass by, his concern grows and his steps quicken.

Dohyun returns to the dressing room and asks the members if they know where she is. Junwoo watches him approach Yunjae, Jeongu, and then Minseong. Dohyun's worried expression, impossible to miss. Junwoo calls out to him, "You okay?"

"Have you seen Hayoon?"

"Last time I saw her, she went back on the bus to get Jihoon's bag."

"Oh no." Dohyun spins around and hurries out of the room.

Junwoo looks back to his phone but his mind is still stuck on Dohyun's reaction. *Did something happen to Hayoon?* He slides his phone into his pocket and stands up. *Did she not come back inside?* He walks over to the makeup table to ask Seojun, "Have you seen Hayoon since we came inside?"

"No, but I was getting dressed before."

The makeup artist instructs Junwoo, "Sit down. It's your turn."

He does as he's told but can't help but sneak a glance towards the door. *Dohyun will find her.*

Dohyun arrives at the glass entrance doors and gazes out, hoping he's wrong. His heart sinks at the image before him. Past the awning, past the security guard, Hayoon is kneeling with one hand on the ground as the rain pours off her face. Her other arm, cradles a bundle against her chest.

Dohyun grabs the shirt of someone passing and shoves the camera at them. He bursts through the door and runs to Hayoon. He grabs her arm and yanks her off the ground. As they pass the guard, Dohyun rams into his shoulder in a fit of anger. He pulls her to the door and slings her into the building.

"What are you doing?!?"

A little flustered, she wipes the rain out of her eyes to see more clearly. "Samchon."

"Why were you outside?"

"Jihoon left his bag on the bus. But then the guard wouldn't let me in."

How is she not angry?!?

She opens the bundle in her arms. "It didn't get wet," she says triumphantly. "I'm going to give it to him."

Dohyun takes his camera from the random person and chases after her.

Hayoon pushes the door open before brushing the wet hair out of her eyes.

Manager-nim sees her and says, "Oh good, you're here. Hand out their lunch for me."

Dohyun tries to intervene on her behalf. "Actually, she…"

Hayoon cuts him off. "Okay. Just give me a minute to give Jihoon his bag first."

Dohyun tightens his grip on the camera. He finds it harder and harder to continually sit back and do nothing as everyone ignores her feelings. She's supposed to be their sister and teammate and yet, they have never once fulfilled their role as big brothers.

Do you not see her drenched to the bone?!?

He straightens his posture and adjusts his frame of mind. *Fine. If you don't see what you're doing, I'll make you see it.* Dohyun changes his strategy. *Time to put my footage to use. ...In a week, I get two days off when the boys go to the Middle East. I'll work on it then.*

"Hey, Hayoon." Dohyun pulls his laptop out of his bag and sets it on the table.

"Mm?" She looks up from helping Seojun adjust his mic.

"I need to take your camera's footage and upload it, to send to the company. I'm going to stay back but you can go out with the boys to watch."

"Okay. It's in my bag."

Dohyun leaves his laptop on the table to make a quick trip to the staff room for lunch before upload.

When he comes back, the room is already empty. He opens Hayoon's bag and pulls out a plastic case with the card inside. He takes a bite of his sandwich as the card loads.

What's this? Dohyun opens the file to see Hayoon in her room. He checks the room for people before playing the video.

"Today is my sixth day living with the boys but a lot has happened already."

Dohyun pauses the video. *A video diary?* He tests his theory by opening the file labeled as Day 16. *What is she doing?* In the video, Hayoon is sitting on the floor in what appears to be a bathroom. The camera's view changes as she picks it up. Dohyun lifts his finger to fast forward when he hears water running but can't bring himself to press the key. He finds himself unable to look away as the blood mixes with water around her feet. *What is that sound?* His professional expertise kicks in as he rewinds the video to isolate the sound coming from outside the bathroom. *Cheering?*

He releases a deep breath and checks the time to gauge how long before everyone walks in. *I need to find the real storage card before they come back.* He pulls the camera out of her backpack and finds the card inside. As the originally desired file uploads, he watches a few minutes.

Is that her room at the house?

Hayoon pulls her bandaged legs up to her chest amongst discarded bandage wrappers. Her eyes shift from the camera to her legs as she lowers her head to rest on her knees. Her lips move but Dohyun can't hear anything.

He grabs his earbuds and turns the volume up on his laptop. He breaks when he hears her whisper, "If this is what it's like to have a family... I don't think I want one anymore."

Dohyun blinks his tears away and closes the video. *Is it like this for her at home, too?* He randomly opens a day to find out.

"This is day thirteen, I think. The boys are in Japan for one more day. I went back to the doctor today. I had to go back because my iron's low. They wanted to test it again. Today, the doctor wasn't too happy. I need to..."

Dohyun is caught off guard when one of the makeup artists opens the door. "Are they coming back?"

"Yes."

He carefully puts the card back in the case and in the exact same spot in her bag.

Dohyun pretends to be busy with the BTS footage she recorded with the group as they come back in. He notices her clothes have air dried to become only slightly damp. Her stomach growls as she sits in the chair beside him.

What did the doctor say? It wouldn't hurt to have more evidence when I go to the manager.

"Hayoon, the company asked me to send a copy of your second doctor's report for their files. Did you go back?"

She freezes, allowing her phone to slip out of her hands to the table.

"Do you have the report with you?"

She silently reaches into her bag and pulls out a piece of paper. She unfolds it slowly but doesn't hand it over.

Is it really that bad that she won't look at me?

Dohyun takes the report from her hands. He reads the visit summary at the bottom. *Sigh. Looks like that video can't wait until they come back.*

He calmly takes a picture of the report before returning it to her. Her grip tightens, wrinkling the paper. *Why is she acting like she did something wrong? It's clearly all their fault.*

She moves one hand to cover her stomach as if it could mask the deep growl.

Dohyun pats her head while saying, "It's okay. I'll be right back."

He heads back to the staff room and straight to the snack table. He inwardly scoffs at the generous layout in front of him. *Even the interns can get fruit, drinks, and snacks whenever they want. But Hayoon...*

He grabs an apple and bottled tea. He surveys the table again to make sure he made the right choices for her.

8

We'll do better.

-Baekhyeon

Day 23

After pulling an all-nighter, Dohyun gives the team manager a call before breakfast.

"The boys don't have any plans today, right?"

"Baekhyeon gave them their split parts for the new track to practice and Junwoo is going to the studio. I think Hakkun and Jihoon might go to the gym later but that's it."

"I need a favor."

"What is it?"

"I need to show the boys a video about Hayoon...but no one else can see it."

"Why? What's wrong?"

"Did you know Hayoon got hit by a car?"

"What?!? When did that happen?"

"During the show's recording. There's a lot you don't know about her."

Manager-nim can detect an unusual tone in Dohyun's voice. They've both been with the boys for years and he's never requested anything.

"...okay. Come by the house this afternoon. I'll make sure all the boys are there."

Baekhyeon greets Manager-nim at the door and looks to Dohyun questioningly. After seeing their expressions, he asks concerned, "Is something wrong?"

Manager-nim moves out of the way to let Dohyun enter and set up. "He has a video for you guys to watch. Is everyone here?"

"Yeah. Kun and Jihoon waited to go to the gym until we're done. What's going on?"

Sigh. "I'm not sure but it's about Hayoon. Did you know she was hit by a car during the show?"

Baekhyeon's face displays complete shock. He doesn't utter a word as his eyes search the room for her.

She comes out of her room and walks over to where Junwoo had pulled up a high stool. There isn't enough space on the couch without squeezing in when all the boys are there. Baekhyeon joins the group as Junwoo gives up his seat for Hayoon.

Dohyun connects to their screen and the team chitchats while waiting. Hayoon notices Baekhyeon staring at her and pulls her sleeves down self-consciously. *Can you still see my scrapes?*

"Okay. Let's get started." Dohyun uses his loud voice to be heard, calling the boys to attention. He avoids eye contact with Hayoon as he tells the boys what they're all there for.

"As you all know, when we were recording for the special episode, I was assigned to Hayoon."

What are you doing? Her nervousness increases as he continues speaking.

"There are some things I thought you should see."

He moves out of the way to stand near Manager-nim and starts the video.

"BTS: Hayoon"

The section title appears as they watch pixels gather to form Hayoon, in her room.

"Looking Back"

> "Today is my sixth day living with the boys but a lot has happened already."

Hayoon's eyes dart over to Dohyun. *How does he know about this?* His apologetic expression meets her fearful one. He mouths, "It's okay."

She continues on in the video to talk about the first few days before she had a camera and how excited she was to have big brothers.

"I always wanted brothers. Even if they tease me, I won't get mad. I've never had a brother or sister to watch movies, or play games, or cook together. My classmate used to tell me stories about her big brother getting in trouble. I don't think his grades were very good. But when she got in trouble, he stood in front of her. He took us to a coffee shop once to study. On the way there, he was making fun of her when a man approached us. He pushed her closer to me and blocked us. Honestly, I was a bit jealous of her. But now I don't have to be. I have eight brothers.

The first couple days, I didn't get to do a lot with them. I went shopping with Jihoon, Seojun, and Yunjae. Seojun has a lot of energy but I don't mind. Since the beginning, he's talked to me the most."

The boys all chuckle at her comment of Seojun.

"When we went shopping, they bought a bunch of snacks but I didn't buy any. I was too shy to ask. Maybe next time I'll be brave enough.

Oh yeah, they played a game to see who had to do dishes. I didn't get to play but it's okay. Junwoo let me play without anyone knowing.

A couple days ago, the boys went to stage rehearsal but I didn't go. There wasn't any room so I had to stay at the house. I'll go next time.

And then yesterday, I rode in the staff van. I was going to find somewhere to sleep until the members arrived but they needed my help. I think that guy thought I was an intern. I helped the lighting crew clean and carry these huge crates. I thought my hands would blister but they were okay. I got to meet Lee Dohyun yesterday, too. He's my cameraman and super nice. He bought me coffee and told me all about the boys.

Today, I rode in the staff van again. I wonder when I can finally ride with the boys. This time, I got assigned to the stage crew. Even though they use pulleys, it's still crazy heavy. The guy who was helping me, he was a real intern. He let go of the rope and I could've sworn it was going to hit the ground. Luckily, Dohyun came and saved me."

She looks down sadly to her hands.

"I got rope burns on my hands and wrist."

She perks up, painting a smile on her face.

"It's okay though. I'm sure they'll heal fast and the boys' stage looks great."

Baekhyeon and Jihoon glance over to Hayoon who moves her hands down to grip the edge of her shirt.

The video switches from Hayoon's video diary to a comparison of what the boys see and what really happens. Hayoon's voice is replaced with Dohyun's voice over.

"What You See"

Hayoon diligently hands out the members' food and drink repeatedly with a smile.

"Hayoon hands out every member's food and drink with care but did you know?"

"What You Don't See"

Hayoon throws the empty bag away.

"There's never been any food for her."

The members finally understand the purpose of this video and their smiles get wiped from their faces.

"What You See"

Hayoon jumps enthusiastically in the barrier zone at the concert and plays a card game with Seojun and Minseong in the dressing room.

Junwoo smiles hearing her holler, "Look at Junwoo oppa!" However, Baekhyeon's smile doesn't return in expectation of what comes next.

"What You Don't See"

Hayoon works with lighting crew, the stage crew and gets ordered around by half a dozen company staff members. Her rope burns and cuts are highlighted by a red circle.

"Hayoon somehow went from a little sister to a manual laborer. She has worked for nearly every department, becoming so exhausted she couldn't finish her bread bought from a vending machine before drifting off to sleep."

Dohyun's voiceover is replaced with the video's audio when he found her in the stairwell.

"You didn't eat?"

The boys sadly watch Hayoon and Dohyun's entire interaction.

"...They'll start to look for you soon."

"Don't worry. They won't look for me."

"Aren't you mad at them?"

Jihoon straightens his posture when he hears Dohyun's question, holding his breath for Hayoon's answer.

"Why?"

"You're supposed to be a part of the group. A part of their family. But you ended up hungry and covered in injuries."

"You can't blame them. Their company decided to give them a little sister. They might not have wanted me. They don't mean to forget me. They're just busy right now. Chasing their dreams."

The boys sitting on the couch, hunch over in shame when they hear Hayoon's answer.

"What's your dream?"

"Me? Hmmm."

"I want someone by my side who thinks I'm worth it."

"Worth it?"

"Someone who thinks I'm worth their time, their care, their protection. You know when you get sick and you just want someone to hold your hand until you fall asleep. Or when something really good happens to you and you just want to run and tell them. They'll pat your head and compliment you."

"Like a big brother?"

"Yeah, like a big brother."

"What about your family?"

"Mmmmm...I don't have any."

Seojun is the first to let a tear fall. He sniffles and looks back to Hayoon with saddened eyes. Jihoon holds Seojun's hand in comfort.

"What You See"

Minseong runs over with the last item card and the team cheers in triumph.

"What You Don't See"

Hayoon climbs up the industrial shelves in the stock room to get their item.

The boys' eyes widen at her impressive climb. Minseong looks to Hayoon and gives her a thumbs up.

BOOM! Hayoon gets hit by the car and rolls on the ground before picking herself up.

The boys are blindsided; shocked at what they saw. Yunjae gasps, covering his mouth. Baekhyeon and Jihoon jerk their heads back to look at Hayoon. Hakkun becomes the second to cry and Seojun lets out a sob. Minseong holds Baekhyeon's hand beside him. Hayoon closes her eyes and turns her head. She winces as she remembers the pain. Junwoo moves a step back and closer to place a hand on her shoulder. They continue watching as she refuses to give up.

"I'm okay. I got to go."

"Stop!"

"I can't."

"Hayoon, you just got hit by a car. You're bleeding."

"Nothing's broken. I need to catch up. I know the last riddle."

"Why are you doing this to yourself? They didn't even tell you when they left the country! They left you behind!"

"They might not want me but they need me to win. I can't let them down."

Dohyun's voiceover talks over their cheering and continues talking as the boys watch the blood fall down her legs.

"While you guys were celebrating, Hayoon left to bandage her injuries without any of you noticing she was gone."

Yunjae looks back to Hayoon as a tear falls down his cheek.

"What You See"

The group successfully completes the two cycles of the word game to win their late coupon.

"What You Don't See"

Dohyun zooms in on Hayoon as she slyly gives Jihoon and Seojun their answers but the group takes the victory picture without her.

"Just like the show competition, you won because of her but when it comes to taking a group picture, she's an outsider."

It continues with Hayoon's video diary.

She wakes up in the middle of the night, unable to sleep from hunger and heads to the kitchen with a grumbling stomach.

"What if I eat this but one of the boys wants it tomorrow?"

She talks to herself as she decides to borrow Junwoo's house key on the hook and walks to the twenty-four-hour convenience store down the street. As she walks down the aisles, she finds the boys' favorite snacks.

"This is Seojun's favorite. Do they have spicy for Minseong?"

She loads her arms with snacks for the boys while her own stomach twists in pain. On her way home, she needs to stop and put down the full bags to rest her red hands.

Dohyun's voiceover asks,

> "When she was taking care of you, who was taking care of her?"

A new scene begins with Hayoon in her room talking about her honest, raw feelings.

> "Today was the first day since my parents died someone told me I can tell him if I'm not okay. Today was the first day in a really long time, I didn't have to be okay."

Hayoon smiles weakly but sincerely.

> "It was nice."

"What You See"

Hayoon stands with a smile backstage, watching the boys at yesterday's event.

"What You Don't See"

Hayoon is kneeling outside, drenched in the rain. Dohyun runs out to get her and pulls her into the shelter of the building. Dohyun's voiceover replaces the video audio.

> "Hayoon was outside in the rain for over twenty minutes. The security guard refused to let her in. She knelt on her hands and knees to protect the bag in her arms, using her own sweatshirt to keep it dry."

Manager-nim hands her the boys' food and she starts to pass it out.

> "Without being able to dry off, she's put to work to hand out everyone's food, even though she knows she won't get any. She willingly serves you and runs around for staff. She never complains. She remembers which coffee goes to each member and what your favorite snacks are. Who remembers what she likes?

Hayoon edges forward on the stool as she recognizes the final scene from her video diary. It happened after she was hit by the car but Dohyun wanted it last in the video. He hopes it will make the biggest impact and force the boys to see how she's struggling.

Hayoon sits on her bed, surrounded by discarded packaging from her bandages. She starts happily talking about the day's competition.

> "I solved five of the riddles. I didn't want the camera to be on me so I gave the answer to Hakkun and Yunjae. All those runs after school finally paid off. We only had to run a mile but I was relieved I could keep up with the boys. I climbed this huge shelf; it was kinda cool. But on the way back...mmm...I got to eat lunch today."

Hayoon tries to change the topic to control her emotions but fails. She pulls her knees up to hug them. Her head looks heavy as it falls to rest on her legs.

> "It was nice seeing the boys so happy they won... but sometimes..."

She blows out a deep breath in her last attempt to stay composed.

> "My legs really hurt. Having brothers isn't what I thought it would be like."

Her voice cracks as she admits defeat. Her pain becomes evident.

> "If this is what it's like to have a family... I don't think I want one anymore."

Junwoo puts his hand back on her shoulder and gives it a comforting squeeze. Seojun sobs softly from the couch. The boys' emotions are all a mix of guilt, shame, anger, and sadness.

She buries her head, covering her face.

> "I'm so tired."

Hayoon picks up the trash around her in bed, pats down her bandages and lays down, curled up in a ball.

Hayoon watches, confused, as the video uses a fast forward effect while she's sleeping. *Didn't I turn off the camera?* The video returns to normal speed.

Hayoon rolls over to face the camera. In her sleep, she starts crying with uncontrollable sadness while clenching the sheets in a death drip. The tears dampen her pillow.

I cried? Hayoon gasps, covering her mouth with her hand. She stares at the screen in disbelief. Baekhyeon stands up from the edge of the couch to face her. She jolts up from the stool and bumps into Junwoo. She grabs a fist of his shirt at her side as the rest of the boys turn to look at her. Half of their faces are stained with tears.

She whispers, "I didn't know."

Junwoo holds her shoulders in an instinctual response from behind.

They look back toward the screen to watch her cry as the audio overlay track begins.

Hayoon continues to cry in her sleep as a short audio compilation of her own words plays in the background.

> "My legs really hurt. I got rope burns on my hands and wrist. They don't mean to forget me. They won't look for me. I'm so tired."

The screen goes black.

The boys, Manager-nim and Dohyun's attention is all on her. She looks from face to face and feels cornered.

"I...I..."

Hayoon runs out of the room, straight out the door. Seojun and Minseong chase after her as the rest of the boys stand.

She runs down the street before getting into a taxi. Seojun stands in the middle of the street, frustrated. Minseong tugs his arm and they head back to the house.

"She's gone," Minseong reports to Baekhyeon when they come back in.

Some of the members are sitting and some standing but all are too stunned to speak.

Baekhyeon breaks the silence to ask, "Did anyone know this was going on?"

They all shake their heads.

Dohyun speaks up. "I spent days shadowing Hayoon but only four minutes of the footage was usable. What you saw in this video is only a fraction of what's on here." He holds up his flash drive with all her files saved on it.

Jihoon asks Manager-nim angrily, "Why doesn't she get food?"

Seojun cuts him off. "Yesterday, we were at the fan event for nearly the whole day! Was she...?"

Dohyun shakes his head no, confirming she wasn't given food.

Baekhyeon asks their manager, "How could this happen?"

Manager-nim didn't know what to say.

Yunjae asks, "How long has this been going on?"

Dohyun answers, "Since day one. Twenty-three days."

Jihoon guiltily admits, "She went back to the bus for my bag. I didn't know she never came back in."

Minseong reflects on the competition. "She ran beside me for half a mile. Why didn't I know she was injured?"

Baekhyeon tries to refocus the group. "It's too late to say these things now. We need to get her back."

"Why don't we give her some time? She seemed just as shocked as we were."

Dohyun supports Jeongu's statement. "She didn't know I took her SD card. She never intended to tell you."

Jihoon asks the group, "Do we even know where she went?"

Dohyun jumps in, "The only time I've seen her genuinely happy is when she told me about hanging with the dance unit."

"The company's locked. She can't get in."

Junwoo confesses, "She's been dancing with me almost every day. I gave her my passcode."

Baekhyeon orders his troops. "Let's go!"

They all rush to the door with Manager-nim.

"I'll find out what's been going on." Manger-nim commands Dohyun, "Send me that video."

Dohyun tosses him a flash drive. Everyone slides their shoes on as they're walking out the door.

"Dance unit in Junwoo's car. Vocal and rap in mine." Baekhyeon tosses the key to Junwoo.

While walking down the drive way, Manager-nim makes a phone call to his assistant. "Emergency staff meeting in an hour. Everyone!"

Both Junwoo and Baekhyeon's vehicles are silent as the brothers are all thinking about Hayoon's video.

A thought suddenly occurs to Yunjae. "Junwoo hyung, you remember when Hayoon helped us figure out that transition? The first time she danced with us."

"I remember."

"Wasn't that the day after we recorded our show?"

"Yeah." Junwoo answers but his mind is focused on finding Hayoon.

"So that means Hayoon was dancing with us after she got hit by a car. ...She must've been in so much pain."

Now, Yunjae has Junwoo's attention. He grips the steering wheel tightly.

"You're right."

Seojun leans forward from the back seat. "You think that's why she always wore a hoodie and sweatpants?"

"Maybe."

Minseong asks, "Why do you think she didn't tell us?"

Sigh. No one answers.

Hayoon pauses her music and slides down the mirror to the floor. Alone, she rolls up her pant legs, revealing her injuries. She checks her arms after rolling up her sleeves. *These ones are almost healed.*

She sees the door open swiftly in her peripheral vision and bolts off the ground. All the members come into the room causing Hayoon to unconsciously step back.

They stop when Junwoo holds his arm out slightly in front of Baekhyeon. He looks down at Junwoo's arm, surprised by his assertive action. Baekhyeon follows Junwoo's calm gaze to Hayoon and understands. Hayoon's eyes are locked on Junwoo, too.

Junwoo approaches Hayoon and stands before her. They forget about everyone else in the room, just like the first time they collaborated on choreography together. He takes her hand slowly and rotates her arm to see her scratch. He feels her start to pull her hand away but he holds firm. His thumb grazes her skin where she once bled. He gently releases her arm to her side and bends down to one knee. Hayoon tries to grab his arm to stop him but his reassuring expression causes her hand to release. She looks up at the members for a brief moment as he's kneeling. Her gaze returns to Junwoo as he smoothes the edge of the bandage gingerly. He looks up to her and asks, "Does it hurt?"

The members all stand, half surprised at Junwoo's action and half guilt-stricken from seeing her wounds.

Hayoon shakes her head, denying the pain.

He stands back up and says just above a whisper, "I'm sorry."

Her eyes go from glossy to watery as she tries to muster up the willpower to not cry. She opens her mouth to speak but only the beginning of a soft sob comes out. Hayoon tries to start again.

"I never blamed you."

Junwoo's sad eyes mix with guilt and pain.

"Hayoon-ah," he whispers, his voice filled with emotion.

Hayoon stares into his eyes and can't stop a tear from escaping.

"Oppa," she whispers, her voice shaking.

She closes her eyes as Junwoo reaches up to wipe her tear away. More tears escape from beneath her eyelashes, cascading down her face.

Junwoo slides his hand around to her neck and pulls her in to his embrace. She wraps her arms around him, releasing long held tension, relaxing against his body.

The rest of her brothers are awestruck by Junwoo's display of affection. He barely shows any affection to Baekhyeon and Jihoon and they've been best friends for years.

Baekhyeon breaks the trance first and leads the way. They encircle her in a group hug and shower her with concern.

"Are you tired?"

"You must think we're horrible brothers."

"We're sorry."

"Does your leg hurt?"

She pulls away from Junwoo to hug Seojun. She continues to turn around the circle, hugging all of them: Baekhyeon, Jihoon, Kun, Yunjae, Jeongu, and Minseong. Seojun pulls her toward him and dries her tears with the edge of his sweatshirt sleeve. They're all chuckling at Seojun's cute action when her stomach growls.

"Are you hungry?"

Hayoon's face blushes as she covers her stomach.

Baekhyeon asks her, "What do you want to eat?"

Seojun shouts, "I want ramen."

Jeongu slaps him on the back of the head, "Nobody cares what you want."

Hayoon pretends to think for a second before she says, "Ramen."

Seojun grabs Hayoon by the shoulders and starts leading the way out. "You see? My sister cares about me." He sticks his tongue out at Jeongu.

As they reach the parking lot, Junwoo hollers out, "Wait."

The boys look back, confused by his outburst.

He makes his way through the group of boys to ask, "Where are your shoes?"

Everyone looks down to Hayoon's feet. Her bare feet fidget in place.

"I..."

Junwoo passes by her and crouches down directly in front her. Hayoon looks to Seojun on her left and he gives her a little shove. "Get on."

She climbs onto Junwoo's back and he stands, holding her legs around him.

Seojun jumps onto Jihoon without warning and yells, "Go!"

Hayoon and the boys are all sitting around the table, waiting for their ramen. Jihoon is in charge of dinner and drops an armful of ramen on the table.

"Hayoon, which one do you want?"

Hayoon looks down the table, "Me?"

"We've got four kinds." Jihoon holds up the options for her to see.

Hayoon looks to Junwoo and Seojun, a bit flustered why he asked her first.

Jihoon tries to help her decide. "Seojun, Jeongu, and Kun like this one. Junwoo, Baekhyeon, and I all eat this one. This one is Minseong's favorite. This one is Yunjae's."

"That one." She points at the ramen and Jihoon opens it to add water.

After Hayoon, Jihoon passes out ramen by sliding it down the table like a shuffle board game. The boys all prepare their ramen, waiting for Jihoon to walk around with the water.

Hayoon uses her phone to count down for her ramen to be ready. The second she pulls off the lid, Yunjae slides her a fork. She stands up and Minseong joins her.

"What do you need?"

She holds up her empty cup. "Water."

"I'll get it." Minseong takes her cup to fill up.

The room fills with conversation as they eat their ramen. Hayoon puts the last bite in her mouth and stands up.

Minseong shoots out of his chair. "Need more water?"

Hayoon feels like something's off. "I'm going to throw it away."

Junwoo takes her empty ramen. "I got it."

As he's walking to the trash, Baekhyeon hands his back to be thrown away, too.

The last few members are finishing up and she stands to go to the bathroom. This time, Junwoo, Seojun and Minseong all stand in unison with her.

She glances around to each of them, caught off guard by their actions. Hayoon points to her room and tells them, "I'm going to the bathroom."

They watch her walk away before sitting down.

Baekhyeon leans across Jihoon to ask Junwoo, "Since when have you been close to Hayoon?"

"You know she comes with the dance unit when we practice."

Jihoon chips in, "Just from watching practice?"

"She doesn't just watch."

Their conversation is cut off as Hayoon comes back from the bathroom. Baekhyeon reminds everyone to clean up before leaving the table. Hayoon offers to help but gets shot down by Jihoon.

"You go rest in the living room."

She finds Yunjae in the living room and sits beside him.

"Is everyone..."

Yunjae puts the remote down and asks, "Is everyone what?"

"Is everyone being nice because they feel guilty?

"We always wanted to treat you well. We don't treat you bad on purpose or because we don't like you. You don't know how nervous Jihoon was you wouldn't like your room. He looked stuff up online for hours and spent way too long in the store trying to pick between two pairs of slippers. Most of us don't have sisters. Even if we do, we've been training and living together as a group for so long that we didn't really grow up with them."

Baekhyeon comes to sit next to Hayoon. "Give us some time. We'll do better."

Junwoo comes to add, "You can tell us when we do something wrong."

The last of the leaders sits next to Yunjae. "Tell us when you get hurt, too."

Seojun scuffles into the room carrying his pillow and blanket with a mischievous grin.

Hayoon blatantly and hilariously asks, "Are we sure he's nineteen?"

They all laugh at her unexpectantly, unfiltered question.

Minseong comes in as they're laughing. He takes one look at Seojun before sprinting down the hall. Two seconds later, he arrives beside Seojun with his pillow.

"Please," he begs Baekhyeon.

Baekhyeon concedes, "Okay. Go get our pillows, too."

Seojun tosses his blanket and pillow on the couch, hitting Yunjae, and runs back down the hall.

Junwoo tells Hayoon, "Get ready for bed and bring a pillow and blanket out here."

Are we all sleeping in the living room together?

Hayoon sits on the couch watching the movie with Seojun at her feet. He reaches the popcorn bucket back for her to take some. She takes a handful without looking away from the screen.

Oh no. Hayoon's stomach churns. Her hand rests on her thigh with the remaining popcorn. Sipping water, she rubs her stomach trying to settle it down. *Oh no!*

Hayoon catapults off the couch and runs to her room. Baekhyeon elbows Junwoo beside him before leaving to check on her.

Baekhyeon and Junwoo poke their heads into Hayoon's room. They listen as the toilet flushes and sink faucet turns on. Baekhyeon steps into the room as Hayoon exits the bathroom.

"You okay?"

"Maybe I ate too much."

"Feel better now?"

"Better."

They head back together to finish the movie.

With the weight of emotional fatigue, Hayoon falls asleep before the movie ends. Yunjae starts to speak when he gets shushed by Baekhyeon. He points to Hayoon. Yunjae clamps his mouth shut to keep from waking her.

Jihoon whispers, "She must've been tired."

"You think she looks skinnier?"

Baekhyeon tells them, "She's one of us now. We need to look out for her."

The boys nod their heads in silent agreement.

Yunjae breaks the serious conversation by asking, "Are we going to watch another movie?"

Hakkun puts his hand out for the remote to pick another one.

Once the movie starts, Baekhyeon's eyes are on the screen but his mind is distracted. As leader of the group, Hayoon is his responsibility but he didn't know anything.

Junwoo notices and signals to Jihoon. Jihoon taps Baekhyeon's leg and they all move to their bedroom.

Baekhyeon wonders why they wanted to leave the movie. "What's up?"

"We should be asking you that. Are you okay?"

He lets out a deep sigh. "Did you guys know about anything that was in that video?"

"I knew she gave Jihoon and Seojun answers but that's it."

"Same here."

Beakhyeon honestly tells them his thoughts. "I seriously failed as the group's leader. They told us she was one of us but did we ever treat her that way? Even once?" Jihoon rests his hand on Baekhyeon's shoulder as he continues. "I'm supposed to look out for our members. So many things happened to her and I never knew. I know she doesn't go on stage with us. We're often separated. But still, she shouldn't have been treated like that."

Jihoon tries to help ease his guilt. "You can't blame yourself. It's not just you. Except maybe Seojun and Junwoo, I don't think any of us paid attention to her."

"I'm going to message Manager-nim about the staff meeting. You guys can head back."

Baekhyeon messages Manager-nim.

"How'd the staff meeting go?"

"Half of them didn't know who Hayoon was. Two thought she was a new intern. I'll call you in the morning."

9

From today on, we're a group of nine.

-Baekhyeon

Day 24

"Jeongu, do you have time to come with Jihoon and I to the company?"

"Sure. Why?"

"We need to put the third row in the SUV but I need to go talk with Manager-nim so I want you to help Jihoon."

"Okay."

"Baekhyeon, how's it going?"

"Some of the boys are still sleeping. I sent Jihoon and Jeongu down to put the seat back in the car. Whatcha got for me?"

"I talked with the staff. We sent out an e-mail notification when Hayoon moved in but it turns out, not everyone reads them. Using the video as evidence, a few staff were given reprimands. The rest were given warnings. We tried to come up with all the things that would need adjustments to include Hayoon. The food problem is fixed but we need to know if she has allergies."

"I can ask when I get home later."

"Do you need help with anything on your end?"

"I can take care of things at home but I need you to contact all our upcoming interviews to make arrangements. From today on, we're a group of nine."

"Okay, got it." Manager-nim writes a reminder on a sticky note.

Baekhyeon continues, "I'll introduce Hayoon at our fan meeting but I need you to coordinate with the media department to make a formal announcement on our social media page."

"I'll talk with Dohyun to see if he can edit together a short clip of Hayoon to post with the announcement."

"She said in that video she solved a bunch of the riddles but it wasn't in the show. Oh, also when she climbed that shelf. Fans will love that."

"I'll ask Dohyun to coordinate with PD-nim to get the raw footage from the show."

Baekhyeon's phone vibrates with a message from Dohyun.

"Have you seen Hayoon's doc report?"

Baekhyeon tells Manager-nim to hold on a second as he replies.

"No. Is she ok?"

"Ask her...soon."

"I need to go." Baekhyeon rushes out of Manager-nim's office to get home.

Baekhyeon kicks off his shoes in the entryway, calling out, "Junwoo!"

"In here," he hollers back from their bedroom.

Baekhyeon walks through the open door, closing it behind him.

"What's up?"

"I got a message from Dohyun when I was at the company." He shows Junwoo the text.

"Did you ask her?"

"Not yet. Come with me."

"Okay." He stands up. "She's on the second floor."

They walk up the stairs and pull bean bags over to sit near her. She smiles in greeting and takes off her headphones.

Baekhyeon asks her, "Are you busy?"

"Not at all."

Baekhyeon stares at her without talking, making an awkward silence. *How do I ask?*

Junwoo jumps right in. "Did you go to the doctor for your checkup yet?"

"Oh." Hayoon's smile disappears. *Sigh. Did Dohyun tell them?*

"Do you have your report?"

"Samchon told you?"

Junwoo asks in a coaxing tone, "Hayoon, can we see?"

They can find out from Dohyun if I don't tell them myself. Hayoon shuts her laptop with a sigh. Baekhyeon and Junwoo stand up when she does.

"It's in my room. Let's go."

They follow her in to her room. She shuffles through a stack of documents in her nightstand and pulls out a single piece of paper.

"Here." She holds it out for them.

Baekhyeon takes the report. His eyes scan the page rapidly before they look over to Junwoo, laced with disbelief and panic. Junwoo rips it out of his hand to read for himself.

Baekhyeon transfers his attention to Hayoon. "Why didn't you tell us?"

She shrugs it off. "You're busy."

Junwoo starts reading the visit summary out loud. "Weight loss. Low iron level. Dehydration. Showing signs of recent malnutrition. Follow-up visit in two weeks."

"It's fine. Not a big deal."

Baekhyeon grabs her wrist. "Let's go."

Junwoo picks up her bag and phone on the way out.

Baekhyeon hollers out, "Jihoon, let's go!"

Jihoon takes one look at Baekhyeon pulling Hayoon toward the door and chases after them. Baekhyeon finally releases her hand as she's putting on her shoes. He grabs the car key off the hook and pushes the front door open.

Hayoon hopes she's wrong but still asks, "Where are we going?"

"To the doctor."

"...Due to lack of adequate nutrition, she could experience fatigue, nausea, headaches. Have you noticed her falling asleep during the day?"

Junwoo answers the doctor, "She fell asleep once on the way home from dance practice."

"Dance practice?!?" the doctor asks in disbelief. He shifts his eyes to Hayoon but she looks to the floor in avoidance. "How long are you dancing for?"

Junwoo responds, "Shortest practice was an hour. Longest was four."

The doctor questions, "How is that possible?"

The leaders all look at him curiously. *How is that not possible? We always practice that long. Isn't that normal?*

He explains, "Given her recent health status, it shouldn't be possible for her to exercise that long without passing out. If you add up the body's normal daily calorie expenditure plus a three-hour dance practice... she would've been burning over double the number of calories than she was eating. It's a miracle she hasn't been hospitalized."

The doctor shakes his head in concern. The boys can feel his disapproval and judgement.

Baekhyeon speaks up, "How can we fix this? Does she need medicine?"

"Not right now. The best way to help her is to make sure she's eating nutritious meals consistently. No skipping meals. If she goes to dance practice, she needs to make up the calories. Stay away from spicy foods and cold foods like ice cream."

Baekhyeon confesses, "Last night, she threw up. Is she sick?"

He checks her chart. "Her temperature is normal. What did she eat before she threw up?"

Jihoon says, "Ramen."

Baekhyeon contributes, "And Seojun's popcorn."

"Both are heavy carbs. She probably just ate too much."

"Ate too much? From one ramen?"

"For almost a month, she's been going long periods of time without eating. Her body adapted. Right now, her stomach might have a hard time processing a lot of heavy foods in a short amount of time. Luckily, it's only been a few weeks. Focus on nutrition and she'll be healthy again in a month. I'll write down some tea recommendations to help soothe her stomach in the meantime."

"Thanks, doctor."

As they are leaving the doctor's office, Hayoon looks like she was scolded. Jihoon puts his arm around her shoulders to comfort her.

She looks up at him and apologizes. "Sorry."

He squeezes her shoulder. "It's not your fault."

Baekhyeon tells Jihoon, "You and Junwoo take Hayoon home. I'm going on a coffee run."

Baekhyeon bangs the door open and yells, "Coffee!"

Yunjae and Seojun are first at the door.

"Take this." He hands Seojun coffees in a carrier. "Yunjae, the rest is still in the car."

The rest of the boys crowd around the table, but not Hayoon. She stays in the living room, pretending to be busy on her laptop. Over the last few weeks, she had mastered the art of being unnoticeable and distracted when yummy things are handed out.

Baekhyeon picks up a coffee. He reaches through the frenzy of members to hand it to Jihoon. He nods toward Hayoon. Jihoon calls out to her, "Hayoon."

She looks up. Baekhyeon's smile briefly subsides at Hayoon's facial expression. It completely lacks any expectation. Jihoon holds up the coffee. It takes her a second to realize what he is saying until he extends it toward her. A bright, sincere, joyful smile spreads across her face. She practically throws her laptop to the couch as she springs up.

Jihoon gives her the coffee and chuckles. *She looks like a little girl who got a present.* He nods toward Baekhyeon, "There's cake, too."

Baekhyeon holds up a cake when she looks to him. She excitedly jogs over. He places the cake in her hand. A small, happy squeal comes out of her mouth causing Baekhyeon to laugh. He pats her head. "From now on, there will always be food for you, okay?"

She looks at him with happy puppy dog eyes and nods. She brings her coffee to her lips to drink.

"Get a spoon."

She reaches out on the table for a spoon and opens her cake. He takes the lid for her. Hayoon takes a bite. "It's good!"

"Do you like strawberry?"

"Mm."

Baekhyeon pushes Seojun out of the way and tells her, "Sit down. Don't rush."

This is the best cake I've ever had. She looks at the members' faces around the table. *Do I really have brothers now?*

Minseong holds out his spoon and tells her, "I wanna try strawberry."

She holds out her cake for him to reach.

"Try hazelnut." He extends his cake in return.

Jihoon walks around to Baekhyeon. "You look like a proud dad watching his kid."

Baekhyeon shoves his shoulder. "Eat your cake."

Day 25

"Are we taking the van or bus today?"

Hayoon switches sides to stretch her right hamstring beside Junwoo.

"Probably the van. But on Saturday, when we go to Daegu, we'll take the bus for sure."

"Isn't the fan meeting Sunday in Busan? Are we coming back Saturday?"

"No. We'll stay in a hotel that night. In Daegu."

"Do you normally have this many fan meetings?"

"Our fans are super important to us. Last time, we had two big events in Seoul. This time, we'll have three slightly smaller events in three different cities. Not all our fans can come to Seoul. We try to go to at least Busan twice a year."

"When's the next fan meeting after this week? I didn't see any more on the schedule."

"Not for a while. After we get back from Busan, we go to Saudi Arabia and then Japan. When we get back, we'll record for our show and prepare for our comeback. Then, we have a few award shows."

Hayoon finishes stretching first.

Junwoo asks her, "Can you tell Yunjae I need him to come back with us tomorrow before everyone else gets here?"

"Okay." Hayoon picks up her phone to message him. "Is it for that slide?"

"Yeah. I want to try it with you ahead of time. That way, if it doesn't work, we can fix it."

"Okay." Hayoon checks the time on her phone. "We got to go."

Junwoo grabs his water and shuts off the studio lights. "Let's go."

"Don't forget to wear your shirts," Jihoon shouts down the hallway.

What shirt? Hayoon sits on the couch, waiting for the boys to get ready to leave.

Baekhyeon and Junwoo walk into the living room with matching team shirts.

Maybe I should wear the same color.

Hayoon returns to her room to find a red shirt in her closet.

She comes back two minutes later but Junwoo notices she changed. He intercepts her on the way to the couch and tugs her wrist down the hall.

"Wait a sec." He cracks his door open to peek inside. "Okay. Come in."

He swings open his door and heads straight for the closet. She shyly creeps a few feet in. She had been in Seojun's room before but this is the first time for the leaders' room. Jihoon is sitting on his bed, packing his bag.

"Where's your old shirt?" Junwoo asks Jihoon while digging through their shared closet.

"Which one?"

"Same one. Before you switched to L."

"Try on the left."

Junwoo flips through a few hangers before pulling one out. "Got it! I'm taking it."

"Black one's in there, too."

Junwoo pulls out another hanger.

"Let's go." He ushers Hayoon out of the room.

As they're walking down the hall, he hands her both shirts. "Wear red today. Wear the black one when we go to Daegu."

"Thanks." They split up so she can change.

Hayoon hurriedly changes into the red shirt and throws the black one on her bed. She doesn't want to be the last person ready. She joins the members in the living room. *Phew. I'm not last.*

Seojun bumps shoulders with Hayoon to catch her attention. "Nice shirt."

She smiles proudly and bumps him back.

In the dressing room, Baekhyeon starts the count off to make sure everyone's present before heading out to the stage.

"One."

"Two."

"Three."

"Four."

"Five."

"Six."

"Seven."

"Eight."

After Seojun, Baekhyeon asks, "Where's nine?"

Before Hayoon can react, Seojun pulls her up from the chair and raises her hand in the air. "She's here."

The boys all stare at her, waiting.

Seojun whispers, "Say nine."

"Nine.?." Her statement sounds more like a question causing the boys to laugh. Baekhyeon leans over to ruffle her hair.

"Let's go."

Baekhyeon leads the group out to start the event. Hayoon joins Dohyun to walk out and shrugs her shoulders. He chuckles and pats her on the back. "You did good."

Manager-nim informs Baekhyeon, "This is the last one before we break."

Baekhyeon nods his head in acknowledgement. He signals to the members and they clean up their areas at the table to leave.

Hakkun watches the members at the end of the line with the last few fans when he notices something's missing. *Where'd she go?* He stands up from his chair to look around. Hakkun tugs on Baekhyeon's shirt to get his attention.

"Where's Hayoon?"

Baekhyeon's casual scan around the stage starts to gain a sense of urgency. He moves over to stand between Junwoo and Jihoon.

"Have you guys seen Hayoon?"

Junwoo's eyes widen at his question. *Hayoon!* His chair squeaks on the floor as he stands up.

Soon, the boys are all looking around like lost puppies for Hayoon. They scan the audience, calling out, "Hayoon." Realizing it's too loud to hear, Yunjae and Seojun try quieting down the fans.

Baekhyeon picks up the microphone and tries again, "Hayoon!"

The hundreds of fans slowly become silent.

"Hayoon!"

The boys search the faces in the crowd, listening for her reply.

"Here!"

Hakkun points to the back right of the crowd, "There."

The brothers all follow his finger to find Hayoon. She's holding up a young child who's waving her hands in the air to get their attention.

Cute. Hayoon has not only one child with her but is completely surrounded by them. She waves the boys over. Like before, the child in her arms speaks for her. "Come here!"

Baekhyeon cheerfully tells Hakkun, "We'll go get her. You guys stay here."

He grabs two bodyguards and runs to Hayoon with Junwoo and Jihoon. The fans cheer as they cross the room to meet up with her.

"Little sister, you found mini-fans to play with." Jihoon plays with the little girl in her arms.

"Can I show you something?"

"What?"

She sets the girl down and tells the children, "Get ready."

They all scurry around into two lines. "5, 6, 7, 8."

To the leaders' amazement, the children start doing the choreography from their latest album's title track.

The members left behind all move to the edge of the stage to watch. The fans closest to them hold up their phones to take a video. When the children finish the chorus, the members clap and shower them with compliments.

A young boy taps Hayoon on the arm and she bends down to hear him. "Can they dance with us?"

Hayoon straightens up to ask Baekhyeon. "Can you dance with them? Just once. Please."

He bends down and scoops the boy up into his arms. "Let's go!"

The children all jump up and down in excitement. When they reach the stage, Baekhyeon, Jihoon, and Junwoo start tossing the smallest children up. Hakkun and Jeongu kneel down to help pull up the taller kids.

The leaders jump up to the stage last. Hayoon stays on the floor and instructs the children where to stand. The music starts blaring over the main speakers and Hayoon claps to count them off.

Hayoon glances back to the hundreds of fans behind her. *Ahh!* Dozens of phone cameras are all pointed in her direction. She ducks down to get out of their cameras' view.

The mini-fans crush their choreography and the audience roars in applause. The boys take time to high-five the kids and help them off the stage.

Junwoo reaches down to help Hayoon up to join them. Baekhyeon catches her shirt to stop her from walking off stage.

He calls back the members. "Don't go yet."

Hayoon stumbles backward when Baekhyeon pulls her shirt in his direction. She pivots around to face him, wondering what he needs her for.

Baekhyeon holds up the microphone and talks over the crowd. "We have some exciting news to share with everyone."

Hayoon realizes what's happening and tries to back away. She bumps into Jihoon and Baekhyeon grabs her wrist to keep her from leaving.

"This is Hayoon. She's the newest member of our family."

She holds her breath and takes a small step to angle behind Junwoo's shoulder.

Baekhyeon continues, "During our break, you can go to our group's page and watch an exclusive video of Hayoon from our latest Peak Season episode. We'll be back soon."

The fans cheer as the members start to leave the stage.

Minseong links arms with Hayoon. "Let's go eat."

A tiny voice calls out, "Hayoon unnie."

Hayoon turns her head back to see a girl reaching toward her from off stage. She breaks free from Minseong without a second thought. Baekhyeon reaches for her wrist but misses as she jogs away.

Hayoon kneels at the edge of the stage in front of the girl. Instead of taking what the mini-fan wants to give her, she grabs the wrist of her outstretched arm to help the mom set her on stage. Now, the girl stands eye to eye with Hayoon.

The boys watch protectively from afar, unable to hear what they're saying.

The girl opens her fist to show Hayoon a hair clip. They speak a few more words before Hayoon lowers down to sit on her heels.

Her brothers smile with pride when the young fan fastens the hair clip in Hayoon's hair. Hayoon gently hugs the girl and allows the mom to take their picture together. She waits until the mom puts her phone away before handing her daughter back to her.

Hayoon stands up, waves, and returns to the group.

Minseong relinks arms with her and jokingly asks, "Is this our fan meeting or yours?"

Dohyun stands abruptly, alerting Yunjae nearby. Dohyun exchanges glances with him and jerks his head toward Hayoon, who's on the verge of escaping.

Yunjae grabs her arm. "Where are you going? Your food is going to get cold."

Hayoon tries to pull away while racking her brain for an excuse. "I...I..."

Jeongu comes over to the couch with an armful of bento boxes.

Yunjae and Hayoon are having a silent stand-off while Jeongu reads out their numbers.

"5, 8, 9. And mine."

Yunjae and Seojun take their food from Jeongu leaving two boxes left in his hands.

9? Hayoon leans over subtly to check the number. 9.

Minseong walks by and stops at a frozen Hayoon.

"What? You don't like it? Here. Take mine."

He reaches over to take her box but she snatches it first.

"No. I like it."

Seojun yanks her down to the couch.

"You're blocking the tv."

Manager-nim starts distributing the coffee around the room.

"Yunjae, americano. Seojun, americano. Hayoon, latte or americano?"

"Huh?" Her pitch rises at the unexpected question.

Seojun teases her by asking, "Did you go stupid? He's asking if you want a latte or americano."

"I..."

Before she can get her words out, Junwoo answers for her. "Americano."

Manager-nim hands her an americano.

Hayoon holds her americano in one hand and bento box in the other. *I get coffee, too! Is this all because of that video?*

She looks over to Dohyun to double check. He smiles in confirmation and gestures for her to eat. Hayoon finally accepts her new reality and smiles giddily.

Baekhyeon stealthily watches their interaction and smiles feebly at her happiness.

Jihoon nudges him and asks, "What's wrong?"

Sigh. "How bad did we treat her before that would make her unable to believe that food is for her?"

Junwoo hears their conversation and tries to comfort him.

"We'll do better." He smiles optimistically.

Baekhyeon's smile slowly brightens, watching Seojun interact with Hayoon.

"Seojun, do you want some of my meat and rice?"

He jokes with her, "I think you worked harder than me, teaching your dance class. Eat lots, little girl."

"My birthday comes first, little brother."

10

Oppa.

-Hayoon

Day 26

Hayoon stares out her bedroom window, feeling frustrated after hanging up a phone call from Manager-nim. *Did I really do something wrong? Why did he have to talk to me like that?*

Junwoo's words echo in her head. *"If you're not good, you can tell me." Can I tell him? Will he understand me?*

She is tired of struggling on her own and decides to find Junwoo.

Hayoon finds him in the living room playing video games with Jihoon and Minseong. *Maybe later.* She detours up to the second-floor balcony.

Junwoo sees her change direction and head up the stairs.

"I'm going to the bathroom. You guys play."

He follows her up the stairs to check on her.

When he steps out onto the balcony, Hayoon is getting ready to put her headphones on. She stops mid-motion when he catches her eye.

Hayoon sets her headphones on the table and faces Junwoo. Her expression tells him, he was right to follow her.

"What is it?" he asks concerned.

She takes a step forward, desiring to be hugged and comforted, but withdraws.

"...I..."

Sigh. She looks off the balcony to the ground below. Her face twists in irritation at herself for finding it hard to admit she needs him.

Sigh. Hayoon turns her head toward him but doesn't lift her eyes. She stares at his feet, gathering courage.

"That day... you told me... I'm not okay."

He takes a small step toward her and patiently waits. She raises her eyes to meet his. Junwoo explores her eyes to discover they're void of fear and hesitancy. He lessens the gap between them once more and reaches up to gently rub her arm. His eyes welcome her in. He leaves the last step for her, if she wants. Hayoon lifts her arms to his back and leans into his embrace. His hands slide across her back to draw her in.

He whispers, "I'm here."

Junwoo moves a hand up to hug her head against his chest. Their natural movements lack even the smallest hint of awkwardness. He feels her muscles relax against him and tightens his grip in response. Junwoo recalls how she suffered alone and kept her emotions buried. He thinks back to the video and wonders why she has no family. *Sigh. One problem at a time.*

"Can you tell me what happened?"

"I got in trouble."

"Why?"

"With Manager-nim. About yesterday."

"Does Baekhyeon know?"

She shrugs. Junwoo steps back to talk with her.

"If the company tells you to do something or says something that makes you upset, you should talk to Baekhyeon. That's one of his responsibilities as leader."

She doesn't look convinced.

Junwoo tries to reason with her by asking, "You can't just go along with what everyone else says, can you?"

She doesn't reply but her expression pleads guilty.

"Seriously? Like with what?"

"Hmmm. Like when Yunjae was handing out drinks and I got soda."

"What did you want?"

"Tea. I don't like soda."

"What else?"

"I love my room and really appreciate Jihoon taking the time to pick everything out."

"But?"

"It's really pink."

"What color do you like?"

"Blue. Light blue."

"Okay. I can help with that. But for now, let's go see Baekhyeon about today's thing."

She grabs his hand to stop him from walking away.

"You can't tell Jihoon about my room."

"I got it. Don't worry."

"Hey, Hayoon, did you see this?"

She leans over to look at Yunjae's phone. "Is that the video Dohyun made from the show footage?"

"Yeah, but have you seen the comments?"

"No. I don't have an account."

"What?!?"

"I don't have social media."

"There are still people with no social media? Huh. When we come back from dance practice, Seojun and I will help you get an account. Here. Look on mine."

Hayoon scoots closer on the couch so they can share the phone.

"They called you a secret weapon. Fan videos from the fan meeting are blowing up, too."

"Isn't that normal for you guys?"

"Not us. You. With those kids."

"Let me see."

Yunjae scrolls up from Hayoon's show video to find it. "Hold on. Let me find this other one. I saw this fan art earlier... got it. This fan made a painting of when that little girl put the clip in your hair."

"Daebak! I can't believe they did that in one day. Can you send it to me?"

"Sure. When Seojun and I help add you to the group later, you can read all the comments."

Junwoo calls from the kitchen, "Hayoon. Yunjae. Time to go."

"You ready?" Junwoo asks the pair warming up.

"Ready," Hayoon answers.

"You're going about four feet in front of the mat. Yunjae, you're going to take her left arm. I'll take the right."

Hayoon and Yunjae move into position.

Junwoo continues, "Yunjae and I will step forward first and slide Hayoon on the ground. Hayoon, you need to roll to your back to slide. When you get up to where we are, we'll lift you off the ground. Your feet will go up and your back will arch over as we throw you. Yunjae, the first couple times, don't let go of her arm until her feet hit the ground."

"Okay."

Junwoo and Yunjae both take her wrists.

"Ready?"

Hayoon responds, "Ready."

The first attempt, Hayoon doesn't get high enough off the ground.

Hayoon asks Junwoo, "Once I start going up, can you support me on my lower back to help me get over?"

"Right here?"

Junwoo places his hand on her near the bottom of her shoulder blades.

"Lower."

He moves his hand down.

"There."

"Let's try again."

During the second attempt, the mat slides on the floor under her. They move too close to the wall ahead of Hayoon.

She yells, "Wait!"

Her big brothers immediately stop, holding her arms back to prevent her from sliding.

"I'll put some mats on the far wall side."

Junwoo lines mats the rest of the way until they hit the wall.

Two failed attempts cause Hayoon to rethink her actions. Junwoo sees her stand silently at the start position and fears she's getting nervous. He swings her wrist back and forth to get her attention.

"I won't let you get hurt. Don't worry."

"I know. Let's try again."

Roll back. Feet up. Tighten core. Arch back. Success!

They all high five with a great sense of accomplishment.

"Again! Again! Again!"

"I think I can get a bit higher this time."

"Ready, go."

Fourth attempt goes better than the third.

Junwoo announces, "Let's get it one more time before we break."

Fifth try starts like the last two but Yunjae's foot slips. He lets go of Hayoon's arm by mistake.

Hayoon cries out, "Oppa!"

Junwoo scoops his arm from Hayoon's back around to her stomach. He pulls her into him to protect her as they fall to the ground. Junwoo grunts as they hit the floor. She rolls off of him toward Yunjae.

"Hyung, are you okay?"

Junwoo ignores Yunjae's question and holds up Hayoon's arms to inspect her. "Hayoon-ah, did you get hurt?"

"I'm fine. Are you okay?"

They all help each other stand.

"I'm good, too."

"Let's go again."

Day 27

"Oppa! Have you seen my earbuds?"

The bus goes quiet after Hayoon speaks. *Oppa? Which oppa? She's never said oppa before.*

Junwoo walks down the aisle and hands them to her. "You left them in the car after dance practice."

"Thank you."

Baekhyeon's jealousy shows itself. "Oppa? You call Junwoo, oppa?"

Junwoo and Hayoon simultaneously turn to Baekhyeon in confusion.

"Huh?"

After spending dance practice with them, Yunjae is the only one not surprised. He decides to add fuel to the fire by telling them, "She calls him oppa at dance practice all the time."

"Why does he get called oppa and not me? I met you first. I'm the oldest."

Hayoon blushes at his question and Junwoo laughs at his immaturity.

Jihoon jumps in, "Me too. Call me oppa."

Her brothers all start pleading their case to be called oppa.

"I designed your room and took you shopping."

"I'm the second oldest."

Soon, even Seojun is complaining.

She barks back at him, "Baby Seojun, you're younger than me!"

The boys all shift their attention to teasing Seojun.

After their group greeting, Baekhyeon starts the fan event by introducing Hayoon to their Daegu fans.

"Who subscribes to our group page?"

The crowd of fans scream in reply.

"Did you guys watch the video we posted Thursday?"

More screams resonate through the room.

"If you haven't seen it, let me introduce you to someone."

Baekhyeon waves Hayoon over from whispering with Seojun. She jogs over to stand beside him.

"This is Hayoon."

"Get away from MPeak! Get out!" A crazy fan starts yelling at Hayoon from the audience.

Junwoo moves at lightning speed. He reaches his arm across Hayoon's stomach to grab her waist on the far side. He pushes her behind himself, moving his hand to her back to keep her close. She stumbles and grabs his shirt to steady herself.

Baekhyeon immediately cuts off the fan as she shouts profanity.

"Security!"

The crazy fan starts walking down the aisle toward the stage as security runs to intercept her.

Hayoon's brothers surround her on all sides. Hakkun stands behind her with his hands on her shoulders. Jihoon joins Junwoo to form an impenetrable wall in front of her. Seojun holds her hand beside her. Minseong and Yunjae flank her other side. Jeongu coordinates with staff to increase security at the below stage barrier.

Security reaches the aggressive fan and forcefully escorts her out of the room. All the members and fans stand like statues, watching her get dragged out.

Baekhyeon orders security and staff, "Get her information. She's banned from all our events and fan sites."

The door shuts behind them leaving the room so quiet you could hear a phone vibrate.

Hayoon peeks around Junwoo to the crowd with a thousand eyes staring back at her. *Oh. That's a lot of people.* She hides herself behind him again.

Baekhyeon looks at his little sister and sighs as he makes a decision that could get him in trouble later. He walks toward the circle of safety and reaches his hand through them to Hayoon. She trustfully takes his hand and allows him to pull her out to stand in front of Jihoon.

He addresses the sea of fans without letting go of Hayoon. "We apologize for the interruption. We love our fans and respect your opinions."

Fans start getting their phones out to record one-by-one.

"If your bias is Kun or Seojun, it's okay. If you think our last album wasn't that great, it's okay. Or if you didn't like our outfits at the last award show, it's okay. Everyone is different. Even among best friends, you might have different personal styles or opinions. Those differences make us beautiful and unique. However! It is NOT okay to threaten or attack my members because of those differences."

Baekhyeon glances over to Hayoon. She smiles with gratefulness for her leader's protection. He gives her hand a squeeze.

"Hayoon is one of us. We will protect her. We don't want to kick people out. Truthfully, this is the first time we've had to blacklist someone. I hope it's the last. We know our fans want what is best for us. Trust me when I say, Hayoon is the best for us. At first, we thought maybe the same as some of you. We've been together for years and then suddenly have a new family member. And she's a little sister. Some of us maybe even thought she would be a burden or distraction."

She drops her head at the sound of those heavy words. *Burden? Distraction? Am I?*

Baekhyeon chuckles half-heartedly and shakes his head at just how wrong they were.

"It turns out, she's the one who takes care of us. She always puts the members before herself and never complains."

He didn't intend to make a lengthy speech today but there it is- the truth. He puffs out a long breath to try and compose himself. He strokes the back of her head as he continues, "Even when she's hungry or tired or injured..."

Hayoon whispers, "Oppa."

Oppa? Baekhyeon loses it at the tone of her voice when she finally calls him oppa. He understands now. For Hayoon, calling them oppa isn't about age or status. It's about trust.

He looks away from the audience to pull himself together. Unfortunately, he's met with the emotional gaze of his members who share the same guilt.

Suddenly, someone yells out through the silence, "Unnie!"

Baekhyeon's arm flies out in front of Hayoon in defense. She gently lays her hand on his forearm.

"It's okay. Give her a chance."

I hate when people judge me before giving me a chance because I'm an orphan. I don't want the members being on defense against their fans and not trust them. This was my choice. I knew who they were when I agreed. I can do this!

In her most courageous moment of fighting stage fright ever, she steps forward. She keeps moving until her arm is fully extended and her fingers slip from Baekhyeon's grasp. Four feet in front of the members, she can feel the heat of stage fright creep up her neck. She stands there, vulnerable, looking into the crowd.

"Hayoon unnie!"

She locates the source. A girl, a few years younger than herself, is holding up a poster that reads, "We love you, Hayoon."

"Hayoon unnie! We love you!"

Hayoon's stage fright recedes slowly yet significantly like the tide. She joyfully points to the poster while looking back at her brothers.

"Look!"

More encouraging shouts from fans fill the room. Her happiness becomes contagious. The boys run up for a group hug around Hayoon.

Baekhyeon leads the way to a room down the hall from the hotel's lobby. Manager-nim is toting takeout bags in both hands.

"They said we can use this room to eat but there won't be enough chairs."

Baekhyeon turns on the light and comments, "Seven chairs are enough."

Junwoo, Hayoon, and Seojun come in together discussing their upcoming album's choreography. Junwoo claims a chair while Hayoon and Seojun help Manager-nim take the food out of the bags.

Manager-nim leaves the food to the maknaes and claims a chair on the opposite side of the room to work on his laptop.

Jihoon comes in with the rest of the boys.

"What'd we get?"

Seojun enthusiastically replies, "Chicken!"

Jihoon sits beside Junwoo and Baekhyeon pulls up a chair beside Manager-nim to collaborate on comeback plans. Seojun slides two plates over to Minseong and shares his chair.

"Hayoon, come sit."

She circles around the table to Junwoo and distributes plates to herself, Jihoon, and Junwoo.

"Sit."

Jihoon pushes his left leg against Junwoo's right leg, making a human chair for her.

Seojun holds his phone out in front of Hayoon's face. "Did you see this?"

She reads the fan post as she chomps down on her chicken.

"They called you the family princess."

Minseong tugs his arm. "I want to see."

Seojun retracts his arm and turns the phone around for Minseong.

"Hashtag the guardians. Hashtag princess protectors."

Jihoon unlocks his phone to check their page.

"Baekhyeon, the video of you from earlier is blowing up."

Baekhyeon pops his head up from Manager-nim's laptop.

"Good or bad?"

"Good. Really good."

Minseong tells Hayoon, "Some fans asked why you don't have an account. They want to follow you."

Seojun admits, "Shoot. I forgot to help you set one up. Let's do it later."

Hayoon is busy eating but grunts in agreement.

Hayoon, Seojun, Yunjae, and Minseong are all hanging out on the pool deck when they realize it's past curfew. Hayoon starts freaking out and runs to the elevators, pushing the button repeatedly.

Yunjae tells her, "Chill out. I heard Baekhyeon tell Jihoon earlier they were going to have a meeting after we ate. They're probably still in his room."

They ride the elevator up seven floors and run smack into their leaders when the door opens. Baekhyeon's fatherly demeanor towers over his curfew-breaking trouble makers.

Seojun whispers into Hayoon's ear, "Act cute."

Her eyes ask, "Are you kidding me?"

Seojun whispers, "Trust me. It'll work."

Hayoon observes her guardians' expression. *They don't seem angry. Sigh. Might as well try.*

She reaches out to take Baekhyeon's hand and cutely swings it back and forth. "Baekhyeon oppa, we didn't mean to. Can I go back to my room? I'm really sleepy."

Minseong hides his smile behind Yunjae. *She's good.*

Jihoon's eyebrows rise and Junwoo clenches his jaw to stop his smile. Baekhyeon sighs in defeat.

"Go."

"Goodnight," Hayoon responds merrily.

The curfew-breakers all sprint off to their rooms before he changes his mind and punishes them.

Baekhyeon shakes his head grinning. "I should be angry she played me... and yet, I feel kind of proud."

Jihoon and Junwoo chuckle beside him before turning into their own rooms.

Day 28

"Ugh," Hayoon grunts when Seojun sits in her lap. "You're too heavy. Get off."

"You called me fat!" Seojun exclaims. "Yunjae, come help me."

Before Hayoon can run away, the members jump on top of her.

The guardians walk into the dressing room after checking the event stage. Baekhyeon counts heads to make sure everyone is present before he debriefs them on the fan meeting schedule.

"...Where's Hayoon?"

He hears Hayoon weakly say, "Here."

Baekhyeon looks around from the boys on the couch to the makeup table to the snack table.

"Where?"

A hand raises up from under the pile of members on the couch.

"I'm down here."

On top of her, Seojun, Minseong, Yunjae, and Jeongu all crack up laughing. Baekhyeon pushes Yunjae to the ground and Jeongu rolls over to expose Hayoon. Junwoo pulls her up, slides onto the couch and yanks her back down on top of him.

Hayoon leans back dramatically, acting like she was dying after being crushed. He plays along, patting her head like a little girl.

"You nearly smothered her to death."

Baekhyeon tries to reign them in. "Alright, alright, settle down. We need to go over some safety rules for today."

Yunjae picks himself up off the ground to sit on the edge of the couch.

Baekhyeon grabs a chair from the table and flips it around to sit, facing the boys. "The fan meeting today is bigger than yesterday. And because of the space, security is going to be harder to manage off-stage. After we greet the fans, they're going to play a short video from our concerts. Once that's over, we need to move to our table positions for the fan signing. Listen up for the order. Kun, Jeongu, Jihoon, Junwoo, me, Seojun, Minseong and then Yunjae. You can keep a few small gifts from fans on the table if you want but there will be a box behind you for most of it. Try not to put the fan's gift in the box until after they move down from you. None of you should leave your designated area without informing security."

Yunjae asks, "Where's Hayoon's designated area? Will she be with us?"

"She has the largest perimeter that includes the whole stage and off to the side. Hayoon, you can't leave the stage today. There's an event here tomorrow so there will be people in this back hallway by the dressing room that aren't our people."

Seojun loops his arm through Hayoon's. "Come help me."

She agrees but Jeongu still smacks him on the head.

"She's not your servant, stupid."

Hayoon sincerely offers, "If you guys need anything, tell me."

Baekhyeon finishes up, "After the fan signing, there will be a short Q&A and then we're done."

The boys split up to watch the video off to the side so they won't block the fans' view of the screen. Yunjae waves Hayoon over from behind the curtain to watch the video with him. The fans up front scream when they see her sneak out to Yunjae. Hayoon gets startled by the unexpected reaction.

Baekhyeon glances over to see what caused the fans to react. *Guess they all know who she is now.*

Minseong reaches out to squeeze Hayoon's shoulder in support. She ducks into him.

Across the stage, Junwoo shifts his weight over, wanting to go to her.

Baekhyeon places a hand on his arm and whispers, "She's okay. They'll take care of her."

He observes Junwoo curiously. *Why is he protective of her? Is it because of the Daegu fan meeting? Earlier than that. Because of the video? But we all saw the same video. Is it because they hang out at the dance studio?*

The video ends and the fans line up by ticket number to come on stage. Hayoon tags along with Seojun. She helps him and Minseong with their boxes.

Fifteen minutes in, two teenage girls hand Junwoo a poster size picture from their last Peak Season episode to sign. While Junwoo is signing, the taller of the two girls asks, "Is there going to be a fan event soon where Hayoon is going to sign, too?"

"You want Hayoon to sign this?"

"Can she?"

Junwoo told them, "Hold on a minute."

He looks down the line to where Hayoon is organizing Seojun's box for him.

"Hayoon-ah!"

She jogs over to him.

"Need my help?"

He gestures toward the girls. They hold out a gold marker in her direction.

"Can you sign your picture for us?"

Hayoon's caught off guard by their question.

"Me?"

Junwoo places his hand on her lower back and guides her over to share his chair. Hayoon takes the marker and slides the poster over to sign under her picture.

Do I write my full name? I don't have a signature. She checks how Junwoo signed and follows his lead.

The girls gush over their poster and ask, "Can we take a picture with you?"

Junwoo answers for the both of them, "Of course."

He pulls Hayoon in close for the picture. When the fans move on to Baekhyeon, he rubs her back in reassurance.

"You did good."

Hayoon leaves Junwoo to go back to helping their maknaes.

A few minutes later, there's a young fan in front of Yunjae that doesn't seem to want to leave. She keeps looking back, up the line.

Yunjae asks her, "You okay?"

She takes her bookbag off and opens it to reveal a stuffed animal butterfly.

"Can you give this to Hayoon unnie?"

Yunjae sweetens his tone and tells her, "I think she would like it more if you give it to her yourself."

She pulls it out of the bag and sets it on the table to put her bookbag back on.

"Hayoon. Come here."

He moves his leg parallel to the table to make a bench for her to sit.

"She has something for you."

The adorable little girl holds out the butterfly sheepishly.

"For me?"

She nods her head and reaches out further to put the stuffed animal in Hayoon's hands.

"I have two brothers. My parents always give me their old toys from when they were little. I didn't get to choose my own pretty toys until I got bigger. You live with all boys so I wanted to make sure you got to have pretty toys, too."

Hayoon is touched by her kindness. She can't be more than eight and yet, she shows such compassion for others. Hayoon hugs the butterfly to her chest.

"Thank you. I love it!"

"I couldn't decide between the butterfly or a flower. If you like flowers better, just wait until I get more allowance and I'll buy it for you."

Hayoon reaches across the table to hold her hand.

"You bought this with your allowance?"

Minseong and Seojun start watching their cute interaction.

She proudly responds, "I saved up for almost two weeks."

"Wow, two weeks? That's a long time. You made the right choice. I love butterflies!"

Hayoon looks down to the line at the end of the table she isn't allowed to cross. *Sigh. I want a hug.* She thinks back to what Baekhyeon said, *"without informing security."*

She pats the girl's hand and says, "Don't move."

Yunjae signs for the next fan as Hayoon runs over to a body guard and explains the situation. He points to the girl and nods in approval. The bodyguard escorts Hayoon back to the table.

Hayoon opens her arms and approaches the forbidden line.

Baekhyeon sees movement out of the corner of his eye and shoots out of his chair. *Hayoon!* His eyes map out her trajectory to the fan waiting patiently past the line.

Yunjae looks over at Baekhyeon when his chair slides back and waves to get his attention. He gives their leader a thumbs up and Baekhyeon relaxes. *Hayoon's going to give me more stress than Seojun, isn't she?*

Hayoon kneels and hugs her butterfly fan tenderly. She notices two boys standing off the side, watching them.

"Are those your brothers?"

"Yeah, they brought me because my mom is busy."

"Are they good big brothers?"

"They tease me sometimes but they're not bad."

Hayoon chuckles at her honest response. The girl points to the members.

"Are they good brothers?"

Hayoon looks down the table at each of the members. "The best." Her smile grows radiant.

The bodyguard warns her she needs to go back soon.

Hayoon pulls out her phone and hands it to the guard. "I have to go but let's take a picture first. Tell your mom to go on our group page to find me." After their picture, Hayoon sends her back to her brothers.

Hayoon is helping clear the stage for the Q&A when Jeongu snatches the princess crown off her head and runs away. She chases him all over the stage, behind the curtain and back onto the stage. Yunjae and Minseong join in and fans start to cheer their names.

"Give it back. A fan gave that to me!"

Off to the side, Manager-nim is holding a whole bag of Hayoon's gifts from fans.

His assistant asks, "What's in the bag?"

"Hayoon's gifts." Half-jokingly he adds, "Next time, we should give her a spot at the table. She practically ran a marathon going back and forth."

They turn their attention back to the members' game of tag.

Hayoon finally catches up to Jeongu and jumps on his back to get the crown back. The fans all scream, making Hayoon self-conscious.

Staff finish setting out the last two chairs and call Baekhyeon over. Baekhyeon rounds up the members for the Q&A. They all sit in their table order and he hands out microphones to Jihoon and Yunjae. Baekhyeon keeps one microphone for himself and signals the fans to quiet down.

He raises the mic up to read the first question but stop midway.

"When is your..."

Hayoon. Why isn't she on stage? Baekhyeon spots Hayoon standing next to Manager-nim and his assistant.

He holds the mic away from his face and takes a step off the high stool, leaning toward Manager-nim to summon him over.

"I told you, for interviews, we are a group of nine. We need one more chair."

Baekhyeon stays standing as they bring over a chair. He instructs them to put it between himself and Junwoo.

While the members are adjusting the chairs to fit one more, Baekhyeon orders Junwoo, "Go get her."

Hayoon hesitantly joins her brothers. *Huh. It's not so nerve-racking if I just have to sit here. I can do this.* She listens peacefully to the fans' questions, becoming more comfortable with every passing minute.

Day 30

"Listen up."

Baekhyeon waits while his members take out their earbuds.

"We have ten minutes until we get to the airport. Our bodyguards just texted me; our travel plans got leaked. Put away your stuff and be ready to go before we get there. Keep your bags close and stay together. Manager-nim has already checked us in so we'll go straight to security."

The boys start packing up their phones, headphones, and earbuds.

As they arrive at the airport, their bodyguards are waiting for them. The boys naturally fall into a line with Baekhyeon and Jihoon in the lead. Behind them, stood Hayoon, Junwoo and Seojun. Yunjae and Minseong follow Junwoo with Hakkun and Jeongu bringing up the rear.

The second the sliding doors open and they step into the airport, they are flooded by fans. Junwoo grabs Hayoon's hand in protective instinct. The guardians realize quickly, the number of bodyguards they have is not enough.

The fans get closer and Hayoon is accidentally pushed. Junwoo jerks her hand back and she spins in to face him. He releases her hand to embrace her back. Junwoo hands off his bag to Seojun to better protect Hayoon.

The members are gridlocked. The fan pressure on every side is making it impossible to advance forward.

Junwoo lowers his head to ask Hayoon, "Are you okay?"

She tries to hide the fear she feels from being a trapped introvert in a huge crowd. *I'm okay. It's going to be okay. Breathe.*

"Don't be scared. I got you."

He looks all around them to assess the crowd. *We need to move forward. Can Hayoon push through with the fans? Should I put her on Jihoon's back? He's wearing a bookbag. She won't be secure. ...I'll have to pick her up.*

Junwoo exchanges glances with Baekhyeon and Jihoon. They nod in understanding.

Junwoo turns his head back to yell at Yunjae, "Let's go!"

He hoists Hayoon up and she wraps her arms around his neck in automatic response. She locks her legs around his waist and keeps her head down. Junwoo pulls her in tight.

Yunjae puts his ball cap on Hayoon to cover her face. Yunjae and Minseong both stay close to Junwoo, keeping a supportive hand on Hayoon's arms.

Hayoon feels Seojun slip away and calls out to him.

"Seojun!"

Junwoo takes his left hand from Hayoon's back to grab Seojun and prevent him from getting separated in the chaos. Minseong latches onto Seojun from behind.

The boys break through the mob and enter the security line. Baekhyeon stays at the entrance to count heads while Jihoon leads them forward. They reach the ID checkpoint and Junwoo lowers Hayoon to the ground.

He takes the hat off and brushes her hair out of her face.

"You good?"

"I'm good."

Junwoo hands the hat back to Yunjae and checks with him. "You good?"

"Yup."

Seojun returns Junwoo's bag and says, "Thanks for grabbing me."

"Thanks for taking my bag. Are you okay?"

"That was crazy."

The boys pass through security without a problem and go straight to the VIP Lounge.

Baekhyeon, Hakkun, Jihoon, and Junwoo gather at a table together. The maknaes start playing cards nearby.

"As much as we love our fans, the priority in these situations needs to be member safety."

Baekhyeon's gaze shifts to the younger members. No one speaks it out but they all know who has become the primary concern when it comes to security.

Their leader points out their weakest point. "Right now, except myself, there's no consistency to everyone's position. Whoever you're talking to when you get out of the van is who you end up walking by. But I don't think we can rely on this working anymore. We have more fans and travel to more countries than we used to. I think we need to break out of the two-by-two lines and change to something that will keep us safer and together."

Hakkun adds, "I agree. Two-by-two is too spread out. It's easy to break apart."

"How about everyone tries to give me two new security formations before we board the plane so I can review them onboard?"

Baekhyeon checks his watch.

"We've got an hour. Let's get to work."

Hakkun and Jihoon take their bags over to a couch to work. Baekhyeon and Junwoo stay at the table.

"Junwoo…"

Baekhyeon trails off when he sees Junwoo's eyes locked on Hayoon. He taps the table in front of him.

"Hey. What are you thinking?"

Sigh. "I was thinking about when the company sees the fans' posts if we'll get in trouble for what I did."

"For picking up Hayoon?"

"Yeah. I don't want her to think it's her fault if we get in trouble."

"You made the best choice for that situation. I've got your back. If the company has a problem with how we protect our members, I'll deal with it. For now, let's focus on these plans."

"Let's stop over there."

Baekhyeon points to an empty gate sitting area and Manager-nim helps him herd the boys to gather away from the other deboarding passengers.

"Who needs to go to the bathroom?"

Jeongu and Minseong raise their hands.

"Go ahead. The staff need a few minutes to collect our bags and load the bus."

One of the bodyguards goes with Jeongu and Minseong. The remainder of the group sits down to chill. Baekhyeon shares the new plan with Manager-nim for when they're on the move. The head bodyguard provides his input on where his men should go.

"Okay," Baekhyeon says in his leader voice. "Let's line up. Jihoon and I will be up front with a bodyguard. Next line, Yunjae, Hayoon, and Jeongu. Behind them, Seojun, Junwoo, and Minseong. Kun, you're in the back with Manager-nim."

Jeongu and Minseong jog back over and fall in line.

Yunjae takes Hayoon's bag off her back to carry and Junwoo gives his to Seojun. Hayoon anxiously looks to Junwoo directly behind her. He nudges Yunjae's arm.

"Switch hands."

Yunjae switches Hayoon's bag to the outside and holds her hand. She exhales deeply to try to relax. Sometimes, Hayoon is a strong, capable, independent young woman who never gives up. But in times like this, her introverted personality makes her seem like a scared little girl who needs protected.

Junwoo massages her right shoulder and reassures her, "There won't be as many fans here."

The group leaves the terminal where fans are waiting. Unlike at their departure, the fans in Saudi Arabia are fewer and not as aggressive. Baekhyeon and Jihoon lead the way into a hallway that, despite its large width, creates a bottleneck.

Due to the congestion, the members slow to a crawl. Hayoon is squished in a member sandwich. Junwoo uses the opportunity to place his hands on Hayoon's waist to remind her, she's not alone. He can feel her tense body relax.

It's okay. My brothers won't let anything happen to me. There's no reason to be scared.

II

I'm here.

-Junwoo

Day 31

Minseong is livestreaming from the dressing room before sound check. Hayoon stabs a piece of watermelon and offers it to Minseong from behind his phone. He bites the watermelon off the fork and reads fan comments.

"Whose hand is that? It's Hayoon's."

She feeds him another piece.

"Hayoon, the fans are asking why you haven't accepted their follow requests."

"Huh? What's that?"

"Seojun helped get you an account, remember?"

"Yeah, I remember. I posted the picture with that cute little girl who gave me the butterfly. Her mom messaged me, too."

"Did you confirm any follow requests?"

"Any what?"

"Open your account on your cell phone. Click this." Minseong yells at her, "Hayoon!"

Kun and Jihoon run over worriedly.

Minseong flips his camera view so the fans in his live could see her screen.

Jihoon leans over to look, too.

"Woah. That's a lot of requests."

Hayoon looks confused.

Minseong explains, "This little red number means this many people want to follow your account. They want to look at your posts and get notifications when you post something new. Click the number and you can accept them."

Minseong notices the number of fans watching his live increase. They either think Hayoon is adorable or are asking for her to accept their request.

He pulls her close to him so the fans can see her. "What do you have to say for yourself?"

Hayoon answers innocently, "Sorry. I promise I'll accept you all soon."

He snags another piece of watermelon.

"What kind of watermelon is this? Sweet."

"The kind that grows from the ground," she answers sarcastically.

He steals the whole container and runs away.

She chases after him shouting, "Jihoon and Seojun didn't get any yet. Give it back!"

Minseong runs around the dressing room, down the hallway, and around the stadium floor before he runs out of breath. He holds up his hand to stop her.

"Aren't you tired?" he asks panting.

"Nope. I have eight brothers; I can't be weak."

She sticks her tongue out at him when she snatches the watermelon back.

The comments in his livestream are flying across the screen. He laughs lightheartedly while reading the comments and asks, "Was anyone rooting for me?"

Hayoon is watching Kun's solo stage as her brothers zoom past her. They duck down to run under the stage to get into position on the lift. *Red?!?* Hayoon freaks out. Her eyes dart around to find a solution.

"Samchon! Give me your sweatshirt!"

Dohyun asks bewildered, "What?"

She uncharacteristically barks at him, "Give me your sweatshirt. Hurry!"

He unzips his sweatshirt and Hayoon rips it out of his hands, taking off under the stage.

Jeongu joins the rest of the group and realizes he put on the wrong outfit. He hears Hayoon hollering after him.

"Jeongu!"

Hayoon?

"Take it off!"

Jeongu stares at her, dumbfounded.

"You're wearing the wrong shirt. Switch with me."

Jeongu snaps out of it and drops to his knees to take his shirt off without hitting his head.

Baekhyeon takes the sweatshirt from Hayoon's hand to help. Jihoon helps Jeongu pull the shirt over his head.

Hayoon kneels and whips off her matching team shirt, exposing her high-neck sports bra. Baekhyeon drapes the sweatshirt over her shoulders and tosses her shirt to Jeongu.

"Five seconds," the stage crew manager calls out.

The boys all climb into position. Hayoon steps back out of the way, sticking her arms through the sleeves. Baekhyeon nervously checks his members to make sure everyone is on their mark.

Hayoon returns to Dohyun's side as Junwoo starts to sing.

Phew. Made it.

Day 33

"Did you guys get to rest yesterday or did you practice?" Dohyun asks Hayoon.

"Little of both. Practiced 'til three."

Manager-nim splits away from Baekhyeon to stand with them.

Baekhyeon turns his mic on to start sound check.

"Let's get started."

The members assemble backstage to practice their entrance.

"Do you want to watch from backstage or the floor barrier tonight?"

Hayoon answers Samchon, "The barrier."

As they're conversing, Kun's mic slips from his hand to the stage floor and breaks apart on impact.

Baekhyeon covers his mic to tell him, "Get it fixed!"

Someone from the sound crew strides out to meet him off to the side. They only have forty seconds until his solo and the notes are too high for Baekhyeon.

Hayoon shifts her attention from Kun to Junwoo. He's motioning for her to take his place.

Are you crazy? She refuses animatedly.

...35 seconds. Junwoo insists.

...34 seconds. Hayoon throws her jacket at Manager-nim and naturally slides into formation during a position change.

The members can't believe what's happening, especially the vocal and rap units. Hayoon matches the energy and style of their choreography perfectly! She blends right in. Her brothers get hyped, dancing alongside her.

...12 seconds. Kun is low-level panicking when Hayoon looks back to check his progress. *He's not going to make it.*

Hayoon looks over to Junwoo and gestures to Minseong's microphone. *Get me his mic!*

Junwoo blindly trusts Hayoon without hesitation and without knowing her plan. He takes the mic out of Minseong's hand and smoothly hands it off to Hayoon during a transition.

...3 seconds. With no audience and an urgent situation, Hayoon's stage fright has no chance to take effect. She lifts the mic up to her chin and belts out Kun's solo.

No one, including Junwoo, can believe what is happening. The members' eyes widen and jaws drop in shock. Kun completely forgets about the broken mic in his hand.

Hayoon's voice is raw and unpolished but incredible. She hits every note with ease; not an ounce of strain can be detected.

Manager-nim asks Dohyun hopefully, "You're recording, right?"

"Oh yeah."

Hayoon finishes Kun's solo, unaware of the members' mental breakdown behind her, and continues into the dance break.

She can even do the dance break?!? Baekhyeon exchanges a questioning glance at Junwoo as they dance.

Junwoo smirks in response. *You idiots actually thought she was only watching when she came to the dance studio. Ha.*

As the professionals they are, the members wait for the audio director's okay after the song ends.

"Let's take a fifteen-minute break."

The second he releases them, the boys all run over and jump on their sister in a boisterous attack. A million questions are flying out of their mouths.

"You can sing?!?"

"You can dance?!?"

"Hayoon, that was awesome!"

Her shyness overwhelms her at the sudden realization of what she did. She covers her face.

Her brothers usher her back to the dressing room, chatting nonstop. In the room, they disperse to do their own thing.

Hayoon sits on the couch and opens her bag with shaking hands. She is pulling out her earbuds when Junwoo sits beside her. He wants to tell her how amazing she is but knows, that's not what she needs right now. He pats his leg and lifts his arms out of the way for her to lay down. She lays her head on his leg and turns on her side to hide. Junwoo strokes her hair to soothe her.

He softly says, "I'm here. It's okay."

"Pass a fork."

Yunjae throws a fork down the table to Baekhyeon.

Hayoon's mouth is full of food when Jihoon asks her, "When did Junwoo teach you our choreography?"

Junwoo answers, "I didn't."

Baekhyeon becomes intrigued. "So how does she know it?"

"She learned it from watching us."

"Seriously?"

Yunjae proudly reports, "Hayoon can dance all of our parts to any song."

Baekhyeon asks a follow-up question, "So when you guys go to the studio, she practices with you?"

Junwoo responds, "Hmm. Not always. That one day, Seojun was practicing vocals, she filled in for him. Mostly, she helps me with new choreography. You know that choreography I just finished for our next album?"

"The one you showed me yesterday?"

"Yeah. That was her."

She waves her fork in front of her, denying it.

Junwoo adds, "If we weren't an all-male group, I'd be worried about my lead dancer position being threatened."

Baekhyeon concurs, "After today, I'm worried about my lead vocal position, too."

Hayoon blushes from the shower of compliments. *Do they really think I did well? No one has ever said things like this to me before.*

Day 35

"The first of three games also has three rounds. Each team will send one member to compete and our guests will select the challenge category."

Hayoon listens to PD-nim explain the game but can't help thinking it's not fair they get to choose all three categories AFTER the players have been chosen. *Is it because it's our show and they're guests? Why can't we know the category before we choose the players?*

PD-nim points to the categories on the board. "Intelligence. Strength. Speed. You cannot choose the same category more than two times. The team who wins the most points, wins the game. Teams, please send your first players."

Her brothers huddle up to discuss who's going to play.

Huh? Hayoon's ears perk up at the familiar sound of Chinese.

She leans over to Seojun and asks, "Are they not Korean?"

"Two are Chinese, one is Japanese and I think two are American. The rest are Korean."

An international group. Interesting. Unbeknownst to anyone, Hayoon studied Chinese as her second elective for six years.

She tunes her ears in to their rival's discussion.

Her brothers decide to send Baekhyeon. They start to break their huddle but she grabs the front of his shirt.

"Wait."

Hayoon appears to be zoned out but then pushes Jeongu. *Strength!*

"Go!"

They stare at her wondering what the heck is going on.

"Trust me."

Baekhyeon tells Jeongu, "You go."

She's right. The opposing team chooses strength and Jeongu brings back a win.

Next round, the members are still deliberating when Hayoon blurts out, "Baekhyeon oppa."

They give her a curious look but she rebuts, "I don't have time to explain."

Baekhyeon makes eye contact with the members and no one voices opposition.

The international team chooses intelligence. It's not easy but Baekhyeon brings back their second win. The third round is double the points and has the possibility to push the game into a bonus round.

This time, the boys don't bother opening their mouths.

"Talk," Hayoon commands them.

They start talking about the most random assortment of things, waiting for their princess to give her orders.

Speed.

"Seojun."

No stares. No questioning. No delay.

They crush the competition. PD-nim congratulates MPeak and explains the second game. Hayoon gets confused by his instructions but gets that it's a strategy game.

Jihoon tries to help her understand. "It's like capture the flag but there are side missions."

Both groups move to their planning tables with a map of the area.

Yes! The international team relies on Chinese again to talk strategy freely without alerting her brothers. *...I'm too far away.*

Hayoon moves around the table to stand closer to their team. She stays out of the huddle, pretending to drink her water bottle, to hear better.

Got it! She returns to the opposite side of the table and holds her palm up for Baekhyeon to give her a marker. She rotates the map and draws three circles on the field.

"They're going to concentrate in these three regions."

They assume she heard them talking but it doesn't occur to them what she heard wasn't Korean.

Baekhyeon modifies their plan according to the intel she provided. They decide to break into three groups and attack all three regions at the same time. Baekhyeon sends Hayoon with Jihoon and Junwoo to the largest central region. He takes Yunjae and Seojun to the east. Hakkun leads the group with Jeongu and Minseong to the west. Within a fraction of the game time allotted, all three regions of the international team fall in defeat. Mpeak dominates for the second time!

The game points aren't weighted evenly so the international team still has a chance if they crush them in game three.

The teams arrive at a game show stage setup for the final game.

"The third game is simple. Music trivia from around the world. The first team to hit the buzzer, gets to answer. If you are wrong, the other team will get a chance."

A *speed game*. Hayoon relaxes in her chair to let the extroverts take over.

"This next question comes from China."

She perks up to listen to the question. *I know this!*

The other team smacks the buzzer before Hayoon can tell Seojun the answer.

"Eight."

"Correct."

No, it's not.

Hayoon tugs on Baekhyeon's shirt impatiently and whispers, "They're wrong."

"What?"

"They're wrong."

Baekhyeon stands up to challenge their answer. Before her leader has a chance to clarify, the member who answered previously, insults him.

He tells his group mate in Chinese, "He has no idea what he's talking about. It's eight. Idiot."

Idiot?

Hayoon stands abruptly, sending her chair skidding back.

She responds angrily in rapid Chinese, "What right do you have to say that about him? He's not wrong! Your answer is wrong."

Everyone on set snaps their head in her direction.

"This song was released in 2018. The nineth member didn't leave, making them a group of eight, until the end of 2019. The answer is nine."

Hayoon looks to PD-nim and switches fluidly back to Korean to explain it to him. She finishes talking but no one flinches out of their frozen state.

"Look it up," she demands.

Baekhyeon pulls her in to a side hug and rubs her arm to calm her down. She puffs out in frustration, "He called you an idiot."

One of the staff holds up her phone to confirm, "She's right."

The international group's leader asks astonished, "You speak Chinese?"

It dawns on Hayoon why everyone is staring. And they are ALL staring at her.

Seojun asks the same question again, "You speak Chinese?"

The rival team's maknae asks curiously, "You guys didn't know she spoke Chinese either?"

Her panicky eyes meet Baekhyeon's and she buries her face in his shoulder. He holds the back of her head, providing refuge to their shyest member.

"Why didn't we know you spoke Chinese?"

She turns her head to answer, "You didn't ask."

Baekhyeon laughs at her blunt and honest answer. *She's right. We didn't ask.*

"Dance, sing, speak Chinese... is there anything else we don't know?"

She shakes her head. Baekhyeon hands the embarrassed Hayoon off to Junwoo, kicking their chairs closer.

"Hayoon." The international group's Chinese members approach her. "Can we have your number?"

How can I say no? She glances over to her guardians and motions to Junwoo's phone. He tosses it over.

She unlocks it and tells them, "My phone wasn't working so I'm sharing Junwoo's until we have a break to buy a new one."

They add each other.

Baekhyeon summons her over, "Hayoon, time to go."

Her brothers are all waiting for her. Junwoo offers his hand out for her to hold. She jogs over to take his hand and gives back his phone. He raises a questioning eyebrow and she smirks mischievously.

"You have some new friends."

"I do or you do?"

"Since we're sharing a phone until I can buy a new one, we do."

Beakhyeon, Jihoon, and Minseong overhear their conversation and laugh. Baekhyeon puts his arm around her.

"Isn't our little sister smart?"

She jokes back, "I have all the men I can handle."

"Thank you for fitting us into your busy schedule."

Baekhyeon responds to the interview host, "Thank you for having us."

"You've had quite a few posts go viral lately. Baekhyeon, your speech at the Daegu fan meeting gained a lot of attention. Your fans started using the hashtags 'princessprotectors', 'theguardians', and my personal favorite, 'dontmesswithMPeakfamily'. The fans are all very curious about Hayoon."

The host respectfully asks Baekhyeon, "I noticed, with the exception of Peak Season, Hayoon has been kept out of the spotlight. Would it be okay if I asked her a few questions?"

Hayoon looks over to Baekhyeon at the end of the couch behind her.

"Of course you can."

She shifts her attention to Hayoon.

"After watching the home footage you took, the fans have some questions for you about living with the members."

Hayoon nods.

"Which member has the messiest room?"

"Minseong and Seojun."

"Who's the best cook?"

"Jihoon."

"Which member are you the closest to? Or which member do you hang out with the most? The fans speculate it's one of your so-called guardians (Junwoo, Baekhyeon, and Jihoon) or Seojun."

"Depends on the situation."

"What do you mean?"

Hayoon elaborates, "If I want to go on a coffee run, I'd choose Jihoon. If I want to play games, I'd choose Minseong or Seojun. If I want a late-night snack, I'd choose Yunjae. But if I had to choose one member I'm the closest to, I'd say Junwoo."

The host asks her, "Why Junwoo? Some of the members have been together since they joined the company or they spend more time together in the same unit so it makes sense they would be close. But you met all of them at the same time and don't have a unit team."

Yunjae opposes, "She has a unit team!"

"What unit?"

Hayoon explains, "I'm not an official member, it just sort of happened that way."

All four other members of the dance team overlap each other, defending her position on the team.

The interviewer laughs at their defense of Hayoon.

"I'm guessing it's the dance team."

Hayoon tells her, "When I first came, I was crazy shy. I didn't tell anyone I love dance. When they divided up to practice in their teams, Seojun and Junwoo invited me to go with them. I went and just kept going back. Junwoo is the lead dancer so we naturally spend more time together."

Junwoo is sitting directly behind Hayoon and puts his hand on her shoulder as he speaks.

"Hayoon is an incredible dancer. But because she's shy, most of our members don't even know how talented she is. There are times when I'm making choreography and moves just aren't connecting. She finds a way to make it work better than I could've done. I rely on her a lot."

She reaches up to her shoulder to squeeze his hand.

Yunjae chimes in, "She doesn't go on stage with us but she's as much a part of this team as any of us."

The host comments, "Some fans have noticed when you guys are in a dangerous situation, like the fan meeting or airport, Junwoo is always by your side. Why is that?"

Baekhyeon speaks up to tell her, "Hayoon didn't choose who she walks with. Myself, Kun, Junwoo and Jihoon considered many factors when deciding where all the members would stand. In fact, Hayoon told us to put her in the back to make our safety the priority. But the fans have been saying for a long time that MPeak is like a family and like family, we protect our own."

He glances over to silently ask Junwoo's permission before continuing. Junwoo nods in approval.

"That being said, Junwoo has a very strong protective instinct when it comes to Hayoon."

Hayoon leans back against Junwoo's legs as Baekhyeon speaks.

"I don't know if you've seen the full video of what happened at the airport but we found ourselves in a situation where there wasn't enough security. Fans were pushing from all sides and we risked getting separated or injured. Junwoo's body reacted before anyone had time to think about it. Because of that, we got out safely."

The interviewer interjects, "We actually have a picture from that incident."

She holds up a tablet with the viral picture from the airport of Junwoo carrying Hayoon.

Baekhyeon tells her, "When you're in a dangerous situation, it helps if you have a central point. The point that draws the group together. If everyone is working on their own, it can cause problems. Since Junwoo instinctively protects Hayoon, she naturally becomes the security focal point. Our teamwork has become stronger since she joined us."

The host switches her attention to Junwoo to ask, "Why is it that you're so protective over Hayoon? I'm sure all the members would agree; they would protect her, too."

Junwoo answers confidently, "I know our members would protect her. I think it's because she's on the dance team. I'm more... possessive isn't the right word. Hmm. How do I explain it? When you dance with someone, there's a higher level of trust you need to have with that person. There are difficult moves that I work out with Hayoon before teaching them to the group. If we don't have trust and mutual understanding, it wouldn't be possible."

She turns to Hayoon and asks, "Do you agree? Do you trust him?"

"I do. Just like how his instinct is to protect me, my instinct is to run to him."

"If you say it's because of the trust you have from dancing, then if the lead dancer was another member, would you be running to them instead?"

Hayoon pauses to formulate her thoughts and emotions into words. She signals to Baekhyeon, asking for support to say what she wants.

He gives it. She looks straight back to Junwoo and he gives her shoulder a squeeze.

"Probably not."

"Why?"

"Remember how I answered at the beginning? I said it depends on the situation. For example, the members that I would choose to play pranks with, are the ones whose personalities are more mischievous. Our interests and personalities play a big role in who we are. Those things are unique to us."

Her brothers are listening and nodding in agreement.

"There is no one else like Junwoo oppa, regardless of his role in the group. His position as leader rather gave us the opportunity to grow and create choreography together."

Junwoo complements her answer by adding, "We come from different dance backgrounds so we're used to bouncing ideas off of each other. We are able to both teach and learn. Whether we're growing in our relationship or improving in dance, it can only benefit the group."

Baekhyeon adds his support, "I'm excited for the fans to see the next comeback. The choreography is going to be better than ever before."

The host applauds their answers and turns the tables to ask, "So who's the mostly likely to create mischief?"

"Seojun!"

The rest of her brothers erupt in laughter and continue the interview.

Hayoon and Junwoo are the exception. They seem like they are separated in their own world. She looks back into his eyes. He moves his hand up from her shoulder to rub her temple with his thumb. His warm smile tells her, *you did good.*

"Before you guys leave, I have a quick challenge for you."

Seojun extrovertedly asks, "What's the prize?"

"Everything you need for a barbeque, including ten pounds of meat."

The boys get excited but Baekhyeon settles them to ask, "What's the challenge?"

"I heard Hayoon subbed in for Kun at the sound check in Japan."

Yunjae accidentally throws his little sister under the bus. "She can dance and sing! She's really good."

Jihoon warns Yunjae, "Shut up."

"We're going to play five of your songs. Hayoon has five seconds to start dancing once the music starts. If she correctly dances ten seconds for four out of five songs, you win."

Hayoon tugs on Junwoo's shirt. He asks, afraid to know the answer, "Does she have to dance alone?"

The host tries to be lenient. "The rest of you can dance behind her but she can't look back."

Kun asks for clarification, "From any of our songs?"

"The current concert set."

"That's almost two dozen songs!"

Baekhyeon takes a half step forward to intervene on Hayoon's behalf but Junwoo stops him.

"She can do it."

Junwoo gives her a confidence boosting nod, trusting in her whole-heartedly.

"Can you do it?" the host asks Hayoon.

"I'll try."

Baekhyeon doubts Junwoo's judgement call but stands down.

The dance unit take positions behind her while the rest of the members watch next to the host. To Baekhyeon's surprise and relief, Hayoon knocks them out one at a time. The vocal and rap teams cheer her on, marveling at how she's learned every song in such a short time.

Mission success!

12

Why won't you let us help you?!?

-Jeongu

Day 36

Whistle! Whistle!

Baekhyeon falls out of bed and smacks his roommates to wake them up.

Seriously?

He shuffles down the hall, banging on the boys' doors to wake them up.

"Hurry up! Line up!"

The members hustle, half-asleep, to put on shoes and sweatshirts before running outside.

PD-nim announces through a megaphone, "2 minutes! If you're late, you get punished."

Jeongu grumbles, "We just fell asleep."

Kun grouchily says, "I hate morning challenges."

Baekhyeon is first to arrive in front of PD-nim. Junwoo and Jeongu step into line behind him. Seojun and Minseong crawl out together behind Kun.

Junwoo asks Baekhyeon, "Did you wake Hayoon up?"

"I banged on her door."

As Baekhyeon finishes talking, Hayoon stumbles out of the door.

Hayoon! Alarmed by Hayoon's sleep shorts and crop top, Junwoo leaves his second-place position to go to her. He can tell right away, something isn't right. Even after dancing for three hours, she wears no less than a t-shirt.

Baekhyeon looks back when Junwoo steps out of line. *What is she wearing?*

Hayoon! Yunjae jogs up from behind Hayoon and drapes his sweatshirt over her shoulders.

She pushes the sweatshirt off without fully opening her eyes. She staggers, veering off to the right. Junwoo lunges forward to catch her as she collapses. He cradles her in his arms on the ground.

Being the increasingly devoted brothers that they are, the members all spring into action, abandoning PD-nim and the show.

Junwoo can feel the heat from Hayoon's body in his arms and reaches up to check her forehead. He worriedly tells Baekhyeon, "She has a fever."

Baekhyeon feels her forehead for himself and Yunjae covers her with his sweatshirt.

Baekhyeon says authoritatively, "We need to get her inside."

"I can't get up like this. Jihoon, you take her."

Jihoon repositions himself to slip his arms under Hayoon. Minseong helps support her as he lifts her up. The boys ignore the existence of their film crew and carry Hayoon inside.

Seojun hurries ahead of Jihoon to pull Hayoon's blanket over so he can set her down. Junwoo tucks the blanket around Hayoon and adjusts her pillow.

Jeongu comes in with the thermometer. Junwoo tries to get out of his way but Hayoon has a death grip on his arm. Jeongu hands it over for Junwoo to use.

Baekhyeon orders the members, "Yunjae, medicine. Seojun, water. Jeongu, get the extra blanket out of my room. Kun, go talk to PD-nim. Ask if we can reschedule filming today."

Kun turns to leave but Baekhyeon calls him back. "Wait. Try to find a nice way to tell him the recording from earlier needs to be deleted. Hayoon's footage can't be used."

"39.5," Junwoo reports.

Baekhyeon walks into Hayoon's closet to find a sweatshirt. He pulls it off the hanger and tosses it to Junwoo. Jihoon climbs onto the bed from the other side to help him lean her up and put the sweatshirt on. Instead of laying her down flat, Junwoo props her up against him to wait for Yunjae to bring the medicine.

Yunjae, Seojun and Jeongu come back in a flurry. Jihoon jumps off the bed to help Jeongu arrange the blanket.

Junwoo coaxes Hayoon to swallow the medicine and tips the cup up for her to drink. She blinks her eyes to try and fix her dizzy vision. *Who are you?*

"Take another drink of water."

Hayoon recognizes his voice and clings onto him.

"Oppa."

Kun comes back to report, "They can give us an hour but we can't reschedule."

Yunjae objects, "Someone needs to take care of her."

Kun tells them, "I asked for leave for Junwoo. But PD-nim said he can only get leave for today. Tomorrow..."

Junwoo asks his roommate, "Can you get my phone from our room? I'll call my mom to come tomorrow."

Minseong adds in, "My mom has this soup she always makes when I'm sick. I'll call her to bring some over."

Jeongu pulls out his phone and says, "I'll have my dad bring tea from his shop that helps the body recover."

Their leader processes his thoughts out loud.

"Mineong's mom is bringing soup. Jeongu's dad is bringing tea. Junwoo's mom is coming to take care of her tomorrow. After tomorrow's show, we have two days off. Then, two days of filming and then holiday. 39.5..."

Manager-nim knocks on the door frame, "Everything okay? Does she need to go to the doctor?"

Baekhyeon gives deciding authority to Junwoo.

"If her fever gets any higher, she'll need to go to the hospital. For now, let's wait and see."

Junwoo picks up his blanket and pillow and takes his phone charger out from the wall.

Baekhyeon pauses his movie to ask, "How's Hayoon?"

"The same."

"Are you going to sleep in there tonight?"

"Yeah, I'm afraid her fever will go up during the night."

"Leave the doors open so I can hear if you need me. Do you want us to help move your mattress in there?"

"Can you?"

"Jihoon! Jeongu! ...Can you move Junwoo's mattress into Hayoon's room?"

"Got it."

"Junwoo, you know you have to move it back out before anyone comes over right?"

"I know. I won't forget."

Day 37

"Junwoo! Mom's here!"

Junwoo leaves Hayoon to greet his mom.

"Hey mom, did you bring the camera?"

"I brought it. How's she doing?"

"She still has a fever. She's woken up a few times but not for long."

"Jihoon's mom said she's going to come in a few hours and Minseong's mom is bringing soup around lunch time. What time will you get back from filming?"

"Not sure. Hopefully before dinner time."

Junwoo's mom walks around the bed to feel Hayoon's forehead. She straightens the already straight blanket and strokes her hair.

"Poor thing."

Junwoo plugs the motion activated camera into the wall and links it with the app on his phone.

"Will it notify me when it detects movement? Even in the dark?"

"If you turn on notifications, it will."

He sits on the edge of the bed by Hayoon, leaving the chair for his mom.

He tries to wake Hayoon softly, "Hayoon... Hayoon."

She groggily opens her eyes and answers, "Oppa."

"Try to stay awake for a minute, okay? This is my mom. We have to go so she's going to stay and take care of you, okay?"

Hayoon pulls the corner of the blanket back and tries to lift her heavy head.

"What are you doing? Lay down."

Junwoo's mom guides her head to rest on the pillow and tucks the blanket back in.

"You said we have to go."

Junwoo's mom tells her, "You're not going, sweetie. The boys will go. You need to rest."

She addresses Junwoo, "You go. We'll be fine. Jihoon's mom will be here soon to keep me company."

He looks at Hayoon worriedly.

"If anything happens, call me, okay?"

"Don't worry. I raised you fine, didn't I?"

"Okay... I'm leaving."

He dashes out to get ready and leave.

Junwoo kicks off his shoes and calls out, "Mom," as he walks towards Hayoon's room.

"Son, you're back."

He greets Jihoon's mom, "Hi, mom."

"How was filming?"

"It was fine. How's Hayoon? Did she wake up?"

"She woke up around lunch time. We fed her a little bit of soup but she's still pretty out of it."

Jihoon's mom adds, "She kept saying she could do it when we were trying to feed her. Maybe it's because she doesn't know us. Why didn't her family come?"

Junwoo sits on the bed and strokes her hair.

"She doesn't have any. ...She's like that with us, too."

"No parents or siblings?"

"No. You said you guys watched her first Peak Season episode, right?" He keeps his eyes on Hayoon the whole time he's talking. "When she left the store, she got hit by a car. No one had a clue until her cameraman told us days later. *Sigh.* ...She's been through a lot since she moved in but never told us."

"Son, give her time."

Baekhyeon, Jihoon and Seojun saunter in to check on her.

177

"How's the patient?"

"Not any worse at least."

Jihoon's mom stands up to tell them, "I need to head home to make dinner for your little brother. I'll come back tomorrow."

Jihoon and Baekhyeon walk her to the door.

Out of nowhere, Hayoon grumbles and starts kicking the blanket away. Junwoo grabs the blanket before it hits the ground.

"Hayoon, what's the matter?"

Junwoo's mom asks, "Do you need to go to the bathroom?"

She mumbles, "I have to get ready for dance practice."

"What?"

"Time for dance practice," she says while trying to lean up.

Junwoo's mom chuckles and asks her son, "What kind of a strict dance leader makes her afraid to miss practice even in her dreams?"

He guides her back down and tells her, "Hayoon, there's no practice today."

She clutches onto his arm.

"What is it?"

"Oppa, I want to go upstairs."

"It's chilly out and you're sick. Wait a few days, okay?"

Completely out of character, Hayoon acts cute and begs him.

"Oppa, I want to go outside. Please."

Seojun laughs satisfactorily. *I taught her that.*

How am I supposed to say no to that?

"Seojun, grab her blanket."

"Son, are you sure that's a good idea?"

"Just for a few minutes. Can you heat up soup for her while we're gone?"

He scoops Hayoon up into his arms. Seojun grabs her blanket and follows them up the stairs to the second-floor balcony.

Junwoo sits down with Hayoon in his lap like she's a six-year-old little girl. Seojun folds the blanket to half it's size and places it around her shoulders. He relaxes into the other chair.

"I forgot how nice it is up here."

"Hayoon comes up here a lot."

Seojun seriously asks, "Do you think we made her sick because we didn't take good enough care of her?"

"Maybe her body was just tired."

Junwoo readjusts his arms. Seojun watches him with appreciation.

"I'm glad I'm the mischievous fun brother and not the caring one. It looks like a lot of work."

Junwoo swings at him but he's too far away.

"Hey. Mischievous fun brother, go get the soup from my mom and bring it up here."

"Uhh?"

"Go."

Seojun goes back inside, laughing, to get the soup.

Hayoon stirs in his arms. He leans over to look at her furrowed brows. *Nightmare?*

He whispers close to her ear, "I'm here. It's okay."

She latches onto his arm like a koala bear. He hugs her head into his shoulder with his other hand and kisses the top of her head. *When will you trust us enough to tell us when you don't feel good? Did you already feel sick at the interview? Sigh. I should've noticed.*

Day 38

Hayoon reaches for the water on her nightstand but Minseong beats her to it.

"Do you want water?"

"It's okay. I can get it."

Minseong hands her the mug and hovers beside her. He waits until she's done drinking to set it back on the table. Seojun walks carefully in while concentrating on the steaming bowl in his hands.

"Jihoon hyung said our moms are bringing you lunch. Probably soup. He made you porridge for breakfast. Since your fever came down a little and you're awake, you should try to eat."

Hayoon reaches out to take the bowl. Jeongu stretches a hand out from where he sits in a bean bag chair in the corner.

"Careful!" Jeongu says as Seojun moves the bowl away from Hayoon.

Seojun tells her, "I'll help you."

"It's okay. I can do it."

Seojun rejects her, "It's too hot."

"Then set it on the nightstand. I'll eat it in a bit."

Seojun does as she wants and Jeongu settles back down into the chair. Hayoon tosses the blanket off her legs and drags them off the edge of the bed. Minseong and Seojun drop their phones on the ground and jump up to assist her.

"Where do you want to go?"

"Bathroom."

"We'll help you."

"I can do it."

With a decent amount of effort, she walks over to the bathroom. *You can do it. ...Aish. I can't do it.* Her head starts spinning. She falls into the door frame and slides down to her knees. Minseong and

Seojun leap over to pick her up off the ground. Jeongu rockets out of the bean bag.

"Sorry. I thought I had it."

They support her back to bed. Minseong picks her feet up to slide them back under the blanket.

"I can do it."

Jeongu huffs out in frustration. He can't contain it anymore.

"Why won't you let us help you?!?" He explodes at Hayoon.

Minseong utters in surprise, "Hyung."

Hayoon is taken aback and curls her fingers around the blanket. Junwoo has the fastest reflexes and arrives at Hayoon's side seconds before Baekhyeon and Jihoon.

Baekhyeon questions, "What's going on?"

Junwoo darts over to comfort Hayoon on the bed. Although it's gone down, her fever is still hanging on at thirty-eight. She finds her emotions hard to control in her fragile state. Her lip quivers as Jeongu's question puts her on the verge of tears.

Seojun loosely grabs Jeongu's arm and warns him, "Hyung, don't."

"No, I'm going to say it. Every time we try to do something for you it's, 'I can do it,' or 'It's okay.' I know we didn't take care of you before but we're trying now. Why won't you give us a chance?"

Hayoon lowers her head. Junwoo rubs her back and Baekhyeon moves closer on the bed to take her hand.

"If you don't like something we do, you can tell us."

She weakly responds, "That's not it."

Junwoo encourages her, "If you have something you want to say, say it. We won't get mad."

"Why won't you say anything? Waste of time."

Hayoon lifts her eyes to see Jeongu storm toward the door.

"Don't go."

His feet stop but he continues to face the door. Hayoon takes a deep breath.

"I wanted to tell you when I didn't feel good. I want to tell you when I'm thirsty. I want to tell you I want someone to stay with me until I fall asleep. ...But it's not that easy."

He turns around in a fury demanding to know, "What's not easy?"

Hayoon's suppressed emotions boil up inside of her.

"For the last six years, who did you expect me to tell?!?"

Jeongu's frustrated expression disappears at her sudden confession. Hayoon leans away from Junwoo's warmth and toward Jeongu's stone face. He instantly regrets his quick temper.

"I had no one! When you're sick, your mom coaxes you to eat medicine. When you're hurt, she'll bandage you up and give you candy to make you feel better. But me? I'm different. When I was hit by a car, I had to bite on a towel so I didn't scream out in pain as I cleaned my own cuts!"

I'm such an idiot. She's not pushing us away. She just doesn't know how to accept our help. How could I forget she's alone? Stupid. Stupid. Stupid.

"Hayoon."

Hayoon's emotional outburst weakens her. Her labored breathing alerts her brothers to her declining condition. Baekhyeon helps guide her back in to Junwoo's embrace.

"That's enough. You need to rest."

Hayoon crumbles into Junwoo, exhausted. Baekhyeon signals to Jihoon to take Minseong and Seojun out of the room. Jeongu hesitantly sits at the foot end of her bed.

"I'm sorry, Hayoon. I shouldn't have yelled at you. ...You're not alone anymore. If you want something, you can tell us, okay?"

He's right. ...I didn't mean to make them feel bad.

"Jeongu oppa."

He inches forward toward his little sister.

"What do you need?"

"You know that coffee shop on the way to the company? I want to eat their blueberry muffin."

"I'll go now."

Baekhyeon hollers to an already gone Jeongu, "Take my car."

Junwoo smiles affectionately at Hayoon and lowers her to lay down.

"Get some sleep. I'll be here."

Day 40

Hayoon watches as a bunch of women approach Junwoo and Baekhyeon. *She looks kind of familiar.* Junwoo points over to Hayoon and the ladies scurry toward her.

"Hayoon, do you remember me? I'm Junwoo's mom. This is Jihoon's mom."

Hayoon stands to greet them, "Im...Eomeon..."

"Call me eomma like the rest of the boys."

The word gets stuck in Hayoon's throat.

"...Eomma."

"Sit. Sit. Sit. This is Yunjae's mom and Seojun's mom. Baekhyeon's mom couldn't come today but she sent porridge for you."

She holds up a thermos as proof.

A man comes over to stand under the canopy tent with them. He holds up a black bag and asks, "Where do you want the camping lounger set up?"

Too many people. Hayoon grips her tea bottle tensely and looks for an escape route.

Jeongu jogs over to the tent and greets the moms with hugs. He stands behind Hayoon and places his hands on her shoulders firmly.

"We have to start filming soon. Why don't you set up the lounger over there and take a seat for a while? When we take a break, I'll bring Hayoon back to you."

They act according to Jeongu's plan. Hayoon exhales the breath she'd been holding in.

"Thanks, Jeongu oppa."

Oppa? That's the second time. He grins giddily behind her. *She accepts me.*

"I got you. ...But you know they'll all be waiting when we take a break?"

"Mm. It's okay."

He occupies the chair next to her.

"You know, when your fever was really high, Junwoo and Jihoon's mom took care of you all day? Minseong's mom brought you soup. My dad sent tea from his shop."

"Really? ...I didn't know."

"Seojun's mom came to check on you, too, but you were sleeping. Baekhyeon's family sent a whole bunch of fruit for all of us to eat. ...A lot of people care about you, Hayoon."

"But they don't know me."

"It doesn't matter."

Hayoon looks at him confused. *How could it not matter? I'm a stranger to them.*

"Starting back from when we were trainees I think, we stopped having only one mom and dad. I think Jihoon's mom was the first one to treat all of us like her own. Being trainees isn't easy. We would go months without seeing our families or over a year for some of us. One member's mom became everyone's mom. Last year, Yunjae's mom got cancer. The only reason Yunjae could stay with us was because he knew, with all of our families, she would never be alone. The second you became our little sister, you became their daughter."

Nearly inaudible, Hayoon whispers, "Their daughter."

Baekhyeon calls them over to start filming.

During filming downtime, Seojun starts randomly laughing in the middle of the stage. Minseong follows his gaze to Hayoon under the canopy tent.

Minseong calls out, "Jihoon, come look at this."

Baekhyeon and Jihoon both stroll over to see what Minseong is pointing at.

Chuckling, Jihoon says, "Yunjae, bring me my phone."

Yunjae picks it up from the bench beside him. Jihoon opens the camera and takes several shots of Hayoon to post.

Hayoon reclines stiffly in the camping lounger in the middle of the moms towering over her. One is holding tea out for her; one is holding up a spoonful of porridge; and another is unfolding a blanket to lay on top of her.

Yunjae laughingly comments, "Exactly whose moms are they?"

"What hashtag do you think I should use?"

"MPeakmomentourage"

"1daugher>8sons"

Hayoon makes eye contact with Junwoo and Jeongu. Junwoo pushes his hands down in front of his torso as he exhales, signaling her to relax. Jeongu nods, encouraging her to speak up.

"Eomma, can I wait to eat the porridge? Can I have fruit instead?"

"Of course you can sweetie. Apples, strawberries, or peaches?"

Hayoon cheerfully answers, "Apples."

Junwoo's dad slides over the freshly cut plate of fruit. His mom picks up an apple slice with a fork and hands it to Hayoon.

I did it. Yummy.

Jihoon snaps another picture of her proud, satisfied smile. He reads out loud as he types, "#MPeakprincess."

13

I'm taking you home.

-Junwoo

Day 41

"Are you Hayoon?"

Hayoon glances over to someone she had never seen before. *Who's he? A member from the other group?*

"Hayoon," Jihoon calls to her sternly.

Understanding Jihoon's undertone, she obediently runs over to him. He gestures back to Junwoo, exuding a protective mother bear demeanor. She passes behind him to take Junwoo's hand.

Baekhyeon reads the room quickly when he enters with PD-nim. He strides over to stand with Jihoon in a unified front. His unsaid message clear, *don't mess with our girl.*

Their competitor's leader understands his warning but chooses to challenge it.

PD-nim announces, "Let's get in position. MPeak on the left. Our esteemed guests on the right."

Hayoon jumps on Yunjae's back, steals Seojun's hat, and they run away. Junwoo jogs after them.

Baekhyeon walks with the flirty leader who comments, "You guys seem like a lively group."

"Makes work more fun."

"Maybe we should get a little sister, too."

Sure enough, his sights are on Hayoon.

Baekhyeon subtly sends Jihoon to catch up with Hayoon and the other boys.

PD-nim puts his megaphone down to get housekeeping out of the way before they start.

"Mpeak has two more members so they can choose one of your members to compete with them."

The opposing team's captain tells them, "I've seen your other episodes and Hayoon's team always wins."

The brothers exchange worried glances and Junwoo steps closer to Hayoon.

"We choose your secret weapon, Hayoon."

Me?

Yunjae squats down for Hayoon to slide off his back. Junwoo grabs her waist to help her down safety. She walks out from around Yunjae and out of Junwoo's grasp.

She fakes a positive attitude and joins the other team. During filming, their leader constantly tries to speak with her or get close to her but she doesn't give him the chance.

When the episode ends in their defeat, Hayoon does a horrible job of hiding her excitement to return to her brothers' company.

Baekhyeon summons her over, "Hayoon, let's go eat."

Hayoon starts to leave but stops midway. She turns back to tell them, "You were wrong... what you said earlier. In the other episodes, we didn't win because of me. We didn't win because I'm smarter or better. We won because together, we are smarter and stronger."

Her obvious smirk tells him, *I know what you tried to do today but it'll never work.*

She turns back to her brothers all waiting with prideful smiles. Junwoo holds his hand out again and she jogs over outstretching her arm to take it. Minseong takes her free hand. Kun comes up behind her, massaging her shoulders.

"Tired?"

"Nope."

Her smile lights up, walking amongst her stronger and smarter family.

Seojun jumps on Jihoon to ask, "Hyung, what's for dinner?"

Day 42

"See you later," Jeongu bids farewell to Hayoon and Jihoon as he shuts the door.

Now, only Jihoon and Hayoon remain. He slips on shoes while asking Hayoon, "What are doing during break?"

"I have plans uptown." *Going to the dance studio counts as plans, right?*

"Be careful traveling. Don't forget to lock the door. If you need us, text us, okay?"

"Okay. Bye."

"Hayoon?"

"Yunjae oppa, what are you doing back?"

"I forgot my charger. My parents are waiting outside. We're on our way to the airport."

Yunjae flies through the house to yank his charger out of the wall.

"I'm leaving. Bye."

"Have a safe flight."

Yunjae gets into the car, sticks his charger in his carry-on bag, and unlocks his phone to their group chat.

Yunjae: "Did you guys know Hayoon is still at home?"

Jihoon: "Doesn't she have plans uptown?"

Yunjae: "Idk but she's here now."

Kun: "It'll take me four hours to get back."

Yunjae: "Our flight's sold out."

Junwoo: "It's late today. I'll go pick her up in the morning."

Baekhyeon: "Let me know when she's with you."

Minseong: "Junwoo, you sure? I can pick her up tomorrow night."

Junwoo: "My mom wanted to disown me when I came back without her. We'll pick her up before breakfast."

Minseong: "Okay."

Baekhyeon: "Keep me updated."

Day 43

Junwoo gently rubs Hayoon's arm to wake her up. She grumbles as her eyes crack open.

He strokes her hair and tells her, "Hayoon-ah, time to wake up."

She groggily opens her eyes the rest of the way and asks, "Why'd you come back?"

Junwoo pulls her by the arms up to a sitting position.

"Come on. Let's get you up and packed. We don't have a lot of time. I dropped my mom off to run errands but she'll be done soon."

She moves in slow motion to dangle her legs off the bed. Junwoo tosses her duffel beside her and starts opening drawers to fill it with clothes.

She shakes her head awake and inquires, "Why are you packing my bag?"

"I'm taking you home."

He tugs her arms to get her standing. "Hurry and get ready. Mom's waiting for us to eat breakfast." He pushes her in the direction of the bathroom.

She stumbles forward while processing what he said. "Huh?!?" She spins around to face him.

"We're going home. I'll finish packing your clothes. Hurry and wash up."

Hayoon's energy level shoots up and she bounces off to wash her face.

Day 50

Baekhyeon checks with Jihoon in the kitchen, "Need help?"

"No. Ready in five."

Baekhyeon picks up the juice pitcher from the counter. He fills up the members' cups so it's ready when they come in. Minseong, Seojun and Kun all come in at the same time.

"Seojun, go wake up Hayoon. Her and Junwoo got back late last night. She's probably still sleeping."

Seojun comes back chuckling two minutes later, dragging Hayoon behind him.

"She hasn't opened her eyes yet but I got her."

Baekhyeon walks around to them as Seojun drops her in her chair. He ruffles her hair as she rubs her eyes with the back of her hand.

"You really are a little princess, aren't you?"

She smiles cutely up at him with drowsy eyes.

"Did you have fun at Junwoo's over break?"

Her messy hair flutters up and down as she shakes her head.

"What'd you do?"

"Eomma took me to get my hair cut. We went shopping and we went to the dance studio every day."

Seojun butts into the conversation to ask, "On break, you went to the dance studio? Every day?"

Hayoon nods enthusiastically, "It was super fun. We worked on the next album's choreography and oppa danced contemporary with me!"

"Contemporary? Junwoo?"

"Time to eat!"

Day 51

"Eh?"

The unexpected halt of their music causes Hayoon and Junwoo to stop dancing. They look over to the sound system to Baekhyeon.

"Yunjae and the others?"

Junwoo answers, "They headed out to pick up dinner."

"Good. I gotta talk to you guys."

He walks over to them and sits on the floor, motioning for them to do the same.

"I just came from Manager-nim's office. He had a meeting this morning with the director to talk about fan comments that came up during break. The company has decided it would be best for you two to put some distance between you during the show and public appearances."

Hayoon asks puzzled, "But haven't there always been girls jealous of my being in the house?"

"When it was fans' jealousy of you living with all the members, it was unavoidable and more of an 'oh, I wish I could live with my favorite idol, too' type of thing. This time is different. The attention is focused on just you two and it's more of a directed attack. It started after our last interview but got more aggressive after fans found out you went to Junwoo's house for break. The company wants to minimize the impact."

"With all the brothers? I can not be in the next show."

"Uh... it's only with Junwoo."

Junwoo processes what he's hearing silently. *They want to separate us.* His tall, broad stature becomes shrunken beneath the weight of Baekhyeon's words.

Hayoon hangs her head.

"I know it's not fair. But it's only for the show and public appearances. You probably shouldn't come to the studio with just the two of you anymore, either. Try not to focus on it. ...I need to head back to the recording studio to help with the guide tracks. I'll see you guys later back at the house."

Baekhyeon looks back to them as he walks out of the studio. *Should I have fought for them?* When the company told him, it didn't seem like a big deal. But now, he realizes he didn't consider the emotional impact as much as he should have. He closes the door and peers through the break in the frosted glass to listen to what they would say.

Junwoo reaches out for Hayoon.

"You okay?"

"Honestly..."

She lays her head on his leg, looking away. He puts a comforting hand on her upper arm. She sighs deeply and covers her eyes with the inside of her elbow. He waits patiently for her to sort out how to express what she feels. Even if she doesn't say anything, it's okay. He already knows.

"I don't understand why we're being punished because of other people's hate."

Junwoo rotates Hayoon so she's facing him. He holds her close, massaging her head with his thumb.

She gazes up into his eyes and shakingly admits, "I don't want to be separated from you." *You were the first person to see me. The first person who believed in me. The first person I trusted.*

Junwoo bends his legs to raise her head higher and pulls her up into his embrace. He confesses, "Me either."

Baekhyeon walks away regretfully.

Junwoo never showed how he felt and Hayoon never trusted anyone. Now, I'm breaking them apart from the person who changed all that. Hopefully, it's not too late to fix later.

Day 52

During breakfast, neither one of them sits at the table to eat. They both stay in the kitchen, making up excuses to do unnecessary things. They move in sync but there was a heaviness in the air. She washes the dishes; he dries. He opens a high cabinet; she ducks under his arm to put a cup away. All the while hardly a word is uttered. Their brothers weren't told about separating them but they can tell something is massively off.

Junwoo picks her up and sits her on the counter next to her untouched plate. He hands her a fork and gives her a look that tells her she's forbidden from coming down. She nibbles at her food even though she has no appetite. He understands the emotion behind her sad puppy dog eyes and playfully pinches her cheek to make her smile.

After breakfast, it seems like they are getting ready in slow motion. Junwoo leans against her door frame as she brushes her hair. She looks into the mirror's reflection to him.

"Ready?"

He holds out his hand to her and she takes it with a forced smile. They walk out to put their shoes on and find Baekhyeon waiting for them.

"Let's go."

Baekhyeon holds his hand out for Junwoo to hand her over. Reluctantly, he releases Hayoon. *It feels like I'm abandoning her. Does she feel that way, too?* Junwoo rubs his neck in frustration and follows them out.

Jihoon senses the severity of Hayoon's mood change and checks on her when they take five. Hayoon always has a positive attitude and is never tired. Today, she looks drained and weary. He sits in the chair across from her.

"Hayoon, are you doing okay?"

"I'm just tired. It's fine."

Jihoon holds her hands in front of them.

"Are you sure that's all?"

His concern for her makes it hard to keep a brave face. If there is anyone she can be transparent in front of, it's the guardians.

With pain in her eyes, she asks, "Did we do something wrong?"

Jihoon's heart aches for her. He reassures her, "You're not wrong. Neither one of you did anything wrong."

"Then, why?" She slouches over, unable to hold herself upright. "We work so hard for the company and fans. We spend every day in the studio working to perfect choreography. Is it so wrong to support and depend on each other? Why don't they want us to be happy?"

"Hayoon, listen to me. You can never let other people's hate make you doubt your relationship with him. We know how hard you work and this isn't fair. All your brothers support you."

He pulls her hands up to help her stand and hugs her. "It's going to be okay. We'll find a way out of this." Jihoon looks over to Junwoo, who has been watching concerningly. *Don't worry. We've got her.*

He leaves Hayoon to find Baekhyeon.

"We need to fix this. You and I both know how rare their bond is. We can't let this continue."

Baekhyeon agrees, "You should've seen them in the dance studio when I told them. Is she okay?"

"For now, at least. But she might not tell us if she isn't. The one person she would tell, she can't talk to."

"Sometimes I forget she didn't choose to be an idol like the rest of us. This is a whole new world for her. Must be hard."

"I'll keep an eye on her."

Hayoon kicks off her shoes and heads straight to her bedroom with the emotional exhaustion taking its toll. Junwoo looks after her longingly.

Baekhyeon takes the bag out of his hand and tells him, "Go."

Junwoo never looks away from the direction Hayoon disappeared into. He takes long, quick strides to go to her.

Without knocking, he slowly opens her door. He steps into her room soundlessly and shuts the door behind him. Hayoon is sitting on the bed, lost in her thoughts, and never hears him come in.

He calls out to her tenderly, "Hayoon-ah."

She looks over with clouded eyes. When she sees it's him, her eyes come alive as she lifts herself off the bed. They walk toward each other at the same time like magnets were pulling them together. He kisses the top of her head as she grabs fists full of his shirt back.

"I don't like this," she whispers to him.

"I know. I don't like it either."

"There were so many things I wanted to tell you today."

"Come here."

They sit against the wall side-by-side and talk about everything they couldn't say during the day.

Baekhyeon knocks on the door and pops his head inside. "Time to eat." When he sees their condition, he enters the room and squats in front of them. "Don't worry. I'm trying to find a way out of this. Wait a little bit longer, okay?"

Day 54

"How many more shows do we have?"

"I think two more. Maybe three. But then when we prepare for our comeback, we won't film at all."

Sigh. Two more. I just have to get through two more.

"Hayoon!"

Baekhyeon waves her over while talking on the phone. Seojun keeps walking to catch up with Minseong.

Baekhyeon holds up his pointer finger. *Wait a minute.* She turns away to give him privacy for his conversation.

"Okay. All done."

Hayoon spins around to face an oddly cheerful Baekhyeon.

"Hayoon, did you know you have a fan page?"

"Me?"

"You actually have three. One, fans made exclusively for you. The second one, fans made for you and me, Jihoon, and Junwoo called 'The Guardians' Fans.' But the third is for you and Junwoo. Turns out, there are a lot of fans who have been paying attention to you guys since the fan meeting. After he carried you in the airport, the fan page blew up. They're all waiting for our next comeback to see the choreography you guys made together."

"So...?" Hayoon asks hopefully.

"So, the company decided to take back what they said before."

Hayoon could barely stop herself from hopping up and down with joy. She spots Junwoo across set and looks back to Baekhyeon for permission. *Permission granted.*

She takes off at full speed, catching the attention of her brothers, including Junwoo. He looks past her to Baekhyeon. He nods in confirmation.

Kun stops talking midsentence at the appearance of Junwoo's rarely seen brilliant smile. Yunjae, Jeongu, and Jihoon all turn to see what sparked it. Right then, Hayoon jumps into his open arms and they close around her.

"Let's get started," PD-nim calls them to set with his megaphone.

Junwoo bends down a half foot to set Hayoon on the ground and turns his back to her so she can jump on.

14

No matter where they take you,

I will find you.

-Junwoo

Day 55

"Baekhyeon oppa, what's a fan picnic?"

"It's like going on a picnic with friends you haven't seen in a long time. The fans bring blankets to sit on and we pass out sandwiches, fruit, gimbap and a gift bag. We did it once last year and it was fun. It's only like fifty fans. They'll ask us questions while we eat for an hour and then it's over."

"Do we get gimbap, too?"

Baekhyeon laughs, "Are you hungry?"

"Starving."

"My question is for Junwoo. Did you come up with the choreography for your next comeback?"

Junwoo takes the mic from Baekhyeon to answer, "Hayoon and I worked on it together."

Another fan shoots up her hand after hearing his answer. Baekhyeon points to her and security walks over to hand her a mic.

"Can you upload the full video from the Japan sound check? Yunjae said Hayoon can sing but in the released BTS it only shows her dancing."

Hayoon drops her fork in panic. Baekhyeon leans over to whisper in her ear.

"There were venue staff there that day who recorded it on their phones. Even if we don't post it ourselves, fans will find it. It's better if we post it first to prevent anyone from editing it before posting."

"I understand." *Sigh.*

Baekhyeon holds the mic up to respond, "I can post it on our page. But before I do, I hope fans will keep in mind that Hayoon did what she did to help us get through sound check. She had only been with us a month and was never taught to sing or dance. She was never a trainee. She's never even met our dance or vocal coach. That being said, what she did was amazing. In MPeak, no one else can hit those notes except for Kun. I'm excited for you guys to see it. Next question..."

Baekhyeon chooses a young girl in the second row. Security hands her the mic and she nervously holds it with both hands. She says three words and pulls the mic away from her mouth to talk to the woman beside her.

Are they Chinese?

The members wait patiently while they try to read the Korean translation. Hayoon feels bad for the girl as she struggles to remember more than one word at a time. She taps Baekhyeon's arm. She points to herself and then the mother daughter duo.

"Go ahead."

Baekhyeon snaps his fingers at their body guard to get his attention and sends him off stage with Hayoon.

She briefly communicates with the mom in Chinese before lifting the girl over the first row of fans. Hayoon kneels beside her and asks what she wants to say. She translates three to four words at a time, repeating it twice. Seojun wants to answer her question but he rambles on too quickly for Hayoon to translate.

Hayoon shouts without a microphone, "Seojun!"

He abruptly stops and the fans explode with laughter. He looks like a kid who got caught eating cookies before dinner.

"Slow down. I can't translate that fast."

"Hayoon, did you see our page? That mom, the one that speaks Chinese, she posted a video of you helping her kid. It's only been an hour and our group page has over a hundred new fans. Check your page. Hyung posted the sound check video, too."

Minseong joins the conversation, "I saw that, too. I looked up the mom. Looks like her husband is a big deal."

Hayoon opens the app to check her page. Yunjae snoops over her shoulder to see.

"Hayoon!" Her brothers stop their conversations in the van to stare at her. Yunjae announces, "You have twice as many new fans as the group."

Everyone pulls open their page to see what the fuss is about.

"Your number of fans are catching up to ours."

"There are thousands of comments on the Japan video."

"This fan wants to know if she's going to debut for our comeback."

Hayoon denies it, "Not gonna happen."

"This fan wants her to do our next comeback dance challenge with Junwoo."

"This one said the same with Baekhyeon, Jihoon, and Junwoo."

Baekhyeon asks, "Hayoon, what do you think?"

"Ummm... I can probably do the dance challenge. No one watches when you record it, right?"

Seojun chimes in, "I want to do it with her, too."

Yunjae jealously adds, "If Seojun gets to do it, I do too."

Baekhyeon ignores them to ask Hayoon, "Hey, can you answer this fan's question? It's getting a lot of attention."

"Which one?"

"The one about why you told her what to say instead of translating for her?"

Hayoon scrolls through the comments. "Found it."

As she typing out her response, Yunjae asks thoughtfully, "Why did you do it like that?"

Hayoon reads her response as she types it. "I wanted to give her a voice; not become her voice."

"Wouldn't it have been faster if you spoke for her?"

"Maybe. But it was worth the time for that little kid."

Jihoon supports her decision, "She's right. We always say the fans are the most important to us. Today, Hayoon showed everyone it's true."

Manager-nim tells the members, "Today, we arranged a surprise for you. We canceled your evening practice and your parents are waiting for you inside. In a while, you'll all go out to dinner together."

The boys cheer loudly but Hayoon tries to mask her emotions. She is genuinely happy her brothers' parents came to spend time with them. But there was an undeniable twinge of sadness, knowing no one would come for her.

As the boys disperse to find their parents, Hayoon hangs back to not attract attention. She buddies up with Dohyun who lets her help record the BTS. She looks through the camera to a familiar face, Junwoo's mom. *What's she doing? Junwoo is right in front of her but she looks like she lost something.*

Hayoon moves her view from the camera to the scene in front of her. Junwoo's mom interrupts Jihoon's mom to ask if she knows where Hayoon is.

Did she say my name?

Junwoo's mom tugs his sleeve. "I can't find her. Weren't you just with her? Where'd she go?"

She's looking for me.

Dohyun asks, "What's the matter? What are you looking at?"

Hayoon answers with warmth growing inside of her, "My family."

Junwoo is helping look for her when he hears Hayoon yell out, "Eomma!"

Junwoo's mom holds her hands out to grasp Hayoon's hands as she jogs over.

"Where have you been?"

"I was talking with a friend. Sorry."

"You're not working too hard, are you? You need to take care of yourself so you don't get sick."

"Don't worry. I'm doing well." She smirks at Junwoo. "But Junwoo works the dance unit really hard. I might die of exhaustion."

He hugs Hayoon from behind, hanging his arms down over her shoulders.

"Hey, I heard that. Mom, she's lying."

His mom smacks him playfully and pulls Hayoon away from him. She hugs Hayoon's waist in a side hug.

Junwoo jokes, "Ow! How can you hit your son?"

"Why can't I? You bully my daughter, you deserve it."

Day 56

"PD-nim, we can't start yet. Baekhyeon isn't here."

"Baekhyeon won't be coming. He's watching the monitors from inside. For today's challenge, you need to successfully complete it without his help."

The boys unconsciously inch closer together. Junwoo takes Hayoon's hand and Jihoon puts his arm around Yunjae's shoulders.

"Your company has some concerns about Hayoon's role in the group."

Hayoon's brothers tense up in fear of what PD-nim will say next. Seojun moves up in the group to take Hayoon's free hand.

"They're considering moving her to a rookie group."

Junwoo's hand tightens around Hayoon's.

"Today, Hayoon will not be competing with you guys. She'll be with staff at the audio tent across the field. Your challenge will be divided into a physical task and a knowledge task with ten questions. If you fail at any point, Hayoon will be taken away."

The members are in shock.

"Can he really do this?"

"The company agreed with this?"

"How can you do this when Baekhyeon isn't here?"

PD-nim waits, letting their reactions play out. Truth is, the challenge was designed for them to fail.

"Time to get started. Hayoon, my assistant is going to take you to the audio tent."

Her brothers circle around her, promising to win and bring her back. Junwoo holds her head in his hands, forcing her to focus on him.

"Trust us. We will bring you back."

Her eyes fill with tears but she puts on a brave smile to tell them, "Mm. I trust you."

Junwoo pulls her head forward to whisper in her ear, "No matter where they take you, I will find you."

He releases her to follow the assistant. After five feet, she turns back to ask, "If I can't come back today, can you tell Baekhyeon oppa it's not his fault? He's the best leader and big brother."

Inside, Baekhyeon slams his fist on the table. He raises his voice at the staff blocking his door, "How can you mess with them like this? I want to call our manager!"

At the audio tent, Hayoon watches the monitors as her brothers compete in the physical task. The staff watching with her, comment on how impressed they are with the boys' unity and quick progress. Jeongu's veins are protruding from the physical strain of helping everyone else but he refuses to give up. Minseong slips with only a meter left. Hayoon holds her breath. Kun grabs his wrist and pulls him back up. *Phew.*

They passed! Only one more left.

"Time for part two. You can discuss each question before answering but only one member can answer. Question one, what was the date of MPeak's debut?"

Hayoon stares at the monitor but can hardly hear with the pounding in her head. *Nine more...eight more...*

PD-nim questions how the boys knew an answer he was sure they would fail.

Yunjae tells him proudly, "Hayoon taught us."

Six more...five more... four more...

The audio director murmurs to himself, "They weren't supposed to last this long. How is this possible?"

"It's because of her," their makeup artist comments.

They look over to an anxious young woman who somehow changed every one of their lives in a matter of weeks.

Ding. "Incorrect."

Seojun shouts emotionally, "How are we supposed to know that? That isn't fair."

PD-nim motions at a car behind the audio tent. The boys watch in distress as two men get out and walk toward Hayoon.

Junwoo screams, "No!"

Junwoo tries to go to her but is held back by show staff. Kun and Yunjae start arguing with PD-nim. More staff jump in to hold back the boys trying push through to Hayoon.

Hayoon looks from her struggling brothers to the men approaching her from behind. Without thinking, she takes off, running across the field.

"Hayoon!" Junwoo yells out to her.

Jeongu wedges his body between Junwoo and security. He breaks Junwoo free and shoves him forward.

"Go!"

Junwoo sprints out to save Hayoon. Their terrified eyes lock on each other as the gap between them narrows.

PD-nim panics with how out of hand it's becoming. They never meant to use force but the number of staff involved keeps growing uncontrollably.

Junwoo reaches Hayoon and they collide together.

"I got you. It's going to be okay. I'm here."

Desperate not to be separated, he embraces her tightly, making it hard to breath. Even so, neither one of them is willing to lessen their grip.

During the chaos, Baekhyeon is left unattended and escapes. He arrives on set with the determination to put an end to this nonsense.

"That's enough!"

Hayoon is sobbing in Junwoo's arms and the boys are in various stages of emotional distress.

Baekhyeon screams, "That's enough!"

Staff and members stop fighting and grow silent. In all the years Baekhyeon was leader, he had never once yelled like this.

"You can't do this to them!" He aggressively points to Hayoon. "She's already lost her family once! Was that not enough for you?!?"

PD-nim has nothing to say for himself. He knows he was wrong. "I'm sorry. It wasn't supposed to happen like this. Hayoon isn't really leaving."

Baekhyeon barks back, "No, she's not!"

Kun and Jihoon draw the brothers close together by Baekhyeon.

PD-nim directs his words to Junwoo and Hayoon, "Hayoon isn't leaving."

They don't seem to hear PD-nim so he walks closer. Junwoo spots him in his peripheral view and looks up fiercely as he jerks Hayoon further away. Hayoon claws at Junwoo's back in response. Her sobs can be clearly heard twenty meters away.

Junwoo tries to comfort her, "I'm here. I'm here." He presses his lips firmly to her head and adjusts his arms to pull her tighter.

PD-nim looks to Baekhyeon apologetically.

Their brothers jog across the field to tell them it's over. They try to tug them apart.

"It's okay now."

"Hayoon isn't leaving."

"Junwoo, you can let go."

"It's over."

Some part of Hayoon's brain comprehends what they're saying. Her legs go weak and she falls to her knees. Their brothers support them as Junwoo falls with her. Minseong and Yunjae try to wake Hayoon from her unresponsive state. She blinks herself free and reaches out for Junwoo like a toddler. Although she loves her brothers, she feels overwhelmed with them swarming around her. She needs her anchor. Jihoon helps Junwoo pull her into his arms on the ground. She lays her head on his shoulder to calm down.

Seojun is kneeling behind Junwoo and wipes her tears. He tells her quietly, "It's okay."

She nods and reaches her own hand up to blot at his damp face.

Baekhyeon strokes her head and massages Junwoo's neck.

"No one will separate us. Everything's okay now."

Minseong rubs Hayoon's back. She pulls her head off Junwoo's shoulder as if to say, *I'm better now.*

They help each other stand up. Jihoon leads Hayoon away to rest with Seojun, Minseong, and Yunjae. Baekhyeon gives Junwoo a hand up and follows with the rest of the members. Baekhyeon puts a strong arm around Junwoo's shoulders and asks, "Are you okay?"

Junwoo ignores his question and says to Jeongu, "Thanks for breaking me free earlier."

Kun and Baekhyeon exchange worried glances across Junwoo. They've never seen him so distraught before.

Baekhyeon's group joins Jihoon's group inside and Yunjae moves from his seat by Hayoon to make room for Junwoo. Hayoon hugs Junwoo's arm with her right hand and rests her head on his shoulder. On her left side, Jihoon locks her hand between his. Baekhyeon sits in a chair in front of Junwoo.

PD-nim solemnly walks in to talk with them. He invites Hayoon up to stand with him.

Junwoo darts his arm across Hayoon and locks her in. Baekhyeon stands in front of them. Their normally relaxed leader, coldly and firmly rejects PD-nim.

"She's staying here."

PD-nim apologizes, "I'm sorry for today. It wasn't supposed to happen like this. Hayoon has only been here for two months, I didn't think... I didn't know. I'll admit this game was set up for you to fail. We thought we could take Hayoon away and then have a happy reunion in a few days. Your company never had the intention of taking Hayoon away. They agreed to let us test the members without Baekhyeon and test Hayoon's impact on the group. That's it. I didn't know you guys had become this close."

Baekhyeon throws respect for elders out the window and harshly says, "You went too far."

"You're right. I'm sorry."

"Can we go home now?"

"Yes. Sorry."

On the way home, Hayoon is still hugging Junwoo's arm while sleeping. He strokes her hand in his with his thumb. Junwoo hears a soft sob come from Hayoon and looks over to see a tear slide down from her puffy eyes. She wakes up scared and looks to Junwoo with the most pitiful eyes.

"I don't want to go," she whispers.

His heart physically aches from feeling her pain. He holds her face securely in his hand.

"You're not going anywhere."

Their brothers watch as he pulls Hayoon into his lap to hold her. She lays her dreary head against his shoulder. He rubs her arm to soothe her back to sleep. Jeongu passes his jacket up the aisle for Junwoo to wrap around her.

Yunjae is staring out the window, lost in his own thoughts. He asks without expecting an answer, "Why would they do this? Hasn't she been through enough?"

Junwoo zones out with the emotional trauma weighing down on him. Baekhyeon moves to the seat next to Junwoo.

"Are you doing okay?"

Junwoo honestly admits emotions he would've normally kept hidden.

"I've never been so terrified in my life."

Junwoo shifts his gaze from Baekhyeon to Hayoon's sleeping face.

"If they try to take her, what are we going to do?"

His tone is dripping with desperation and helplessness. They know full well they have little control when it comes to their company's decisions.

Baekhyeon confidently replies, "We're not going to let that happen. Nobody here is willing to let her go, okay?"

Baekhyeon looks around at the faces of his members. *How are we going to recover from this?*

Junwoo carries Hayoon into the house and lays her down on the couch. None of them want to be by themselves; they gather on the living room floor.

Minseong breaks the silence, "When I saw the car doors open, I thought we were done for."

"Does anyone know why she doesn't have a family?"

Seojun emotionally retorts, "She has a family!"

Jihoon hushes him to keep from waking Hayoon.

"You know that's not what I meant."

"Maybe we should buy our own house. One that's not owned by the company."

Kun agrees, "That's not a bad idea. But we might have to divide into two."

"You guys keep talking. I need to cook dinner."

"I'm going, too."

The boys split up to deal with the day's stress in their own way. Jihoon heads to the kitchen with Baekhyeon. Jeongu changes clothes to box in the exercise room. Kun and Yunjae research houses. Minseong and Seojun go to their room to relax.

"Baekhyeon," Junwoo calls him back into the living room.

"What's up?"

"I want to go to the bathroom and change. Can you stay with Hayoon? I don't want her to be alone when she wakes up."

"No problem. Go ahead."

"When she was sick, she told me her dad used to kiss her head every morning when he came out for breakfast. If she starts crying in her sleep again, you can..." *Would he be willing...?*

"I got it. Don't worry."

"Can we sleep in the living room tonight?" Seojun asks.

"Sure. Grab your pillows and blankets after you clean up your plates."

Junwoo hands his and Hayoon's plate to Seojun. He takes Hayoon's wrist and leads her to the back yard.

"Warm up."

He enters the house and comes back two minutes later with a Bluetooth speaker.

"Ready?"

"Mm."

Junwoo knows exactly which song they need and scrolls through his playlist to find it. With the first note, Hayoon's tired expression shows a hint of a smile. When she dances this song with Junwoo, she feels safe.

Once the music begins, their brothers slowly trickle outside. They watch them from afar in awe. The boys suddenly understand their bond; they can feel it. It's the type of strong palpable chemistry that most people don't ever get to witness, let alone have for themselves.

So, this is why they were in the studio every day?

He really can dance contemporary?

Why does it look like they've been dancing together for years?

Watching them dance together, it's like he's... like his dance has life.

I get it now. Why they got so close so fast. All their feelings, the ones stuck inside. They're the same.

Kun whispers, "We can never let them be separated."

The choreography brings them in close proximity to each other and he stares into her eyes. *She's scared.* Completely in sync, they stop dancing and stand face to face. Junwoo runs his fingers into her hair, holding her head close.

"You don't need to be scared. I will always protect you. We will always protect you."

Junwoo sees one of the boys move out of the corner of his eye. *Perfect timing.* "See?"

He turns Hayoon to face her brothers. "Your family won't leave you."

Seojun shouts, "Group hug!"

The boys are lying in the living room reminiscing about their pre-debut days long into the night. Hayoon sleeps fitfully in the middle of them. Baekhyeon is retelling the story of when they almost burned the house down cooking Korean bbq when Hayoon startles awake. She gasps for air, staring at the ceiling. Junwoo props himself up on his forearm to face her. He brushes her hair behind her ear causing her to turn her head toward him. She bites her lip but can't stop a tear from falling and disappearing into her hair.

I can't..." She shakes her head, unable to finish.

He grabs her neck and pulls her in. Her brothers are so quiet, she forgets they're there. She tries to hold back her tears by clenching Junwoo's shirt front. He covers her fist with his hand.

"It's okay to cry."

Her eyes lift to his and she discovers they're a shimmering gloss from held back tears. She draws her hand up to rest on his face; her thumb delicately strokes under his eye. More so than her own pain, seeing the pain deep in his eyes pushes her over the edge. She cries without reserve. At the sound of her cries, Seojun holds Minseong's hand. Yunjae, Baekhyeon and Jihoon huddle closer together, linking their arms. Listening to their little sister cry, their own tears start to silently wet their pillows.

Junwoo can feel her pain and knows, her tears are not from one threat. They come from all the suffering she's had no choice but to endure alone. Maybe even the pain from before she met them, all comes cascading out in her tears. The whole time she's crying, Junwoo holds her.

As her crying finally subsides, she can hear the boys sniffling. She pokes her head up to look behind Junwoo.

"Are you okay?" she worriedly asks.

They chuckle at her cuteness and crawl over to sit around Hayoon. Baekhyeon wipes the tears from her face.

"Feel better?"

She nods and genuinely smiles. Hayoon spots Jeongu wipe a tear from his chin and can't believe it.

"Jeongu oppa, you cried?"

Hayoon's brothers tease stone-faced Jeongu and she wipes his tear off with her thumb. Jeongu swats them away self-consciously.

"I'm going to sleep."

He poutingly pushes Seojun out of the way to lay down.

Jihoon jokingly tells them, "Whoever wakes up first has to make breakfast."

Hayoon settles onto her pillow and Baekhyeon helps fix her blanket. Junwoo interlaces her fingers with his, making her feel safe. Within two minutes, she falls asleep soundly with the incredible weight she secretly shouldered, lifted away.

Day 57

Click. Click. Click.

Hayoon drowsily rubs her eyes. *Where's Baekhyeon oppa?*

Click. Click. Click.

She heads to the dining room to find Baekhyeon ticking away on his laptop. He hears Hayoon's footsteps and looks up from his computer with a warm smile.

"I thought you'd sleep longer."

Baekhyeon rises out of his chair and walks over. He rests his hand on the back of her neck and lightly kisses the top of her head, just like her dad used to.

"Are you alright?"

She smiles weakly and confirms, "I'm okay."

He reaches through the pile of food to get an americano. "Have some coffee."

"Thanks." She takes a sip and her smile becomes more convincing. "I'm going outside."

He ruffles her hair and tells her, "Come back to eat soon."

Hayoon quietly steps around her sleeping brothers to the back door. She basks in the rising sun, still feeling the lingering fatigue from the day before.

Soon after, Junwoo wakes up in a mild panic when he finds the space beside him is empty. Luckily, when he stands, he spots her out on the patio. He sweeps up his blanket and heads outside to join her.

Junwoo wraps the blanket around her shoulders and is thanked with a tender smile. They continue watching the new day begin together.

"Thank you for fighting to save me."

He tugs her elbow to bring her in front of him. "Come here."

He hugs her from behind and rests his lips against her head. Junwoo closes his eyes, treasuring the fact that she was still by his side. He barely lifts his lips from her hair before promising her, "I will always protect you. Everything's okay now."

Hayoon places a hand on his arm across her. No space lies between them. Enjoying the tranquil morning, they recharge in their embrace.

I hope I can stay in his arms forever.

She takes a drink of her coffee and offers it to Junwoo without words. She tips it up when his mouth comes into contact with the cup. She lowers the cup back down and he turns his head in to kiss her hairline. Hayoon leans into the kiss, her face reflecting the sun's warm rays.

Happy sigh. His body feels so warm. Just what I need after everything nearly disappeared.

Baekhyeon enters the living room to see Jihoon watching Junwoo and Hayoon outside. He offers his coffee out in front of Jihoon. He takes a long drink while deep in thought.

Without looking away from Junwoo's back, Jihoon admits, "If they ever find out how close their relationship really is, it'll be trouble."

Baekhyeon sighs in agreement. "That's why they have us."

Jihoon takes one more sip of the coffee before handing it back.

"Let's go eat."

"Did you already leave to get coffee?"

Hayoon shakes her head and replies, "Baekhyeon oppa went out to get breakfast."

"What did he get?"

"My favorite."

"He spoils you too much."

She leans her head back against him and teases, "And you don't?"

Junwoo smirks at her question. There's no need to answer an obvious question.

"Did you eat?"

"Not yet. Should we go eat?"

She spins around to face him. He guides her head to his shoulder as her arms encircle him.

"Mm. I'm hungry."

He takes her coffee in one hand and her hand in the other to head inside.

In the dining room, Baekhyeon holds out a chair for Hayoon. Junwoo sets her coffee down in front of her and sits on the other side of Jihoon.

They're not sitting beside each other? ... recovering faster than I thought. What a relief.

Baekhyeon talks with Junwoo about their comeback choreography. Hayoon digs in to the food, eating hungrily.

Jihoon laughs at her, "Hayoon, slow down. Here, drink some juice."

"Kun, help pass these out."

Manager-nim sets the takeout on the table between Kun and Jeongu.

"The next couple days' schedule has a few changes. But first, I want to apologize for yesterday. My meeting ran late so I sent my assistant."

Baekhyeon cuts off his explanation to ask, "Did you know what they were going to do?"

Manager-nim confesses, "I knew he was going to separate you from the group and test them but I didn't know about Hayoon."

Baekhyeon threatens, "If something like that happens again, we won't play along."

"It won't. PD-nim came to my office this morning to apologize. There's a lot about Hayoon he didn't know. When he found out about the car accident and her family, he felt horrible. Which brings me to the schedule change. As an apology, he's offered to send you on a minivacation. The company has added an interview for you tomorrow morning. But after the interview, you'll leave to the vacation house. You'll be there tomorrow afternoon, the full next day, and then come back after breakfast the day after."

"Why have the interview?" Baekhyeon inquires. If it's to do damage control and pretend like the members are okay with what they did, then he's not willing.

Manager-nim understands what he's implying and answers, "You won't be given a script. Obviously, we hope you won't be too ruthless but you can honestly talk about what happened. After the show is released, we're going to need to give your fans an explanation anyway. They think it's better to be proactive and do it now."

"Are they filming during vacation?"

"No. PD-nim is not going. I'm not either. This is purely for you to relax and recover. One BTS camera will be coming to shoot some action shots of your activities but you can choose who it is and send him away whenever you want."

Hayoon shouts, "Samchon!"

Seojun is startled by her outburst and jumps in his chair. Minseong, Jihoon, and Junwoo chuckle at her enthusiasm.

Baekhyeon supports Hayoon's decision.

"Okay, then pack your bags and I'll pick you up tomorrow morning. Enjoy these next few days. When you get back, you'll be busy with choreography and recording for your album. I'll let myself out. You keep eating."

"Oppa." *What is he looking at? Did he hear me?* "Oppa!"

"Huh?" He snaps out of it to give Hayoon his attention.

"Are we still going to the studio? ...Are you okay?"

"Yesterday, if I couldn't get to you in time and they took you away, where would you have gone?"

"What do you mean?"

"I trust we can protect you but if one day, we're not with you and they try to send you away, promise me you'll go to my parent's house. You remember how to get there, right?"

Realizing his seriousness, she sits opposite of him. *He's worried.* She takes his hands. "Hey, I'm okay." She comforts him softly. "You don't have to worry about me."

"Hayoon, you are really important to me." He looks down at their hands. "I need to know you're safe. I need to know where to find you."

Hayoon releases a hand from his grasp and caresses his face. "I understand. I'll go to your house. I promise."

Junwoo reaches into his wallet and pulls out a credit card. He holds it out to her. "If you can't get home, use this card and I can find you."

"I don't need this."

"Give me your phone."

If it will make him feel better... She hands it over. Junwoo opens the case and slides the card in the back before snapping it shut again.

Hayoon tries to make him smile by joking, "Oppa, what's your card limit? I'm going shopping."

He chuckles and arrogantly answers, "More than you can spend."

15

You're stuck with me forever.

-Junwoo

Day 58

"Yunjae oppa, can you get my coffee for me?"

Yunjae stops eating and picks her coffee up from the table with his chips. He walks over to where Hayoon is resting on the couch.

"Here you go."

Hayoon takes her coffee and opens her mouth for Yunjae to feed her a chip.

"Thanks."

A new staff member watches from across the room, raising his eyebrow in judgement. *Did he just feed her? Does she have princess syndrome?*

Seojun bumps against Hayoon as he sits on the couch beside her.

"Hayoon, let's play a round."

"Okay. ...Kun oppa, can you toss me my phone?"

Kun puts down his own phone to deliver Hayoon's. He ruffles her hair dotingly before heading back to what he was doing.

Dohyun sees the staff member glare at her rudely. He scoots over to tell him proudly, "You have no idea how far she's come." He scrolls through his phone files to find Hayoon's video. "The company showed everyone this video at a staff meeting before you came."

Dohyun continues as he watches the video, "She never told anyone. She didn't have anyone to tell. Just carried it all alone."

He realizes his mistake and apologizes, "Sorry."

"It's okay. It took a long time for her to ask for anyone's help. Now, no matter what the boys are doing, Hayoon will always be more important."

"You looked really scared while watching them compete. Did you think they would fail?"

"I knew they would try their best but we're only human."

"If they were willing to let you leave after they failed, would you go?"

Hayoon tries to remain emotionless as the boys interject.

"We wouldn't let her go."

"Impossible!"

"That wouldn't happen."

The interviewer presses for the answer, "Would you go?"

Hayoon looks him dead in the eyes as she answers, "I would go."

Junwoo grabs her arm. She pats his hand and soothingly tells him, "It's okay."

"Don't you always say you're like family? What kind of family would leave each other behind?"

Hayoon confidently answers, "It's because we are family, I would go."

He's confused by her answer and admittingly says, "I don't follow."

"It because I trust them, I would leave. I would trust they had a reason to let me go. I would trust they had a plan to bring me back. But if it was out of their control, I would accept it. I will always support them."

"Wouldn't you blame them? For not protecting you."

"I wouldn't."

Her brothers get increasingly emotional from her response.

Hayoon explains, "A few months ago, I couldn't imagine having someone hold my hand when I'm scared. Or having someone feed me soup when I'm sick. Even if it was only for a short time, they gave me a family."

She tries to hold back her tears as her voice wavers. Kun spins in his swivel chair to face away from the camera. Yunjae holds Jihoon's hand and Seojun's tears stream down his face. Junwoo reaches out for Hayoon's hand. Even in a theoretical scenario of her leaving, they can't accept it.

"For two months, I was happier than I expected to be in a lifetime. But doing what they do, their decisions cannot be selfish. They have the company and millions of fans that are relying on them. If one person has to sacrifice to protect the family, I'm willing for it to be me."

Baekhyeon's hands form into fists and Minseong covers his mouth to stop a sob from escaping. Seojun leans over to bury his face in Jihoon's shoulder. A single tear rolls down her cheek.

"I hope it's me."

The interviewer fans his face with the cue card to dry out his damp eyes. Dumbfounded, he asks, "You're really willing to give it all up?"

"For them, I am."

Junwoo tells him, "It's impossible that our group's success will ever require her sacrifice."

He switches from Hayoon to ask Baekhyeon, "You seem pretty emotional. What do you think about all of this?"

Baekhyeon's expression betrays him as he tries to answer with a level tone. "Honestly, this never should've happened. I could not be prouder of how they worked together during the challenges and how they protected each other. I'm extremely proud of them. But they never should have had to go through something like this in the first place. Especially Hayoon. She's had to deal with a lot since she joined us. So much more than anyone outside of our group knows about. Seeing her scared and crying like that... I feel like I failed them as leader."

Hayoon objects, "That's not true!" She confronts his guilt with compassion. "You have never once failed me. I have always thought you were the absolute best leader for this group. If it wasn't for you, I wouldn't even be here. That day I met you at the company, when you convinced me to move in, you gave me a better present than a lifetime of birthdays."

Seojun tries to lift the mood by jokingly saying, "Hey, you heard that. That means we don't need to buy her birthday presents anymore."

The members laugh while blotting the remaining dampness from their faces.

Hayoon knocks on the guardians' bedroom door before pushing it open.

"Oppa? Minseong said you were looking for me."

"Come sit."

Jihoon, curious about dinner prep without him, asks, "How's dinner going?"

"Yunjae and Jeongu left to get spices. Kun said the kitchen here doesn't have anything."

Baekhyeon takes over the conversation.

"We wanted to ask your opinion about something."

"What?"

"We're talking about buying a house. It's hard to find a house in Seoul that can fit nine people so we'll have to split up into two."

Jihoon continues, "We can split into houses by unit; the dance unit in one house and vocal and rap units in another. Or us four can live in a house together."

Junwoo asks her, "What do you think?"

"Hmm... There are times when living as a unit would be convenient but Junwoo and I often get back after everyone else. Even though we're on different units, us four have the most similar work and rest times. For now, living as a dance unit would make more sense but since it's buying a house and not renting it, the future seems more important. The dance unit house would be more... lively? They're extroverts and younger. They're always laughing and playing games. The house with us four would feel more... like a complete family. We have fun together but also rely on each other. You three collaborate a lot as our leaders, too. Can we buy two houses next to each other? Then no matter how we split up, it's convenient to go in and out of both houses.

"That's a good idea. Even if the houses were on the same floor, that'd be fine, too."

Baekhyeon thinks out loud, "It might make more sense for us to buy a house together since we're older and have more savings. We can buy one house now and then the others can work on buying their house a little later."

Junwoo adds, "Hayoon, you're younger and just started at the company so you don't have to put in as much. Us three have enough."

She bluntly says, "I have money."

All three guardians look at her surprised.

"How much do you need? Two hundred million won? Two fifty?"

Jihoon's jaw drops.

Bewildered, Baekhyeon asks, "Where'd you get so much money? Rob a bank?"

Hayoon looks at the ground, thinking how to answer. "My family..."

Junwoo is the first to realize it came from her parents. He gently massages her neck and she raises her head with a thin smile.

"Some of it was used for my schooling but there's still a decent amount left. When I turned nineteen last year, I got it all. I haven't used much."

Baekhyeon jokes with her, "Wow, our little sister is rich."

Jihoon tugs on her arm like Seojun would do. "So, for my birthday in four months..."

Hayoon slaps his hand in teasing rejection. Baekhyeon shoos them out to help with dinner.

"I'm going to plug in my phone."

Junwoo hangs back to wait for her. As she's getting the charger out of her backpack, she pauses to look up at Junwoo.

"Oppa?"

He walks in to listen better.

"No matter how we divide the houses, I will live with you, right?"

Pabo. Don't you know you're my priority? He grabs her chin playfully and says, "You're stuck with me forever."

"Good. I hate doing dishes so you can do them."

He wrestles her neck and flicks her on the forehead. "What'd you say? Eh?"

"Ow. Ow. Ow. I give up. You win."

She plugs her phone in and they head downstairs to help their brothers with dinner.

Day 60

"Don't run off after you eat. Put your plates in the sink and go to the living room for a team meeting."

Seojun, Hayoon, and Minseong collect the plates to drop in the sink. The rest of the boys head straight to the living room.

"Our comeback is in three weeks and the award show is just over a month away. We need to record in just one day for each song. If you have questions about your parts, ask Kun or myself before you show up at the studio. Tomorrow, we record the title track. We'll learn choreo the two days after and then we'll be back in the recording studio. We might have to use the guide track for the first choreo day but that's fine. At the end of the week, Junwoo, Kun, and I have a promotion interview in the afternoon. While we're gone, Jihoon's in charge. Review your parts because when we come back, we need to record three songs in two days. Questions?"

Kun raises his hand before saying, "I might be late on the second day if the song isn't finished yet."

Baekhyeon defers to Junwoo, who responds, "That's fine. Hayoon can take your place and then catch you up when you come."

Eh? Me? ... Yeah!

Baekhyeon reminds them, "We'll be extremely busy until after the award shows so make sure we're staying healthy and focused. Help each other."

16

The answer is her.

-Baekhyeon

Day 66

"I'll order the coffee. You can sit down."

Hayoon leaves Jeongu in line to take a seat near the front window to wait. Jeongu orders and moves over to the pickup counter.

"Jeongu-ssi."

As soon as Jeongu hears his name, the coffee shop door opens. A hoard of people bombards Hayoon with cameras and phones in her face. She's completely caught off guard as they all start talking at the same time.

"What was the reason behind your parents' car crash?"

"Did the company hide your training to increase MPeak's popularity?"

"Is it true you knew the company's plot to cheat fans?"

Jeongu pushes through the crowd and grabs her wrist to run away. They chase them for five blocks before Jeongu can hail a cab. They hop in and Jeongu calls Jihoon to find out what happened. The entire way home, Jeongu never lets go of Hayoon's hand.

"Jeongu oppa, why were those people asking that?"

"Someone posted online that you coming to live with us was all a set up. Jihoon's looking into it. It seems like they think us not knowing you can dance and sing is all fake. That the company planned it to get more attention for us. There's Jihoon."

They pull up to the curb in front of their house and Jihoon is waiting for them outside. They slide out of the car and Jeongu hands her over to Jihoon.

"Are you okay?"

"I'm okay." She puts on a brave face as they enter the living room where everyone is waiting. "Oh, your coffee!"

"We don't need it. I'm going to call Baekhyeon."

Jihoon stands in the hallway to call Baekhyeon, where he can still see her. Hayoon opens her laptop to find out what all the fuss is about.

She's immediately blind-sighted by a news article about her parents' death. Seojun slams her laptop shut and take it away.

"Don't look."

He hands her the tv remote and walks toward his room to store her laptop.

Jihoon stops him to ask, "Why'd you take her laptop?"

Baekhyeon can hear Seojun through the phone as he angrily says, "Those jerks posted about her parents' death."

Jihoon can hear Baekhyeon order Junwoo and Kun, "We need to leave, now!"

On the other end of the phone, Baekhyeon's fierceness scares them into grabbing their stuff and running toward the door to get back home.

"Jihoon, we're coming back now. Send the original post to my phone and Manager-nim's phone. Keep Hayoon offline and don't let the boys post anything."

Manager-nim, Kun, Junwoo, and Baekhyeon jump into the car to rush home. Baekhyeon opens the post Jihoon sent him and hands his phone to Junwoo.

"Hayoon was attacked by reporters today. You might want to call her."

Junwoo rapidly reads the post while unlocking his phone.

"Oppa," Hayoon says weakly. "How was the interview?"

"Hayoon-ah, are you with Jihoon?"

"I'm in my room." Her voice wavers as she asks, "When are you coming home?"

"I'm on my way."

Baekhyeon and Kun watch Junwoo as he fights to calm his voice regardless of his tense body.

"I'll be home in an hour. Don't go online. If you need something, tell Jihoon, okay?"

"Okay. Drive safe."

Junwoo hangs up the phone and lowers his head in frustration.

"I should've been there."

Baekhyeon tries to help calm Junwoo despite his own anger.

"Jihoon and the boys are all home with her. She'll be okay."

Junwoo slams the car armrest and repeats louder, "I should've been there."

Baekhyeon hates one of their own is being attacked but as leader, he needs to try and remain level-headed. He places a firm hand on Junwoo's shoulder and silently accompanies him.

Junwoo bursts through the door and kicks off his shoes as he's walking. Jihoon and Seojun rush to the door when they hear it open.

"Where is she?" he demands.

"In her room."

He hurries to her door and takes a deep breath before opening it slowly. His heart nearly stops, finding her huddled in the far corner of the room. Baekhyeon peeks in to check on her before gently closing the door behind Junwoo.

Junwoo crouches down in front of Hayoon. He puts one hand on her knee and strokes her hair with the other.

"I'm here."

With two words, he cracks through her brave façade. She reaches out for him and murmurs, "I didn't lie to the fans."

He hugs her strongly, ready to fight the world to protect her.

"I know. You didn't do anything wrong."

Junwoo coaxes her to lay down and rest before going out to find Baekhyeon.

In the living room, everyone is discussing what happened.

"When will she catch a break? It's been one thing after another for her. If I was her, I might've given up a long time ago."

"What do you think the company's going to do? Will she get suspended until they clear it up?"

"They can't just get rid of her, right? She's one of us."

Baekhyeon shakes his head in disagreement. "She's not the same." *Deep sigh.* "I didn't tell you before because I didn't want it to impact how you treated her. Her contract is short term. She was brought in by the company because our fan base wasn't growing as fast as they wanted. They thought, living with us, she could show our fans what we're really like."

Seojun gets worked up and exclaims, "But they can't use her and then throw her away!"

Yunjae agrees, "She's already a part of the family."

Minseong adds, "What about everything she's done for us? Does none of that matter?"

Baekhyeon logically says, "Even if we only look at it from the company's point of view, she still has value."

"She's as good of a dancer as any of us."

"We all heard her sing at sound check, too."

"Her vocals are no joke."

Kun realistically comments, "But she doesn't perform."

Jihoon points out, "But in the show, she's a huge reason the views have been so high lately. Maybe that will help her stay."

Baekhyeon checks his phone and reports, "They want us all down there tomorrow morning."

Late that night, Junwoo, Baekhyeon, and Jihoon are sitting around talking in their room. Junwoo says, "There's something I need to talk about with you guys." He pulls out a bank card and drops it on the bed.

"What is this for?" Baekhyeon asks seriously.

"On this card, is the exact amount I need to cancel my contract."

"You want to leave?" Jihoon asks astonished.

Junwoo shakes his head solemnly. "I've never wanted to leave."

"Then what's going on?"

"That day we almost lost her, I realized how little control we have living under our contract." He looks at them desperately. "I hope I never have to use this card but she can't leave." He adds resolutely, "I have to protect her."

"Is this because of that post? It's only a rumor. Everything's going to be fine."

"You and I both know, one rumor in this industry can ruin your career. Even if people find out it wasn't true, it could be too late."

"Even if the company kicks her out, our families will take care of her."

"That's not good enough! We have seven months left of this contract. I hate those stupid dramas Yunjae watches where one person has to wait months or years. I won't do that to her. While she's waiting, she's going to see us on tv and think we're happy without her. If she leaves, she's alone. But if I leave, there are still seven of you."

Baekhyeon picks up the card and holds it out. "This is a last resort, got it?"

"You're okay with this?"

"Either we all stay or we all sign somewhere else. All of us."

Junwoo never expected their acceptance of it, let alone their support. He feels embarrassed from underestimating their friendship and loyalty to Hayoon.

Jihoon sighs, "Looks like I need to save more money. Seojun could never save enough for the contract on his own."

Baekhyeon light-heartedly says with a serious undertone, "Looks like we better come up with a good plan to protect our little princess."

Day 67

The members cluster at one end of the table with Manager-nim. On the opposing side, sits the PR director, legal director, artist management director and social media assistant.

The callous PR director has never supported the idea of bringing Hayoon into the house. He tells them, "I recommend Hayoon stops appearing in public and her social media page suspended. That or we can send her on 'vacation' until we find a way to prove the accusations aren't true."

Baekhyeon tells him, "Personally, I don't agree. Hayoon, what do you want to do?"

"If it's better for the members..."

Junwoo cuts her off. "He's not asking what you're willing to do for us. He's asking what you want, without thinking about anyone else."

Hayoon glances over at the intimidating PR director before staring at her feet. *What am I supposed to do? I don't want to leave but can I say that? What'll happen to them if I stay?*

Junwoo takes her hand and rephrases the question. "How do you feel?"

Hayoon laces her fingers through his and quietly shares, "I don't want to go."

The PR director raises his voice at her, "What'd you say?"

Under the director's provoking, Hayoon exclaims, "I'm not leaving!"

A pride wells up in her brothers and Jihoon strokes her head.

"Do you have any idea how selfish you're being? If you..."

Baekhyeon cuts off his rant, saying, "Let's all calm down. Hayoon's decision is the same as ours. Even if she said she was leaving, we wouldn't agree."

"Her contract is almost up anyw..."

"We're not going there!" Baekhyeon edges on the line of disrespect.

The director's anger explodes, "The plan was never for her to become an actual member of the group! You knew that!"

Junwoo flips around to face Hayoon and block her from his rage. Yunjae covers her ears from behind so she can't hear what's going on.

Baekhyeon commands, "Take her home. I'll deal with this."

Baekhyeon comes back to the house after dark. *No one in the living room? No one in my room? Where is everyone? Would they have gone to practice?*

Baekhyeon creeps open Hayoon's door. *Cute.* All the members are sprawled around Hayoon's room sleeping. She's sleeping in the middle of her bed with her guardians on either side. They lay on top of the covers, holding her hands. Jeongu and Kun brought bean bag chairs down from the landing and the three trouble makers are sleeping side-by-side on the floor. As he's taking a picture, a solution that could fix everything dawns on him. He shuts the door and calls Dohyun for help as he leaves the house.

Day 68

The PR director sits down and Baekhyeon takes his place in front of the company executives. Thanks to Manager-nim, even the CEO is in attendance.

"Thank you, director, for your opinion. Unfortunately, my members and I don't agree with suspending Hayoon." He clicks the screen to start the presentation he made with Dohyun. "Right now, this is the situation at our house. This is our family. I promise, if you take her away, nothing good will come of it."

"When Hayoon first came to our house, she was afraid of crowds and afraid of holding us back. Let's take a look."

He plays the video Dohyun made about Hayoon's suffering. When Hayoon gets hit by the car, the CEO leans forward and wrings his hands together.

"Hayoon's every action was to help and protect us. This is a copy of her doctor's report from the day after we watched this video. Malnourished, dehydrated, low iron levels, weight loss. And that doesn't include her physical injuries which include scrapes on her arms and legs, bruises, and rope burn. But no one knew because she never complained."

The CEO interrupts to ask, "Do you have a copy of that report? I want to see it."

Baekhyeon gestures to Dohyun and he hands it over.

"After this video, things changed a lot. We found out Hayoon is an incredible young woman with amazing talent." He clicks through the presentation, pausing along the way to watch short videos. "At her first fan meeting with us, she found a bunch of children and turned them into mini-fans. In the time we were signing autographs, she taught them the choreography to our last album's title track. As a result of the viral post, we gained over two thousand more fans.

At the next fan meeting, because of how kindly she interacted with a young girl, we gained more positive attention and she ended up with thousands of people following her page.

Junwoo found out she could dance and started collaborating with her on our choreography. She helped Junwoo create every single track's choreography for our next album. Not only that but when there's a risky move Junwoo isn't sure will work out, she tries it first to make sure it's safe for our members. No matter how many times she falls, she gets back up and says "again."

The last time we went to Japan, Kun's mic broke during sound check. Let's watch what the result was."

He plays the video from sound check and the CEO asks the PR director accusatorily, "Why haven't I seen this before?"

Baekhyeon continues, "During a performance, Jeongu changed into the wrong outfit and there was no time for him go back. Hayoon was the first one to notice and ran under the stage to take off her own shirt to give him.

Even if you don't consider her impact on us, then you should consider the impact she's had on millions of fans. Here are her current number of followers, shared posts, and fan comments. Peak Season views have also increased by twenty percent. After the negative post, her fans have been showing her support from all over the world.

Now that you know how important she is, let me switch gears by telling you what you'll lose if she's gone. For one, you'll lose a choreographer. We'll also lose her huge international fan base as well as her Korean fans. Peak Season views will go down and PR will be even worse than it is now. Not to mention, all of us."

The CEO blinks with wide eyes in disbelief.

"Kun holds the copyrights to half of our songs and our contract is up for renewal in seven months. Over half of us can buy out our contracts today and the rest will follow when it expires. We've already purchased a house."

The PR director snaps, "Are you threatening us?"

"No. I'm telling you honestly what will happen. You gave us a sister and she became a part of this family; an irreplaceable, needed member of this group."

Baekhyeon observes the CEO to try and gauge his reaction.

"I know you only brought her in to show the world who we are. But it turns out, the answer to getting more fans isn't us, it lies within what she makes us. The answer is her."

The CEO asks, "What do you think we should do?"

"The company needs to make a clear stand against this post. Find the poster, prove it false, and support Hayoon. Then, give her a long-term contract."

Baekhyeon holds his breath as the CEO considers what he's proposed.

"Bring the boys in. I want to talk to them."

Once the boys leave for the company, Hayoon calls Junwoo's mom.

"Eomma, I think I'm in trouble."

She quickly summarizes the situation.

"It's going to be okay. Baekhyeon, Jihoon, and Junwoo will take care of it. If something happens, call me back, and I'll go pick you up right away.

"Ah, Baekhyeon's calling. I've got to go."

"Okay. I'm going to call Jihoon's mom in case we need to go down there."

Hayoon hangs up and connects to Baekhyeon's call.

"Hayoon, Manager-nim's assistant is going to pick you up, okay?"

"Okay. When will he be here?"

"Ten minutes."

"I'll go wait outside."

Hayoon walks terrified into a meeting room with Manager-nim, Baekhyeon, PD-nim, and the CEO.

"Please sit," the CEO tells her.

"Thank you."

"You know why we're all here, right?"

"About that post."

"This morning, we had a meeting to discuss what to do. But first, I want to apologize for all the difficulties you experienced when you first got here. You never should've been treated like that. I also want to thank you for everything you've done for the boys and their fans."

Oh no. He's going to fire me.

Baekhyeon notices the tension in her arms and rubs her back.

"Are you nervous?" asks the CEO.

Hayoon nods her head and timidly admits, "I don't want to leave."

"Then let's talk about what the plan is moving forward. Dohyun is going to work with the production staff to make a special episode all about you. It'll include interviews with the members, footage from the dance studio, and behind the scenes. I'll leave the details up to Manager-nim and Baekhyeon to explain, okay? I need to head to another meeting but I'll be seeing you again soon."

That's it? Was that the plan? Do I leave after the episode?

Hayoon turns to Baekhyeon and asks, "What does that mean?"

"PD-nim, why don't you tell her about the show first?"

"The special episode is going to air outside of our normal release schedule to coincide with the press conference. After that, the next few episodes..."

"Next few episodes? I don't have to leave?"

Baekhyeon smiles and tells her, "We don't want you to leave. Not now and not in a month when your contract ends."

Hayoon's head is spinning. She can't organize her thoughts and starts stuttering, "I...but...when...I don't understand."

PD-nim tries to help. "We want you to be a permanent member of Peak Season. For many challenges, your team won because of you and you added a new dynamic to the show that we never expected. People are still sharing the video of you yelling in Chinese."

Manager-nim adds, "The CEO saw the sound check from Japan and was really impressed. Baekhyeon showed him a video of you working with Junwoo on choreography, too. He scolded us for hiding you at home all this time. The boys have always said you're on the dance unit but now, it's coming from the company, too. The CEO respects you not wanting to perform on stage yet but he wants to move forward from where we are now."

Baekhyeon tags in, "When one of us is out, you'll dance in their spot for practices and rehearsals so everyone else isn't affected. It's hard for our members to take time out of their schedules to reteach choreography. So, it'll be your responsibility to teach them what they missed. During practices with all the members there, you'll help Junwoo find the problems and fix them. Of course, your collaboration with Junwoo will keep going. But now, you get paid for it."

"So, I don't have to leave? ...and I get to dance?"

Manager-nim happily responds, "You get paid to dance. ...You don't have to dance on stage but you will be an official member of the dance unit. If you want the job?"

"I get to stay with my brothers and I get to dance?" Hayoon says, still trying to wrap her head around it.

Baekhyeon laughs and teases, "Hayoon, this is the first time I've seen you so stupid."

Manager-nim says, "I just need one answer from you. Do you want to join the company and become the 9th official member of MPeak?"

Hayoon beams with joy... but then it fades away.

"What did the members say? What if my being here will hurt you guys?"

Baekhyeon swivels her chair to face him and takes her shaking hands in his. "You've always only helped us. This wasn't the company's idea. It was mine and the dance unit's idea to make you an official member and secure your place in the company. They all voted the same. We want you to stay."

Her radiant smile returns and Manager-nim checks again, "Will you join the dance unit, officially?"

"Yes! ...Where are my brothers?"

"In the lounge at the end of the hall."

She takes off out the door with the three men hurriedly chasing after her. She bursts through the door like uncontainable sunlight. Her brothers stop talking and stand from the couches in anticipation. She scans the room, feeling grateful for every one of her brothers.

Junwoo steps forward and opens his arms toward her. She giggles with pure happiness and runs into his arms. All the boys embrace her in a group hug.

Seojun impatiently asks, "You agreed, right? You're going to stay with us?"

Baekhyeon opens the door to enter and they search his expression for the answer.

"Looks like she's stuck with us for a lot longer."

Cheers erupt from the room. Her brothers all fawn over her. Manager-nim throws Hayoon a dance unit t-shirt.

"Let's take a picture," Baekhyeon suggests.

Junwoo and Yunjae help Hayoon wear the shirt and they cluster together for a group picture.

Hayoon's phone rings in the van on the way home. The boys quiet down for her to answer.

"Eomma. Everything's okay."

Knowing she doesn't have a mom, her brothers become curious. Junwoo listens to their conversation and asks, "Eomma?"

Hayoon clicks speakerphone on.

"How could you boys not take care of Hayoon? What is this talk of someone trying to kick her out of the company? Jihoon's mom and I were getting ready to come deal with it ourselves."

Hayoon chuckles and sticks her tongue out at her brothers. Yunjae's mom calls and he puts it on speaker.

"Yunjae, how could you guys let them attack Hayoon online. What are you going to do about this? You better deal with those haters."

"Mom, I'm your son. What are you yelling at me for?"

"Last episode, Hayoon looked like she was losing weight again."

"Eomma, I'm eating a lot. Don't worry."

"That's my girl."

Yunjae's mom hangs up as Seojun's phone rings. He holds up his phone for them to see the caller ID, 'Eomma'.

Hayoon is sitting on her bed, looking out the window when Junwoo opens her door.

"Can I come in?" he whispers.

Hayoon waves him over. He sits against the headboard beside her and hands her a mug of hot tea. *I knew she wouldn't be able to fall asleep after today.*

Hayoon sips the tea and lays her head on his shoulder. *Sigh.*

"I've always known I would have to leave. ...When I first came, the thought of leaving didn't scare me. But now..."

Junwoo holds her hand, providing support for her to work through her fears.

"On the way to the office earlier, I kept telling myself, if staying would hurt you guys, I was willing to leave. When I was listening to the CEO talk, I thought for sure he was going to tell me to leave."

Hayoon wipes a tear off her cheek. She shakingly confesses, "I was really scared."

Junwoo scoots as close as he can and wraps his arm around her, trying to share her pain.

"What if they change their minds tomorrow? Or someone else posts something bad?"

Junwoo tips up her chin to make her look into his eyes. *Looks like we haven't made her feel safe enough here yet. She's still scared we'll disappear.*

"Hayoon, you are a part of this family. Just like me and just like Baekhyeon. Even if the company didn't decide to make you an official member, that won't ever change. Got it?"

"Mm. ...I"

"You?"

"I can stay with you forever?"

Her eyes make his heart beat in double speed. *Hope, fear, desire, desperation...* Afraid his voice will shake, he responds with a simple, "Mm."

He moves his hand back to gently massage her neck. Hayoon reaches up to rest her hand on his arm.

Six inches from his face, she whispers, "You promise?"

Junwoo tugs her neck closer and rests his forehead on hers. Her hand moves up to grasp his bicep.

"I will never let you go."

Junwoo kisses her forehead and pulls her head in to rest against his neck. She hugs him warmly.

Day 69

Hayoon follows her brothers into a big room with rows of chairs and a podium at the front. She taps Baekhyeon on the shoulder.

"What are we doing here?"

"Press conference."

"Did they find the person who posted it?"

"One of your fans hacked the account and sent the information to the company."

Daebak. My fans are awesome. ...I should ask which fan so I can message them. ...Is that legal?

"Who was it?"

They arrive at their seats. The boys sit in order expect for Baekhyeon, Junwoo, and Hayoon. They sit together at the end by the middle aisle.

"It was someone from another K-pop company's girl group. She was jealous. Said some nonsense about how you didn't do any work but got instant fame."

"Oh. ...She's not entirely wrong."

"Hey, you can't say that. You can't discredit all those hours you spent in your school dance studio and everything you've been through to get here. If you ask me, you deserve it way more than her."

Junwoo leans over to whisper, "There they are."

On the outside of the opposite row, five girls gloomily sit together.

"It's starting."

The girl's PR director gets on stage and switches on the microphone attached to the podium.

"Thank you to the fans, media and MPeak for coming today. As the company representative, I deeply apologize for the harm this post has caused."

He waves the girl on the end up to the stage and gestures for her to stand at the mic.

"I apologize for defaming Hayoon and Mpeak. I was wrong. It won't ever happen again."

She moves to the side of the podium and bows to Hayoon in apology. Their PR director returns to announce her punishment.

"In addition to posting a formal apology, she will be suspended for the next two months. This includes their comeback and award shows. We will delay their comeback by two weeks in order to rerecord and rework choreography."

Hayoon tugs on Baekhyeon's sleeve.

"Hmm?"

"I have something to say."

Baekhyeon signals to their PR director. He covers the mic as Baekhyeon tells him Hayoon needs a minute to speak. He nods in understanding and Baekhyeon escorts her up on stage.

"Uh... I can't say that what she did didn't hurt my feelings because it did. But I hope everyone will try to understand where she's coming from. She doesn't know me. She doesn't know everything I've been through to stand here today. She didn't see me alone in my school's dance studio night after night, trying to survive after my parents died. She didn't see me nearly collapse the second I walked through my bedroom door after giving everything, trying not to hold back my members. I'm so thankful for my fans' support but she might not know me the way you do. What she sees is what many other people probably think they see. They see someone who didn't train in the company for years but magically ended up on top. I'm sure she feels frustrated and angry. I can't agree with her decision to attack others because of that frustration. However, before the company releases an official statement of her suspension, I hope they will consider more than just her actions. Consider the other members of her group who are innocent. Before, I was always alone. No one cared if I was sick or hurt. No one to celebrate birthdays with. No one to fight over doing the dishes with. No one to work day and night together with to achieve our dreams. But now, it's different."

Hayoon looks from the girl to her members and then to her own. *Exhale. Don't cry. You can do this.*

"Being in a K-pop group is extremely hard work but no matter how hard it gets, you have the other members to rely on and they on you. In our family, whenever you start to fall, there are eight people beside you to pick you up and push you forward. It's not as simple as one person's mistake today. She has four other members who rely on her and need her. Not only just her members but also their fans. Because of this, their fans will need to wait longer for their album. Company staff will have to work overtime, reassigning parts and reworking choreography. Being accountable for your actions is important but I don't want other people to suffer because of one person's mistake."

Hayoon turns to ask their PR director, "Can I make a suggestion? Of course, you don't have to listen to me but what if we can come up with a solution that doesn't hurt the group, the company or the fans but still shows she is being responsible for her actions?"

The PR director offers to hear her out and they move to the back of the stage. Baekhyeon puts his hand on her back as they leave the podium in support and protection. After Hayoon talks for a minute, the PR director calls the CEO to get her plan approved. They return for the director to announce the results.

"We would like to announce a revised punishment. A formal apology will be posted and she will donate half of her personal profits from their upcoming album to support music programs in rural schools."

The young girl gives Hayoon a surprised expression that seems to ask, *Is that it?*

"Additionally, Hayoon has requested for them to eat lunch together."

A reporter asks Hayoon, "Why do you want to eat with her?"

"I want to give her the opportunity to express herself and get to know each other. It might make her feel better if she can tell me her frustrations. Plus, I heard someone say she's the main dancer in her group. I'm sure our members will be relieved if their ears can rest and I talk choreography with someone else for a change."

Hayoon ends the press conference on a comical note.

17

I finally get to dance with him!

-Hayoon

Day 71

"I know you need to go to practice so we'll try to make this fast. Here is your new contract. Read it over. I'll go get your clothes."

Clothes? Hayoon reads through the contract while Manager-nim is gone.

"Okay. How's it going? Questions?"

"Manager-nim, what's this amount for?"

"You can think of it like back pay. It's the company's way of appreciating the work you've done for MPeak, like the choreography you worked on with Junwoo. Speaking of which, your name will be added to the credits with his, too."

"Does Junwoo agree? I just helped."

"It was his idea. IT is working on adding you to the website but it'll take some time to replace the group photos without you. We don't have a photoshoot scheduled for a while."

"That's okay."

"We are working on informing all the team's sponsors you've officially joined and most have already requested to add you to their contracts. This bag has MPeak apparel and sponsor apparel. Because of you, we've been contacted by new sponsors, too."

"What if I drink the wrong thing and they're recording BTS?"

Manager-nim chuckles at her innocent expression. "You don't have to worry. The managers and staff already consider sponsors when they give you food and drinks during filming. In the future, you'll automatically be included in sponsor contracts. Here is your official company badge. There's nowhere you can't go with that. Your contract term is seven months since the boys' contract expires then. You can all re-sign together. The company will officially post an announcement of you joining MPeak at five o'clock tonight. Your page is going to blow up with comments from fans. When you're done with dance practice, try to respond to at least a few fans from each country."

"Okay. Sign here?"

"Yup."

"Done. Can I go? It's dance day."

"All clear. ...Oh wait."

"Huh?"

"Oh, no. It's fine. I got it. Go ahead. I thought I needed your contact form updated but it's already done."

"I didn't update it."

"Baekhyeon took care of it."

"Can I see?"

"Here." Manager-nim slides a few papers across the table.

"How..."

"They all came in person to sign. My office was like a revolving door that day."

Hayoon chuckles while reading the names. All the members and their families signed. Seojun's little brother signed with a crayon, too.

"I found out where Seojun gets his personality from. His mom made us staple her lawyer's business card to the page."

"Thanks, Manager-nim. See you later."

Kun puts down his water and tells Baekhyeon, "I was thinking about breaking out from our normal style."

"For this album?"

"Yeah. I've been wanting to do like a rock ballad."

Junwoo is listening to their conversation while fiddling on the audio system's computer. He butts in to ask, "How about a collaboration?"

"What do you mean?"

Junwoo sits down between Minseong and Kun to join the conversation.

"If you were to sing a rock ballad, you planned on it being the vocal unit's track, right?"

"Probably."

"What if the vocal team sings and the dance and rap units dance? Like a visual of the song's story."

Kun ponders his suggestion while Baekhyeon inquires, "Can it work? We only have a week and a half until our comeback and that's seriously outside of your normal style."

Junwoo smirks and pulls out his phone. "Not for all of us." He plays a video of Hayoon dancing while he explains, "The first day we went to the recording studio last week, Hayoon came with me so we could work on choreography when I was done. I took this video before she knew I was here."

Minseong comments, "She's really good."

Baekhyeon doubtfully asks, "But can she do it? On stage?"

Junwoo looks over to Hayoon laying on a pillow in Yunjae's lap. She laughs with Yunjae at what Seojun was saying.

She's grown so much these past few weeks. I can keep dancing with her, just the two of us, in the studio forever. But I want more for her than hiding within these four walls. I want to know, if we break her out of this cage, how far she'll fly. I want to find out together. This is the chance I've been waiting for.

Junwoo says with conviction, "She's ready."

Baekhyeon excitedly approves, "It'll be incredible if we can do it. Not to mention, the fans have been begging for Hayoon to debut on stage."

Minseong questions, "But can we do the rock ballad, on top of the rest of the album, in only a week and a half?"

Kun speaks up, "I can do it."

Junwoo adds, "Since Hayoon will help, I can do it, too."

"Let's keep it between us for now and I'll go talk to the leadership team while you practice. Junwoo, send me that video."

Junwoo continues dancing while he looks in the mirror's reflection as Baekhyeon comes back. He gives him a thumbs up.

The music stops and Junwoo calls for a break. Baekhyeon, Kun, Minseong, and Junwoo cluster together to discuss the plan.

"What'd they say?" asks Minseong.

"They think the same as us. If we can make it work, it'll be awesome. They'll support us on their end as much as they can. They said they've been discussing possibilities for Hayoon to have a more active role, since her fan base is so big, but they hadn't come up with anything near as good as this. They think it'd be best if we still perform the title track for our first comeback stage and perform the ballad five days later. If the response is good, that gives us enough time to rework our award show lineup."

"Let's talk to her before we go any further."

Baekhyeon calls to her, "Hayoon, come here."

She skips over and leans her hands on Baekhyeon's shoulders. Junwoo takes her wrist and guides her over to sit down between them.

Baekhyeon seriously says, "We have a question to ask you."

Is something wrong? He's serious?

"What is it?"

"We decided to sing a rock ballad."

Hayoon responds happily, "For this album? Did you already record it?"

"Not yet. We need to ask you something before we start."

"Me?"

Junwoo puts his arm around her waist and holds his phone in front of her to play her video. She slightly shrinks into his side as her eyes look from Kun to Minseong to Baekhyeon.

Baekhyeon bluntly says, "We want you on stage."

"What?!?"

"We need you on stage with us. The vocal team will sing. You and Junwoo will lead the choreography."

Hayoon straightens her posture, trying not to immediately reject them.

"So, vocal team will sing and we'll dance?"

Minseong encouragingly says, "You can do it, Hayoon."

Kun adds, "You're too talented to stay off stage."

Junwoo rubs her leg, not needing to say anything.

"I know it's not an easy decision for you to make but can you think about it?"

Performing with my brothers would be fun but what if I fail them? Sigh.

"I'll think about it."

"Okay. That's all I needed to hear. Let's get back to practice."

Junwoo helps Hayoon stand. He holds the side of her head to whisper in her ear, "Don't stress about it."

Hayoon hangs back when the rest of the group heads home. As the boys are getting into the van, Junwoo steps back. Baekhyeon dangles his car keys in front of Junwoo and warns him, "Don't be back too late."

Junwoo swipes the keys and jogs back into the studio to find Hayoon.

In the dance studio, Hayoon pulls her legs up to rest her chin on her knees. She stares at herself in the mirror, questioning herself. *Can I really do it?*

"You can."

Her eyes shift in the mirror to see Junwoo coming up from behind her. He walks around to sit between her and the mirror. He sits down, straddling his bent legs on either side of her.

"You can do it."

"What if I get nervous and forget everything?"

Junwoo grabs her ankles and pulls them toward him to rest behind his legs. He holds her face in his hands.

He warmly says, "You won't forget. Even if you get nervous and your mind goes blank, your body will remember."

Hayoon frustratingly grunts and hides her face on his shoulder. "I just don't know."

Junwoo rubs the back of her shoulders and patiently asks, "You dance with me the most, right?"

"Yeah."

"So, better than anyone else, I understand your ability, right?"

She nods.

"I know you can do this, Hayoon. And you won't be alone. I'll be on stage with you the whole time. We all want you with us. We will not let you fail."

She reaches her arms over his shoulders and he pulls her in to hug. He brings his legs in crisscross to support her as she lays her head on his shoulder. Junwoo rubs her back slowly and says, "No matter what you decide, we will always be here for you."

"Okay. I'll do it."

"Are you sure?"

"Mm."

We're finally going to be on stage together!

I finally get to dance with him!

He leans back and crunches her face excitedly in his hands. At first, she plays along but then swats him away. He teases back and she rolls out of reach.

Baekhyeon looks up from his laptop when Junwoo and Hayoon walk in. Minseong pauses his game.

So?

Hayoon smiles nervously and nods, revealing her decision.

"Yes!" Minseong exclaims.

"Kun!" Baekhyeon shouts, smiling.

18

I have a family.

-Hayoon

Day 73

"Junwoo, when you get home today you need to pack an overnight bag. Early tomorrow, I'll pick you, Baekhyeon, and Jihoon up from the house."

Junwoo anxiously reaches back to Hayoon. She lowers her phone to her lap and takes his hand.

Their costume designer yells, "Is everyone good with this outfit before we change?"

Junwoo ignores her and asks Manager-nim, "Can I not go?" *What if something happens to Hayoon while I'm gone like last time?*

Hayoon stands up beside him and urges him, "You should go. Everything's fine now. Kun oppa and the other members will be home with me."

Junwoo's eyes show opposition.

"Hayoon, you're going, too."

Junwoo and Hayoon simultaneously say, "Huh?"

"I was looking for you earlier but couldn't find you. The show wants the MPeak princess and her guardians. All four of you are going together."

Jihoon and Baekhyeon look over from trying on their wardrobe and exclaim together, "Road trip!"

"We leave at four tomorrow morning."

Uh? Four? Dang.

Day 74

Baekhyeon scurries around the house trying to find which outlet he left his phone charger in. Hayoon hugs her bag, sleeping upright on the couch.

"Ready?" Manager-nim pokes his head in the door.

Junwoo nods to Hayoon and tells Jihoon, "I'll get the bag, you get her."

Jihoon squats in front of Hayoon to pull her hands over his shoulders to piggy back her. He grumbles, "Why can't I carry the bags?"

"You forgot? She was up late last night helping you."

"Oh, right."

Their interview ends before dinner and they head to the gym. Their fans could easily do a blind member test after seeing their workout. Their personalities and gym routines unmistakably linked.

Baekhyeon follows up his light cardio with moderate to heavy weights and Jihoon hardly does any cardio before hitting heavy weights. Junwoo and Hayoon share a workout playlist and run on treadmills next to each other for longer cardio. Junwoo switches to some moderate weights and Hayoon rolls out a yoga mat for body weight exercises and yoga.

Hayoon stands out of a plank at the same time Junwoo finishes weighted squats. They end up in sync, energetically dancing to the same song in their earbuds. The hotel gym quickly turns into a dance studio. Baekhyeon is taking a break between sets to film for his vlog and flips the camera around to the happy duo. Since the music is only in their earbuds, Baekhyeon and Jihoon sing along.

Manager-nim walks in to remind them of the time and chuckles at what he finds. *Hard to believe this is the same girl who hid in the stairwell a few months ago.*

Junwoo and Hayoon are deep in conversation as they return to the hotel from dinner. They each go through their respective doors but don't stop talking. Hayoon kicks off her shoes, grabs her laptop, and walks through their connecting door to Junwoo's room. She crawls on the bed and Junwoo joins her to watch the choreography video together.

Manager-nim knocks on Baekhyeon's door and Jihoon uses their connecting door to answer for him. Manager-nim is holding up a bag of desserts and tells him, "The people from your interview sent it over. Local pastries."

"Thanks."

Baekhyeon and Jihoon walk across the hall with the pastries. Jihoon lifts his hand to knock on Hayoon's door but Baekhyeon asks, "What are you doing?"

Jihoon answers in an, isn't it obvious, kind of way. "Calling Hayoon to eat in Junwoo's room."

Baekhyeon shakes his head as if to say, *pabo*. He uses Junwoo's spare card to open his door and walks in.

Jihoon follows him and lets out an, "Ahhh," in realization.

Hayoon keeps talking as she steps off the bed, onto the chair and sits crisscross. Baekhyeon hands her a fork and opens her pastry. *They seriously never stop.*

Junwoo holds up his fork for her to try his flavor. Hayoon picks up Baekhyeon's out of reach cup to put in his hand and slides her own pastry over for Jihoon to try. Junwoo tries Baekhyeon's cake and reports, "Yours is better."

When Hayoon is full, she leaves the leaders to talk while she settles in Junwoo's bed to watch a drama.

Twenty minutes into her drama, Hayoon falls asleep with her noise canceling headphones on. Junwoo walks over to set her laptop and headphones off to the side. He gently slides her down to lay flat. Hayoon grabs ahold of his arm and he scoots onto the edge of the bed.

Baekhyeon and Jihoon decide to head back to their own rooms. Jihoon considerately asks, "You want me to take her to her room?"

Baekhyeon answers for Junwoo, "No need."

"Let her sleep. I can go sleep in her bed or the couch."

Hayoon wakes up from the bright sun peeking through the blinds. *Ahhh, another great day.* She lies in bed, basking in the sunlight, truly happy. After enjoying the sun for a bit, she rolls out of bed to wake up Junwoo. Hayoon pokes his cheek and he smiles without opening his eyes. He reaches his arms around her blindly for a morning hug.

"Good morning."

He cracks open his eyes and kisses her head for a wordless good morning.

"We have to leave soon."

Hayoon leaves to get ready in her room ten minutes before Baekhyeon comes in to get them. He drops his bag by Junwoo's door and crosses the boundary into Hayoon's room. She's organizing her bag so he kisses her head from behind. "Good morning."

"Morning." She hands him her backpack. "Can you get my laptop?"

"Sure thing."

Jihoon enters Junwoo's room and he orders, "Go get my charger in Hayoon's room."

Jihoon greets Hayoon, "Good morning."

"Morning. Take his speaker, too."

Jihoon grabs it off the table and heads back into Junwoo's room to hand it over. Junwoo mumbles, impossible for Hayoon to hear, "My water bottle."

At that exact moment, Hayoon yells, "I packed your water bottle."

Junwoo smiles at their telepathy. Baekhyeon and Jihoon exchange glances and shake their heads at the pair's crazy chemistry.

"I packed your jacket."

"Duffel bag or backpack?"

"Backpack."

Hayoon appears in the connecting doorway and chipperly says, "Perfect."

"Let's go."

Day 77

"Where's Hayoon?"

Baekhyeon responds, "She asked for leave this afternoon."

Junwoo questions, "Asked for leave?" *Days before our comeback?*

"Manager-nim messaged me earlier. She asked for three hours of leave."

Seojun worriedly asks, "There couldn't be anything wrong, right?"

"I texted her. She said everything's fine. She'll be back by four."

Junwoo isn't satisfied and calls her.

"Hayoon, are you okay?"

"I'm fine."

"Is it the company?"

"No. I just have an errand to run. I'll tell you later."

Junwoo hangs up. They start practice again but he feels bothered by her tone of voice. Forty seconds into the song, his dancing fades out as his brain is whirling, trying to put the pieces together.

Baekhyeon stops the music. "Why'd you stop dancing?"

His eyes jerk up to Baekhyeon. "I know why she's not here. I know what today is." He runs to grab his bag in distress. "I gotta go."

Baekhyeon grabs his arm. "Is she in trouble?"

"It's her parents' death anniversary."

Without discussion, the boys all run to get their own bags and follow Junwoo out to the cars. They're already strapped for time but none of that matters right now.

Hayoon kneels in front of her parents' tombstone telling them about her new family. "I'm not alone anymore. I have eight brothers. They treat me really well. You don't have to worry anymore." Sudden motion catches her eyes and she looks up to see them walking toward her with flowers in hand. "They're here."

Junwoo helps Hayoon stand as the boys crowd around her. One at a time, they bow to her parents and introduce themselves. Baekhyeon confesses that they didn't protect her well before, causing her to get hurt, but that won't happen again. Junwoo holds Hayoon's hand and tells her parents about the person she grew up to be and how proud they would be of her.

Did you hear that mom? Did you hear that dad? I have a family. You can rest peacefully now. I really am happy.

Hayoon rides back in the smaller car with her guardian protectors. Jihoon hesitantly asks, "Hayoon, can I ask you a question?"

"About my parents?"

"Yeah."

"It was a long time ago. It wasn't some crime of the decade or anything, just some bad weather. Our car crashed and my dad carried me out. He gave me to someone that stopped to help us and went back for my mom. I don't remember that much anymore but something happened and another car hit them."

"Your parents must've really loved you."

"Yeah. You know, my mom started teaching me how to play piano before I could talk."

"So that means, you started training from a year old! No wonder you're so good. Impressive, little sister."

Hayoon chuckles at his exaggerated comment.

Baekhyeon glances back and asks, "Hayoon, do you want to go home or back to dance practice?"

"Dance practice!"

He rolls his eyes. "Of course, you do."

Day 78

Their comeback is only five days away and Hayoon is running on fumes. Every time someone is out for recording, she dances in their place. Every time Junwoo steps out to check for errors, she dances in his place. When someone misses part of learning choreography, she teaches them when everyone else breaks. During after hours, she works with Junwoo on the ballad. In two days, she's slept six hours total.

When Junwoo calls for a break, she crumbles to the floor. She grabs Minseong's pant leg and he throws her his sweatshirt to use as a pillow. Even moving to the couch wastes precious time. Their leaders leave the room and Seojun starts messing with the computer. He clicks on their current title track to play through the speakers. Hayoon propels herself off the floor from a dead sleep state and starts dancing from muscle memory. The boys' eyes widen in amazement. Yunjae hits the space bar to stop the music and Hayoon looks around like she is broken from a trance. Realizing they hadn't resumed practice, she melts back to the floor and falls asleep.

Minseong, Yunjae, and Seojun snicker at Hayoon. Seojun hovers his finger over the space bar and mischievously says, "Let's try it again."

Yunjae smacks him and curiously asks, "You think the BTS camera caught that?"

Minseong runs over to the camera to report, "It's still recording." He presses the stop record button and pulls out the memory card. He jogs over to hand it to Seojun to plug into the computer. Jeongu and Kun join them to watch as Hayoon jumps off the floor.

"Bahahaha. That's amazing!"

Baekhyeon and Jihoon come back to check what they're all watching. Junwoo wakes up Hayoon to join the party. Seojun plays it again and they crack up laughing. Junwoo ruffles her messy hair and tells her, "I don't think you have to worry about forgetting the choreography."

Baekhyeon tells them, "I'm going to post it as a short video loop spoiler."

"No, no, no." *...But it is kind of funny.*

Day 80

Baekhyeon announces to everyone, "I know we thought we were done in the recording studio but today will be quick. Most of you just need to record the background vocals for the chorus in the ballad. Hayoon, you'll need to come back again to record for the title track so you can perform the whole award show remix. The order for today is Yunjae, Jihoon, Junwoo, myself, Jeongu, Hayoon, Minseong, Seojun, and then Kun."

Junwoo lowers Hayoon to the couch from his back. Jihoon hands her a pillow and she hugs it while leaning against his shoulder to sleep. When it's Jihoon's turn to record, he lowers her down to the couch and slides the pillow under her head. Jeongu raises her legs to sit down under them. After Junwoo records, Jihoon picks up Hayoon to sit her on Junwoo's lap so he can work with Jeongu. Hayoon looks like the hot potato being passed between members.

Her head rests on Junwoo's shoulder with her legs dangling beside him. Minseong asks Junwoo for his help. He sets the laptop on the table so Junwoo can work while holding Hayoon.

"Junwoo," Baekhyeon calls for him from inside the booth.

Minseong moves the laptop away to pull the mic closer. Junwoo secures Hayoon with a protective arm and leans forward to converse with Baekhyeon. Seojun and Yunjae come back in and gush at the cute image of Junwoo holding Hayoon while working.

Junwoo spins his chair around to look at the computer. *THUNK!* Hayoon's ankle bangs into the table leg. He grabs her ankle with a startled expression but Hayoon doesn't even flinch. The members and staff all look to Junwoo and he looks wide-eyed back at them. *I can't believe I just did that.* They burst into laughter as he leans back to look at her. *She still sleeping?!?* Even the BTS scenes cameraman struggles to keep the camera steady from laughing at Junwoo's expression.

Baekhyeon looks out from the recording booth waiting for Junwoo's reply, completely clueless.

Manager-nim walks in as the members are trying to recover from their laughter. "Coffee! ...What did I miss?" His question restarts their contagious laughter.

Junwoo carefully rolls over to the computer and they get back on track. When Baekhyeon comes out of the booth, he hands Junwoo coffee and a breakfast snack for him and Hayoon. Junwoo rubs Hayoon's back and whispers, "Wake up and drink some coffee. It's your turn next." She leans up and he hands her an americano. "You can't drink coffee on an empty stomach." He hands her a breakfast bread and affectionately massages her neck to help wake her up. She obediently takes a sleepy bite. She puts her straw up to Junwoo's lips and he takes a sip. With bread in one hand and coffee in the other, she leans forward to rest her chin on his shoulder. Seojun is sitting on the couch behind them and she holds out her bread for him to take a bite.

Day 83

Hayoon drags Junwoo to Baekhyeon and tattles, "He says he's not going. Talk some sense into him."

Baekhyeon knows Junwoo is just throwing a tantrum because he's worried about Hayoon. He's never shirked his responsibilities before so he won't now. He jokes, "You can always put that dog camera back in her room to check on her."

"You see! ...Wait. What? What dog camera?"

"The one he installed in your room when you were sick. It's motion activated so he would know if you got up in the middle of the night. His mom took it from their dog."

"A dog camera? ...Are you kidding me?!?" Junwoo runs away as Hayoon chases him down the hall and into the living room. "Do I look like a dog to you?!?"

"Are you sure you're going to be okay? Between yesterday and today, you've performed on three stages. You guys hardly slept last night and we perform the ballad in four days."

"I can sleep when I get there. I'll be back tomorrow evening. Don't get into trouble with Seojun and don't go to the studio after dark by yourself. Call me if something happens, okay?"

"What are you nervous about? Baekhyeon and Jihoon are both staying home with me." She asks but she knows. "I'm going to be fine. If you don't go, you're going to be late."

Junwoo kisses her head. Hayoon reaches up to rest her hands on his waist as his kiss lingers.

He's still worried. "Don't eat only ramen and sleep as much as you can."

"Wait for me to come home."

Day 85

Junwoo's flight gets delayed twice due to weather conditions. At two in the morning, he stumbles through the door. He's surprised to find the entryway light on and Hayoon sleeping on the couch. He bends down in front of her and strokes her hair as she sleeps. *I'm home.*

She groggily opens her eyes. "You're back."

He whispers, "Let's go to bed."

He pulls her wrists to lean her up and lifts under her arms so she's standing on the couch. He picks her up and carries her to her bedroom. Instead of laying her in bed, he sits down with her in his lap. Junwoo rests his head against hers and whispers, "I missed you." He doesn't need her to hear it but he needs to say it.

She turns her head to nuzzle against his neck. "I missed you, too. Are you tired?" She falls back asleep before he can answer. He settles her in bed and tucks the blanket in around her.

He opens his suitcase in the living room and takes out his gift for Hayoon. He steps lightly back into her room and tucks the stuffed animal in bed with her. She hugs it with a smile and he strokes her hair.

Hayoon holds out her stuffed animal, trying to figure out where it came from. *Junwoo! He's home!* She throws her door open and hurries out to find him setting the table for breakfast. "You're back!"

She runs and jumps to hug him. He embraces her before telling her, "Hold tight." He rotates her to his back and she locks her ankles so he can let go. While Hayoon is attached to him like a koala, he continues to set out the plates.

Jihoon comes out to help cook and he hands Hayoon off to him. Jihoon carries her over and puts her feet on her chair. Hayoon talks to Junwoo while standing on the chair, holding her stuffed animal.

Yunjae throws a fake tantrum and demands, "Where's my present?" He tries to swipe her animal and she smacks him in defense.

"Over there." Junwoo nods to the end of the table.

"I have one, too." Yunjae sticks his tongue out at Hayoon mockingly.

Baekhyeon walks in. "You're back. How was it?" He walks past Hayoon and tugs her wrist to get her to sit down.

Seojun loudly comes in and dramatically tells Junwoo, "You're finally back. You need to tell Hayoon to chill out. She never left the dance studio yesterday! Not even to eat lunch!"

Junwoo is walking past Hayoon but pauses at her chair. She fiddles with her stuffed animal, keeping her eyes down. He lifts her chin to make her look at him. She is ready to be lectured but his eyes are calm. *Eh? I'm not in trouble?*

Junwoo smiles at her dotingly and says, "Eat lots."

Seojun is shocked. "That's it? You're not going to yell at her?"

She taunts back, "I was working on choreography. What were you doing after practice? Playing games?"

Junwoo ignores their sibling fight to ask Hayoon, "What were you working on?"

"That weird section after the dance break."

"Figure it out?"

"Mm. Can we go to the studio after breakfast?"

"We'll only have about an hour before everyone else comes."

"Hayoon! I'm using your bathroom," Minseong calls out as he walks into her room.

Baekhyeon shouts like a true father, "Where are your manners? You didn't even ask."

Hayoon waves him off. "It's fine. This is like the twentieth time. He even keeps a towel in there."

"Seriously?"

"Mm. Yunjae and Seojun do, too." She points at Yunjae and teases, "He takes longer showers than most girls."

Junwoo cleverly blocks Yunjae's brotherly smack for Hayoon as he serves her breakfast first.

19

Oppa, my dream...I got it.

-Hayoon

Day 87

Take a deep breath. In. Out. In. Out. I don't have to sing so it's not a big deal. All I have to do is dance. I won't be alone. I can do this! In. Out. In. Out.

"Hayoon, how are you doing?" Junwoo rubs her arm from behind her.

"I'm ...okay."

"Just watch me. I'm here."

I can do this!

"It's time."

Hayoon walks out into the darkness to get into position. The music starts. *5. 4. 3. 2. 1. Jump!*

As the song's final notes ring out, the fans scream and chant Hayoon's name. Junwoo lowers her feet down to the floor as confetti cannons explode on the stage. Hayoon faces the audience as she slowly breaks into a smile. She holds out her hand to catch the confetti. "It's a butterfly!"

"For you."

Hayoon becomes so excited she runs out to the stage extension as more cannons shoot out butterflies. She lifts her open palms upward as the confetti floats down all around her.

The members are all clustered together, watching Hayoon's genuine childlike happiness. The cameras zoom in and she becomes the ending fairy, without even knowing it. She picks up a pile of confetti and throws it out over their fans.

Baekhyeon yells, "Let's go!" and they all take off after her.

Seojun reaches her first and grabs her wrist as they keep running to the farthest point of the stage to say goodbye to their fans.

They're cheering for me! I can't believe they're cheering for me! I did it! ...Let's do it again!

Day 88

Hayoon bangs the piano keys in frustration. "Ugh!"

Kun suddenly opens the practice room door, causing her to jump up from the bench. "I brought you some standard in-ears to try. Even though we rushed yours, they won't be ready until the award ..."

Hayoon's lip pouts as she whines, "Kun oppa, I can't do it." Her shoulders shrug up as she sniffles. Kun pats her head empathetically. She stares at the ground, expecting him to be disappointed. "I'm sorry."

Are we asking too much from her? We just want to perform together. "Come here." He pulls her over to sit on the piano bench, keeping her hand in his. "You have nothing to be sorry for. Do you have any idea how amazing we all think you are?"

"I'm still not good enough." She stares at the sheet music like the notes are taunting her.

"Do you know how long we trained before debuting?" Hayoon shrugs her shoulders at his question. "As a group, we trained nearly every day for a year. A year, Hayoon. And all of us, except Seojun, trained before that. I trained for two years; Jihoon trained for a year and a half. Baekhyeon trained for nearly three years before becoming our leader. You only have a few days. You started dancing with the company at the same level it took us four years to get to. Junwoo is one of the best choreographers in the industry. You not only keep up with him but many times, he's needed your help. None of us doubt whether or not you can do this."

Hayoon hears what he's saying but can't shake her self-doubt.

"Hey," Kun says softly, "we're here for you."

"Will you help me?"

He ruffles her hair and cheerfully responds, "'bout time you asked." He peruses the sheet music. "Okay, let's start here. Ready?" They sing together for twelve measures before he stops abruptly. "What were you crying about?"

She smiles shyly at his compliment. "That's the thing. I can sing with you but I can't do it by myself."

"What about in the recording studio? You were alone then."

"The guide track was playing in my headphones. I can match pitch but I can't find it on my own."

"Ohhh, I get it. Okay. Let's try it again. I'll sing the first two measures but then try to continue on your own." The expected happens and she quits after six measly measures on her own. "I see. You started good but then your voice loses power and ends up a little flat."

"I've sung it a million times and it's always the same."

"Hmm. I think it comes down to two things. You remember a while ago when we were at home talking about the Japan sound check? You said you didn't have time to get nervous. You weren't thinking about it when you started singing, it just happened."

"Yeah..."

"Maybe you have a hard time singing alone because you don't think you're good enough and you're too nervous."

"But in here, it's just me."

"But the reason you're training now is for a live performance. Even though you're alone, you're still thinking about all those people watching you, right? It's not that you can't do it but your stage fright and doubt are getting in the way."

"What's the second thing?"

"The second thing is just that you haven't had enough time to train. Finding pitch can be learned."

"But we only have a few days."

"That's okay. We can raise the volume of your in-ear vocals so that's all you hear when you're singing. You won't need to find pitch; you can match it. Let's go test these ones I brought for you to try. Baekhyeon ordered your custom in-ears but they won't arrive for five more days."

"Will that really fix everything?"

"...Think of it like a bandage. Your stage fright is still there, for now, but we're finding a way to cover it up so it doesn't hurt."

Day 90

"Today, we're talking with the group who, only three days ago, shook the industry with an incredible rock ballad that they composed and choreographed themselves. Welcome MPeak!

"Thank you for having us."

"Is the song you're going to sing for us from your new album?"

"It is but there's a surprise for our fans, too."

"I can't wait to hear it."

The members put in their in-ear monitors and take their mics off their stands to get ready. Baekhyeon looks over at Hayoon to reconfirm her decision, giving her one last chance to back out. He holds up one finger for option one. Hayoon nods her head slightly but otherwise, doesn't move. Baekhyeon gives Manager-nim a thumbs up for him to instruct the sound staff to play the remix of their title track and rock ballad.

The vocal team begins singing their ballad, *Nightmare*. The rap and dance units provide vocal support in the chorus. As the chorus starts for the first time, Hayoon takes in-ears out from under her hoodie and puts them in. Her brothers can't help but smile and look over in anticipation. The radio host catches Minseong give her an encouraging fist bump and he eagerly edges forward in his chair. The chorus ends and Hayoon joins the vocal team for the second verse. The radio host nearly falls out of his seat. Yunjae pulls his mic away from his face to laugh at his expression. The radio station's BTS camera focuses on Hayoon and she looks to Kun. He holds out his hand for her. She holds it firmly and remembers what he said, *Do you have any idea how amazing we all think you are? None of us doubt whether or not you can do this.* She looks down the line of members and their reactions to her singing melt away her self-doubt. Her fear is replaced with confidence by the time the song ends.

Kun helps Hayoon set her mic back on the stand. "You did good. Really good."

The radio host impatiently waits for the members to take their seats around the table before talking. "Wait a minute. So, is Hayoon in the dance unit or vocal unit." The members proudly smile at his compliment hidden in a question. "I saw your performance of *Nightmare* and the choreography was amazing. I heard Hayoon and Junwoo worked on it together so I thought for sure, she's in the dance unit. But just now, listening to you guys sing, I was seriously questioning it."

Baekhyeon answers, "She's in the dance unit. Her and Junwoo have been collaborating for a long time. She was dancing in the studio with him long before anyone knew about it, even the other units in our group. But it was only recently, we convinced her to get on stage."

"What took so long?"

Baekhyeon defers to Hayoon who honestly answers, "Stage fright."

"Woah. I never would've known you had stage fright after watching you perform."

"I was super nervous. But when we started dancing together, my nerves disappeared. But dancing is different than singing."

Baekhyeon comments, "If it hadn't been for Kun's mic breaking at sound check, we might not have found out she can sing. She had no intention of singing and performing with us."

"Why is that?"

"I've never been trained in singing."

"Are you kidding?"

"I was never a trainee or auditioned for a survival show. Even though this style of dance is different, I have at least trained in dance before. And with Junwoo's coaching, it wasn't a hard transition. But when it comes to singing, I'm not confident at all."

"Wah, well you were incredible. Of course, you all were."

Baekhyeon says, "Normally for this ballad, Hayoon's choreography is physically demanding. Even if she was a full-performance member with five years of experience, she wouldn't be able to sing while dancing at the ballad's level of difficulty. We thought this show would be the perfect opportunity for her to try singing."

"I'm sure the fans loved your surprise. Kun, you're the group's composer, right?"

"I am."

"Can you tell us about the story in the ballad?"

"It's about the fight between dreams and nightmares. Or another way to think about it is fighting your fears to reach your dreams. Every time we have a new album, Junwoo has to wait on me to finish writing before he can start choreography. This song was different. It started with their idea and then we choreographed and wrote the music at the same time. So, your question might be better for Junwoo."

"Junwoo, can you tell us about the choreography?"

"Hayoon begins the ballad with mostly all black clothes. As she fights against her nightmares, who are Jihoon and Jeongu, her black clothes get ripped away to reveal white. Yunjae and I represent her dreams. Like Baekhyeon said earlier, the choreography is very physically demanding. There are jumps, flips, and lifts. My favorite part is when she gets suspended in the air and released by staff. I have to grab her mid-air and hold her still while Yunjae unties the black rope wrapped around her leg."

Jeongu pipes in, "Oh, I love that part. After Junwoo saves her, I get to shove her off the platform."

The host comments, "I was holding my breath when I saw you run up from behind. Yunjae, what's your favorite part?"

"I like the part where she gets tossed between dreams and nightmares and Jeongu grabs her ankle."

"Where she kicks over backwards? I loved that part. Baekhyeon, I know you're not in the dance unit but as leader, is there a part of the choreography you thought worked out really well?"

"I think it's one of the best choreographies Junwoo has made, especially considering how little time they had to put it together. After we performed the ballad, a dance company even reached out to ask about Junwoo and Hayoon co-teaching a multi-day workshop. But personally, I like the part at the end. When Junwoo holds her hands crisscross from behind and spins her, lifting her hands overhead. I think it's so cool how her clothes end up all white and she falls asleep in his arms."

"Are the fans going to get another chance to see *Nightmare*? Does MPeak have any upcoming events?"

"Right now, we're focusing on our award show performances. Whether or not *Nightmare* will be in the lineup... they'll have to watch and see."

Day 95

"Are you Hayoon? Can I have your number?"

"Don't you know she has eight fierce brothers? Are you sure?"

Hayoon recognizes him as the flirty leader from the group that came to compete on their show. The man who wants her number scurries off at his warning.

"Why didn't you put him in his place like you did me?"

Hayoon chuckles and says, "Hey, I saw your performance. Not bad."

"I saw the recording of *Nightmare*. I heard it's a front runner for choreography of the year next week."

Junwoo and Seojun come up to Hayoon. "Time to put your mic on." She takes the headset and Junwoo lowers the wire down her back. Seojun puts her right in-ear in jokingly so she can't hear the flirty leader talk.

He asks her surprisingly, "You're going to sing on stage?"

She laughs. "Looks like we're all growing up." She nods to Junwoo. "It's all his fault."

Junwoo rest his right hand on her waist possessively. "Okay. All done."

Baekhyeon leads the rest of the members past them. "Time to roll."

"Artist of the year award goes to MPeak!"

The members jump up in celebration and hurry on stage to receive their award. Baekhyeon looks around from his position front and center. His members are looking around like they're lost, whispering, "Where's Hayoon?"

Baekhyeon talks into the mic, "Sorry. Hold on a minute. We're not all here. Hayoon!"

The award show camera catches her taking pictures of her brothers on stage. She freezes and smiles shyly. *Me? I only performed once.* Baekhyeon calls to their hoobaes at the neighboring table to bring her up front.

To stall for time, Baekhyeon starts talking. "If you only knew how much she contributed to our latest album, this award would say her name and not ours. Do you have a sister of the year award? Although, there's probably not a lot of competition for a little sister adopted by an all-male K-pop group." The audience laughs at his comment as she joins them.

Day 109

Hayoon whispers to Seojun, "Is this our last award show?"

"We were nominated for awards at a few others but this is the last one we're performing at. After this, we'll get ready for the world tour."

"Rookie Artist of the Year Award Nominees..."

"Do you know what countries we're going to?"

Seojun counts on his fingers as he answers, "America, France..."

"Hayoon from MPeak."

WHAT?!?!? Did they just say my name?

Her eyes shoot over to Baekhyeon and Junwoo. *What's going on?*

"Versatile, all-arounder, K-pop prodigy, MPeak's best kept secret weapon."

She grabs Seojun's hand in panic. Yunjae strokes her head on the other side, laughing at her expression.

"Baekhyeon oppa, what's going on?"

The host announces, "And the winner of Rookie of the Year is... Hayoon from MPeak!"

The crowd cheers boisterously and her brothers shoot out of their chairs in excitement. Seojun and Yunjae yank her out of the chair when they jump up. Her brothers' hyper reaction causes the K-pop groups surrounding them to crack up laughing. Baekhyeon shoves her toward the stage. She tries to compose herself but she can't wrap her head around what's happening.

"Congratulations."

Hayoon bows and takes her trophy from the award show hosts. "Thank you." She's still a bit stupefied as she stands behind the microphone. Without thinking, she mutters, "How is this possible?" She looks back to the host and asks, "Are you sure?" The audience laughs at her honest and unconventional response to receiving the award. She searches the crowd for her brothers.

Breathe. "I'm sure you could probably guess I had no idea this was coming. I didn't even know I was a nominee. Our leaders normally speak for me. I never imagined a day would come where I'd be standing up here without them. This award is such a huge honor. If you've seen our interviews, you'd know that becoming a member of MPeak was an accident. But now, I can't imagine my life not being a part of it. I can't imagine my life without our members. I have a little friend who once asked me if my brothers treated me well. She had all brothers, too, so she was sincerely concerned." The audience chuckles in response. "I told her they were the best. Because of them, I'm happy every day. And it's because of them that I have the chance to stand up here. This award might say my name but it's not mine alone. It belongs to my brothers, their families, our staff, and our amazing fans. I promise to work harder in the future to make you all proud. Thank you."

In the silence before applause, Seojun shouts, "That's our girl!"

The crowd laughs as they give her a standing ovation. Not just her brothers but all the groups who had been on their show, all the groups who had seen her perform, and even the group that spread rumors about her were all standing in recognition of her well-deserved award.

Hayoon gazes out into the crowd and her sight lands on Junwoo. His expression is a face she'll remember for a lifetime; his eyes full of pride and affection. She quickly descends the stairs to return to her brothers. The cameras follow her as she practically runs into their arms for a group hug. In the middle of the group stands Junwoo, with a guardian on each side. He strokes her head and whispers, "I'm so proud of you."

Baekhyeon adds as he rubs her back, "Our little sister is the best."

Hayoon smiles proudly at Baekhyeon and Jihoon before turning back to Junwoo. "Oppa, my dream... I got it."

289

I want someone by my side who thinks I'm worth it. Someone who thinks I'm worth their time, their care, their protection. You know when you get sick and you just want someone to hold your hand until you fall asleep. Or when something really good happens to you and you just want to run and tell them. They'll pat your head and compliment you.

www.ingramcontent.com/pod-product-compliance
Lightning Source LLC
Chambersburg PA
CBHW071408300726
48976CB00006B/2022